MAIN CHARACTER ENERGY

MAIN CHARACTER ENERGY

JAMIE VARON

PARK ROW
BOOKS

PARK
ROW
BOOKS™

Recycling programs
for this product may
not exist in your area.

ISBN-13: 978-0-7783-3420-0

Main Character Energy

Park Row Books
22 Adelaide St. West, 41st Floor
Toronto, Ontario M5H 4E3, Canada
ParkRowBooks.com
BookClubbish.com

Printed in U.S.A.

To anyone who needs the reminder to be
the main character in their own life, this is for you.

PROLOGUE

When I met my aunt for the first time, I expected to hate her. After all, she had been the villain in my mom's story since I was a kid. They hadn't talked in nearly twenty years and every time I brought her up, my mom would shut me down. I didn't know what caused their fracture, but my mom's anger was enough to make me believe that Aunt Margot was the problem.

I never wanted to go behind my mom's back and betray her trust, but when Margot contacted me in secret, I knew I had to finally meet my elusive aunt.

It was a shock to me that our first visit felt like a reunion.

I thought she'd be hard-edged and critical like my mom was, but instead, she was warm and effusive. I was pulled into her comforting orbit immediately.

We convened in Malibu on a rainy, moody February afternoon. I was twenty-three years old and hopeful, brash, naive. We ate at a cliff-side restaurant, waves crashing against the rocks below us. I didn't know this would be the start of an annual tradition where I'd meet her for lunch once a year in February, always at the same place, the same order—a sacred ritual just for us.

"Poppy," she said, her eyes crinkling, her hands outstretched for me to grab them. She seemed ready to cry and I sat there feeling slightly guarded and guilty. I wasn't supposed to be here. If my mom knew I was meeting with Margot, she wouldn't be happy. But curiosity had won out.

"Hi," I said, and the one question that had plagued me slipped from my lips before I could stop it. "What happened between you and my mom?"

Her face clouded over for just a fraction of a second before she waved me off and said, "That's neither here nor there. Tell me about you. What do you love, Poppy? What lights you up? Who do you want to be when you grow up?"

There was a magic to Aunt Margot. It was clear immediately. I felt myself open up like a blooming sunflower in her presence. A smile spread across my face, the initial guardedness falling away like petals to the ground.

Looking at Margot was like looking at myself in the future. Long, loosely waved, chestnut-brown hair, hers streaked with natural gray, mine highlighted by caramel coloring. Almond-shaped eyes. Hers, moody gray-blue. Mine, vibrant green. Curvy bodies. Heart-shaped faces, reddened at the cheeks. Full lips tinted a cherry red, and straight teeth.

Where we differed was that she was so at ease in her body. She made me feel stronger, simply because she was so herself. Her body wasn't an apology. She existed as if everything about her were a celebration. She wasn't braced for the world, like I felt I was. When she spoke to the servers at our lunches, they were all mesmerized by her. She had the kind of wide-open soul that invited everyone in. She had confidence that radiated outward. I basked in it, like it was sunlight after an endless winter.

I wanted to be as carefree as her.

I still do. She made me feel bold.

"What lights me up? Writing," I told her, jutting my chin up. "I want to write books."

Her face beamed into a wide smile.

"That's wonderful, Poppy," she said. "Are you writing now?"

"Yes," I told her. "I'm working on a novel. A thriller, actually."

Margot looked delighted.

"I love thrillers, too," she said. "Who's your favorite author?"

"PJ Latisse," I said quickly.

Margot sported a grin and said, "Oh, I love their books."

"You don't think it's silly?" I asked, my voice low. "To want to be an author? My mom thinks I'm wasting my time."

My relationship with my mom was beginning to deteriorate and maybe that's why I met Margot—to rebel against my mom and all her rough edges. I was realizing I could have agency over my beliefs about the world and myself. She'd spent my childhood urging me to lose weight, forcing me on various fad diets, hoping I would become thin like her. But my body was unruly then. Still is. It didn't respond to her shame, but my mind did. And I felt cloaked in it.

My mom believed a thin body, handed over like a sacrifice, made dreams come true. Or at least, a thin body was the initial conduit for a good life. Without it, possibilities limit and dwindle. If I did nothing with my life except lose weight and find some man to marry me, it seemed like that would make my mom the happiest. She had virtually no patience or interest in my dreams or aspirations.

"Silly?" Margot asked, cocking her head to the side. "To follow your dreams? Never."

"Mom says dreams don't pay the bills." I shrugged. "But I have to try, don't I?"

"You always have to try," Margot said with a sharp nod of her head. "It's your life, not hers, after all."

"Hmm," I said, nodding. For years, I'd been writing at night, during stolen time. I'd been reading my whole life and books were my first love. All I'd ever wanted was to be a writer.

"Remember this, Poppy. For some people, it works out,"

Margot said with authority. "You don't know if it will for you until you try. If you love it, don't give up on it. Ever. No matter what anyone says."

"Okay," I said, smiling, feeling supported and buoyed for the first time ever.

"Something I always say: at the very least, do it for the plot. Do it for the story. Be bold in life, mostly because not being bold is boring as hell." Margot tipped her head back in glittery laughter and I felt my chest expand in hope.

"The last thing I'd ever want to be is boring," I replied.

"Good." Margot nodded firmly, then clapped. "Now, tell me all about what I've missed for the last twenty-three years of your life. Don't skimp on a single detail!" Margot's hands framed her jaw and she rested on her elbows, waiting with undisguised glee.

This Margot was the villain in my mom's story? But, she was lovely. I spent the rest of the lunch catching her up, and she listened with rapt interest. It was the most seen and heard I'd felt in a long time.

And so, when she asked if we could meet again the next year, I said yes. And it became our annual tradition. I secreted the visits away from my mom and never told her about any of them. I kept that first lunch—and future lunches—with Margot in my pocket like a precious stone I could rub my fingers on for luck, support, and the unconditional love I longed for.

NINE YEARS LATER

February

ONE

Malibu, California

I have never once wanted to cancel on a Margot lunch until today. Normally, I look forward to these visits for months, but I drive to Malibu in standstill traffic, annoyed and wishing I didn't have to go.

I don't want to hear any well-meaning encouragement from her. I don't want her to ask me about my dreams and tell me to "do it for the plot." I just want to hide and avoid her. I'm at my worst right now and I'm nervous to let her see me like that.

And then I feel guilty that I think that way.

So, I show up, plaster a smile on my face, hug her hard, and sit across from her at our table.

The wind whips across the windows. Through the open door, I can hear waves crashing on rocks, hard and fast and dramatic. It's overcast, and cold, with ominous dark clouds hovering just above the surf.

Perched right on the edge of the rocks off the Pacific Coast Highway, the large windows make me feel as if the restaurant is on the water, a refuge in the vast sea. Fitting, considering these secret visits with my aunt always felt like a refuge for me.

Margot and I get the small talk out of the way quickly, as usual. She tells me about France, where she lives, but gives away very few details. Even after all these years, she's still a mystery. What does she do for work? In the past, she's told me that she works with "artists" but has never explained further, or allowed me to pry for details. What is her life like? I'm certain she's a creative of some kind, but I never get straight answers.

I try to ask her questions about herself, but she deflects. She spends an inordinate amount of time laser focused on me, using every precious second of our visits to impart as much wisdom as she can.

Margot sets down the fork she was using to eat our calamari appetizer. It dings on the table with intent. She folds her hands in front of her and looks at me without blinking.

"Okay, let's get real," Margot says. "How's your writing going, Poppy?"

I take a nervous, long sip of my red wine. This is exactly why I didn't want to come today. Questions like this.

"It's…not going," I say.

Her eyes narrow at me. I don't want to tell her that last month, I made the difficult decision to give up on my dreams of becoming an author. It didn't feel like a decision as much as an eventuality, a conclusion to be drawn after years of disappointment, failure, rejection, and years of paralyzing writer's block keeping me frozen in front of a blinking cursor. I have mountains of student loan and credit card debt. I have no savings. I've been trying so hard to "make it," I never built a life for myself. At thirty-two, it feels like the right time to give up on my dreams. That believing in them is more foolish than going after them. The weight of disappointment feels like it is going to buckle me under.

And instead of reacting to life, I want to be proactive. Giving up feels like making a choice, a line in the sand—I'll find new dreams, a new life. I need to grow up, once and for all.

But, I'm here. Looking at my aunt now, I'm glad I didn't cancel, if only just to be in her presence. She's wearing an eccentric muumuu, with gold bangles on both her wrists and a chunky gold necklace. Her hair is half up in a clip, wild tendrils loosened around her face and backlit by the sea. Everything about her expresses a desire to be seen. Loud colors in expensive fabrics and the self-possession to not apologize for the space she takes up.

"What does that mean, darling? That your writing isn't going?"

"Well, I write all day for my job, and while it's not exactly the type of writing I want to do forever…"

"But, do you like this type of writing? Internet articles? 'Listicles' as you call them?" Margot's tone is without judgment, but it cuts like it is.

"Hey, for a lot of people, Thought Buzz is a dream job. I mean, I get *paid* to write for a living. A lot of people would kill for this job."

"Then, let them have it. You know you can quit."

"I can't just *quit*."

"You really could," she says. "Just because it *seems* like a dream job, doesn't mean it is one for you. You want to write books. That's been your real dream for so long, Poppy."

"I know," I say. My eyes sting. I take a deep breath, lowering my head so I don't have to look at Margot's face. "But I'm done, Margot. You always told me to try, and I did. It's just not working anymore. I think that's clear enough." I scoff bitterly. "It's time for me to give up and accept that not everyone gets to follow their dreams, and that's okay."

Margot erupts into laughter. She wipes away tears before speaking. I feel a touch of annoyance and know that my face betrays it.

"You do realize, darling, that you sound *exactly* like a person who's meant to be a writer." She laughs again. "You have a gift for writing. There's a reason why it weighs heavy on you. It requires you to dig deep to get to it, and that makes it more valuable."

I pause before speaking, and Margot lets the silence hang between us.

"It hurts to have dreams that feel impossible to achieve," I finally say on an outtake of breath.

Margot chuckles again. "Of course it does. It's so much easier to go through life on autopilot. It's the easiest thing in the world. You never have to be disappointed if you never try."

I look up at her, and my eyes are glassy.

"That's exactly it," I say. I laugh sharply, and then quickly rub away an errant tear from my left cheek.

Margot reaches her hand across the table, and it lands on mine. Her face creases.

"Poppy, darling, are you okay?"

"I don't know," I say. "I feel…" I look down at the piece of calamari on my small plate, searching for the right words. "I think I feel…really lost, Margot. Like, I don't even know who I am right now, or what to do, or how to help myself." I exhale quickly.

She strokes her hand across mine, and I look up at her. It's true. Years at a soul-sucking job, watching so many other people get book deals, having to pretend to be happy for authors who land on bestseller lists and publish year after year—it's exhausting. Even more tiring, having to be ecstatic for my own brother who has the publishing reality I've only dreamed of.

And it's not like I have a completed draft of a novel. It's been years since I've finished anything. The tap of my inspiration and hope has run totally dry. If that's not a sign to give up, what is?

"Poppy, you know I love you. You know I think you're the brightest light in any room you walk into," she says. "But, darling, why are you really not writing your book? What's going on? Talk to me."

I take another sip of my wine and my eyes scan the restaurant. There is a famous actress in the corner, sitting with a group of friends, and her presence is distracting. I just saw a movie of hers last week, and she is as stunning in person, if not more so. I shift in my chair, feeling that sharp pang of insecurity, like I don't belong here. I become aware of my body, of the size of my clothing, of the way everyone else shines with thinness and vibrancy in LA. Confidence is such a fickle thing.

"It's not that easy to devote much time to writing. I need money. I have rent to pay. Student loans. Credit cards. Electricity." I feel my head shake. "*Books* don't pay the rent," I spit out.

She looks serious, but the right corner of her mouth goes up, as if she's harboring a delicious secret.

"Life requires risks," she says. "You can stay safe and make money, but you will have regrets. Or you can barrel forward, take risks, invest in your art, and maybe it will work out. Maybe it won't. But you won't regret it."

"I might regret it, if I end up a forty-year-old with nothing in savings and the discards of manuscripts lying around my studio apartment."

"Poppy, you're too talented for that to happen."

"Everyone thinks they're talented," I snap, a lot harsher than I intend it to be.

"Well, darling, not everyone is. For some people, it's easy to give up. There are plenty of things they find just as fulfilling. But do you not think about writing from the moment you get up until the moment you fall asleep? Do you not wake up at 3:00 a.m. staring at the ceiling, anxious about writing?"

"Yes! And that's precisely why I want to be done with it. It's not worth all this...anxiety."

"The thing that keeps you up is inspiration. It's trying to find a way to get past your doubt and disbelief. It's trying to find a way to access you. Writer's block isn't lack of ability—it's fear."

I narrow my eyes at her.

"How do you know all this?" I ask.

She shakes her head and waves me off like she always does when I venture into questions that are personal and revealing.

"Never mind how I do." She deflects. "I just know."

"You make it all sound so simple," I say, my eyes downcast on the table, fingering the stem of my wineglass. "I try to write, Margot. I do. I sit down and stare at a blank page and it taunts me. It's not as easy as you think—to just sit down and write. Everyone says that. 'Just sit down and write!' Unless you're a writer, you just don't get it."

"Of course it's not easy!" Margot says with force, and I jump. Her eyes are fiery as she continues. "It's not supposed to be easy, Poppy. All good things require grit. I've spent my life around artists, and every single one of them—especially the most brilliant ones—struggle to find a way to access their potential. All of them think giving up is easier. But giving up because you don't think you're good enough is simply another pain to endure. Don't make excuses, darling. Not to yourself, not to anyone. Excuses are a great way to be on the sidelines of your own life."

Margot's cheeks are red. And instead of feeling encouraged, I only feel angry. I don't want any hope. I'm done with hope.

"It's too late for me," I say, airing out the most honest thing I feel. "I'm thirty-two. It should have happened for me already, and the fact that it hasn't, maybe that's my answer. Maybe it's a sign. At my age, my peers have either made it or given up, settled down into stable jobs with partners and had a baby or two, a puppy. I have nothing—I don't have the stable life, or the dream career. I feel like a fool sometimes, like someone holding on too tightly to an old dream."

I feel tears sting at the corners of my eyes, like these words are trip wires to my deepest insecurities. That I am not good enough. That I am wrong in some way. That women my size don't get the life they want, ever. That my whole life will feel like a compromise because I'm not thin. That my mom has been right all along.

Across the table, Margot stares at me intensely. The room and the ocean behind her fall away.

"Listen to me right now," she says, her eyes blazing. "You're in the warning zone here, Poppy. You need to be careful. If you don't start taking some risks, you're going to miss out on everything. It's not too late for you. Promise me that when any good thing comes your way, you'll say yes to it. That you're open to good things happening to you." Margot's eyes are glassy, and I worry she's about to cry. She sounds almost panicked, unlike her usual cheerful self. I feel the air shift around us. She needs me to hear her right now.

I wriggle in my chair and feel my hands go clammy. I swallow deeply.

"I promise," I tell her, but only because it feels like something she desperately needs to hear. I don't know if I truly mean it.

"Good," she says, patting my hand, her features softening. "Life is made in the risks, Poppy. Remember that. It's the foundation for the kind of wild and brave life you're meant for, my darling girl. And at the very least, you need to do it for the plot."

Do it for the plot. She says that catchphrase to me every lunch and it used to make me feel brave, but now it just stings.

"Okay," I say, feeling thousands of miles away from the type of person Margot thinks I am. I nod to her, as if I am comprehending, as if I am processing.

"Can we change the subject now?" I ask, forcing a smile. "I'd like to hear about how you're doing. You tell me so little about your own life."

"Well," she says, smiling slowly. "A woman needs her secrets. Remember that, no matter your age."

From there, our conversation swims back to friendlier, lighter waters. Inside jokes, and lunches from years past, and books we've read recently that we couldn't put down, me making notes in my phone of Margot's recommendations, trying to shake off my anger and bad attitude.

I let Margot believe she's hit a nerve. I let her think I am inspired. But unlike other years, her firm kindness feels less like inspiration and more like a stab in my abdomen.

As our annual lunch comes to a close, I walk out into the gray February chill with Aunt Margot at my side. I hug her tightly and tell her I'll see her next year.

She grasps my hands tightly and says, "Remember, you promised me that when something good comes your way, you will say yes to it." She insists, stares me down, like it's vital that I agree to it again. Her eyes are wet.

"What's going on?" I ask.

She wipes away a tear and simply says, eyes locked on to mine, "Just remember."

"Okay, Margot," I tell her, even though I have no idea what she means. I can't remember the last time something really good came my way.

I squeeze her hands in mine. She nods with finality and we part, until next year.

I drive home in traffic, pierced through by our conversation, still uncertain about everything. By the time I get to my apartment, I collapse on the sofa, and start a new Netflix show that I don't pay attention to at all, scrolling my phone instead. I do whatever I can to strike every bit of her encouragement from my mind. Margot was trying to help, I know that, but maybe I am beyond help.

I don't feel bold. Or brave. Or open to good things. Or like the brightest light in any room. I think Margot sees what she wants to see in me. I'm not who she thinks I am. And I'm not going to take her advice this time.

If I'm being honest, part of what has kept me going these past nine years has been Margot's unwavering faith in me, and I feel this sort of hot resentment about that. Like she lied to me that things would work out. They hadn't. And maybe it's a sign of maturity to accept that.

Scrolling my phone mindlessly, I see my older brother, Jackson, has posted a selfie with his newest book. It was Jackson's first book deal that was the initial blow to my confidence. I was twenty-eight at the time, working an undemanding day job so I could write as much as possible. I hadn't known Jackson was also writing a book. Or that he wrote, at all. It was this little secret he had, something that I would come to find out he and my mom shared together. Jackson got injured in high school and lost his football prospects, so while he was healing, he read. A lot. Then reading led to writing, and my mom spurred him on, all while she tried to talk me out of my own writing aspirations.

I remember I was in my small studio apartment in LA looking at dishes piled in the sink when Jackson called with the news of his first book deal. I was already raw that day. I'd received another agent rejection in my inbox only a few hours earlier.

That rejection was one of 150-something agents that had told me no for the thriller novel I'd worked on for three years. I'd been trying to find an agent for a year with no movement at all. Every rejection made me feel smaller and smaller. And then, that year became another year, and one hundred fifty rejections turned into over four hundred.

I never told anyone in my family about the rejections, especially not my mom, who would have looked at me with an I-told-you-so expression. I let the no's pile up, shame coursing its way through me. But that's how the world works, I thought. You hope that someone like Jackson who had everything in high school might peak early, but no, he gets handed everything. Doors are flung open for him. Jackson didn't just write romance novels—he *reinvented* the genre. Jackson didn't just hope to be successful—it was *expected* that he would be. As a man, as a white man, as a white man who fit the all-American mold, to the literary world, it was like he was a gift to them. And in turn, I had to prove myself that much more.

I stood in my kitchen while Jackson told me he got a high six-figure, multibook deal, and I collapsed on the ground without realizing what happened. I choked out a strangled congratulations, told him I had to go, and shook with sobs. It was an outsize reaction, but it felt like he'd stolen something from me.

I'd always compared myself to Jackson and had felt lacking. My cool older brother with his dorky younger sister. In high school, I wasn't Poppy Banks. I was just Jackson's sister, the one who sat cloaked in his shadow. Writing had been *my* thing. My way to distinguish myself. Jackson getting the book deal I'd always dreamed of, it felt like I was never going to catch up. And it leaked all the inspiration from me like a deflating balloon. Everything I would do from that point would be compared to Jackson. He'd taken from me the one thing I loved more than anything else.

And then as the years passed, my mom's beaming pride toward him, her bragging about his accomplishments felt like another betrayal. His debut novel shot to number one on the *New York Times* bestseller list and stayed there for a dizzying fifty-two weeks. And then, there was the movie adaptation. It was just like in high school, but worse. The golden boy of the family and me, somehow always on the sidelines, watching, burning with envy.

The only writing I've done since then is for my job at Thought Buzz. But listicles and clickbait hardly count. At least, they don't count to me. I took the job at Thought Buzz a few months shy of my thirtieth birthday, thinking a different kind of writing would distract me enough that the writing I actually wanted to do would somehow sneak up on me. I thought if I just stretched the writing muscle, the novels would pour out of me. Take the pressure off.

It did not work.

If anything, Thought Buzz made me loathe writing. The commercialization of it. The pretense that it was a dream opportunity, when it was, in actuality, exploitative to its core. Young writers with big aspirations having to scoop out their trauma to serve it up in the form of a personal essay that assholes all over the world would comment on.

Meanwhile, Jackson kept publishing books. Friends of mine got book deals. I seemed to drift into the shadows even more. Which is how I ended up here, giving up. Because, at least, that's a choice I get to make. At least I can go find something else to want that hurts less.

Remembering this all feels like touching a tender wound, especially after my emotional lunch with Margot. I sense that clawing need for escape, disassociation—and quickly.

I start a new thriller show on Netflix, comforted, distracted, and ready to get pulled into someone else's sad story for a while.

So, this is what it's like to give up on the life you thought you'd have—and finally settle for what you've got. To realize your aspirations and dreams are foolish, and grasping tightly on to them is hurting you more than helping you.

It's surprisingly easy to turn off the tap of hope.

That's it. I'm done with writing novels. The decision is made. It's official. Done with hope. I make a solemn promise to myself: no more writing. No more *thinking* about writing, even. I might be disappointing Margot, but this is my life and I'm tired of feeling like this. I can't keep beating myself up. It's over. Clean slate. Fresh start.

I feel a hollow sort of relief wave through me.

AUGUST

Six months later

TWO

North Hollywood, California

It's late morning on a sunny Saturday, and I'm just about to put coffee on when my phone rings. It's my mom. I groan. I can't remember the last time I actually wanted to answer a phone call from her. This will either be a guilt-trip, or a reminder to do something I don't want to do, or something else that June Banks can conjure up to ruin the start of my weekend.

I slap a smile on my face to give my voice the cadence of cheer.

"Hi, Mom," I say.

"Hi, Poppy," she says, her tone unclear. "I have some news."

"Oh?" No doubt it's about Jackson's fourth book-release party tonight, an event I'm dreading. I don't want to go. Just like the three before them that I've attended, everyone will fawn over and congratulate *me* on Jackson's success—it's unbearable.

"I know you didn't know her, but I just thought I should tell you. Margot passed away yesterday."

I gasp, and nearly drop the phone, my hands trembling. My mom delivers the news casually, as if my whole world hasn't been ripped apart. This isn't the moment to tell her that I knew

Margot. I feel like I can't even breathe, never mind speak. I hold back an onslaught of tears.

There's a long silence, the shock of it hanging between us, and I finally hear my mom tut.

"Poppy?" she asks, sounding annoyed. "What's going on?"

My throat is still constricted. I feel dizzy, my vision blurring. Margot is…dead? I just saw her six months ago, alive and beaming and vibrant. This cannot be real. How can this be happening right now?

"How did she die?" I ask, trying to keep my voice even.

"I don't know," Mom says, in a tone that is so cold it feels like a slap. I realize they were estranged, but to be this casual about your own sister's death? It's unfathomable. I feel as though a hole has opened up at my feet, and I am plunging into it. "Poppy, do you want to meet us at the house, and we'll go to the restaurant together tonight?"

"I'm not going, Mom." The words come out calm, steady. And even though it feels like a small decision—to decide I will not do something that hurts me just to please my family—it feels monumental. Because, before my mom even speaks, I know exactly what she's going to say, and I brace myself for it.

"Of course you're coming," she says. "This is a big night for Jackson."

"It's always a 'big night' for Jackson," I say, pacing the length of my small kitchen. My heartbreak has quickly morphed into rage toward my mom.

I hear her intake of breath, a sign that she's winding up a biting critique of me. It says something that our conversations are this predictable, except usually I cower to her and do whatever she wants. But not this time. The idea of going to Jackson's party, knowing I'll never have another annual lunch with Margot—I can't bear it. I truly cannot. I hold back a sob.

"You know, Poppy, listen to me," Mom says, serious. "Don't take it out on your brother that you never became a writer."

I step back in my kitchen as if I've been pushed. My eyes start to sting in the corners. I feel a sick combination of terrifying grief and abject rage.

"You're right," I say, incapable of holding my anger back any longer. "I shouldn't hold it against him that you supported Jackson's writing right away and yet tried to talk me out of my dreams for years. I seem to remember a very supportive mom saying: 'Big girls like you don't get to have their dream lives; do you want to go on Atkins together?'"

She breathes heavily into the phone, like a bull about to charge.

"You're an adult, Poppy, a little too old to blame me for your failings. It's my fault that your life hasn't panned out the way you wanted it to?"

"If the shoe fits," I say, shrugging, knowing I'm being petulant. I feel as if I might collapse to my knees. "Hard to forget when your own mom doesn't support you."

"Support you doing what, Poppy? You're thirty-two, single, and flailing. What's there to support?" I double back. I don't fully understand what has happened between my mom and me, but it feels like there is a massive chasm between us. And no matter what I do or say, that chasm widens. I've tried to be the good daughter, the good sister, always showing up, always shoving aside my inconvenient feelings, but now I realize I will disappoint my mom either way. And I might as well stop disappointing myself, too.

"Great. Thanks for the call, Mom. I'm not coming tonight. I can miss one night of fawning over Jackson. He'll be fine," I scoff loudly. "He has plenty of admirers," I spit out.

"Very mature, Poppy," she says. "I guess I'll see you at lunch Sunday, unless you have a reason to not go to that, too."

I slump my shoulders, and agree, because I can't seem to disappoint my mom twice in one phone call. I tell her I'll see her then, already dreading it. And when the phone call ends,

I slide down my kitchen counter, land on the floor, and fall into pieces. The sound of my sobs echo around me, and I burrow my face into my hands, wiping away fat, salty tears with the sleeve of my shirt.

Aunt Margot is gone?

Gone.

I didn't get to say goodbye. Her last memory of me was disappointment. Our final lunch, I left frustrated with her, for seeing me so transparently. For trying her best to *encourage* me. And nothing has changed since then. I haven't moved forward in any significant way.

In many ways, I'm further down the hole. I quit writing to try to find something else to do with my life, and I haven't done anything. What do I do now? Where do I go from here? I have to just go to work on Monday morning, as if nothing has happened? I have to just carry this alone?

I feel stunned with grief.

I'll never see Margot again.

I'll never be able to tell her how much she meant to me.

I get up from the floor, sit down on the couch, and I sob more.

THREE

On Monday morning, I meet my best friend, Mia, just before work. We often convene at our favorite coffee shop close to where we both work. She has a job in the building next to Thought Buzz. When I arrive, Mia is sitting at a small table in the corner, with two iced lattes. Her light blond hair is cut just above her shoulders, and she's wearing a short-sleeved shirt, which shows off the many tattoos she has on her slender arms. Just seeing her, I exhale. Once I get to the table, she stands up and I fall into her arms. She hugs me tightly.

I spent most of my weekend drinking too much wine, watching too much TV, and doing too little of the things that might have made me feel better.

I look at Mia and feel at least a small bit of comfort. Her eyes are moist in the corners.

"I'm so sorry, Poppy," she says. Mia is the only one I've told about Margot's death. She's the only one who knows about my Margot lunches.

"I feel like I knew Margot, too," she says, wiping at her right eye. "I wish I could have met her."

"Me too," I say. "She would have loved you."

"How are you holding up?"

"Not great," I reply. "I spent most of the weekend in shock, thinking about the last conversation Margot and I had. I feel like she left disappointed in me, Mi." My voice hitches.

"She didn't," Mia says. "I know she didn't. Margot wasn't like that."

I take a sip from my latte through a paper straw and look out the window to my right.

"I don't know what to do, Mia." I look down at the table and make a dramatically anguished face. Mia smiles despite herself.

"About what?" she asks.

"All these feelings. My life. Myself. Everything." I slump down on the chair. "I'm sick of myself. I gave up on the novels, but I still haven't done anything else. I'm just stuck in place."

"Maybe that's a good thing," Mia says. "Maybe that means you're ready to make some changes."

"I just wish I knew *what* to change. I want a direction. I want a sign. I want someone to hit me over the head with something that I can't say no to."

"Don't we all?" Mia laughs. "Everyone wants a path to land on our doorstep, and all we have to do is walk down it and, poof, life is figured out."

"Exactly," I say, smiling tentatively at her. "You get it."

"Of course I get it," Mia says. "Also, your mom's reaction? What was with that? Does she really not care that her sister passed?"

I groan. "I really don't know," I say. "Sometimes I feel like I don't know my mom at all. To not express a single emotion— it makes me kind of worried for her."

"No kidding."

"I'll ask her about it, and she'll probably bite my head off, but at least she'll know I'm thinking of her."

"Good luck," Mia says, and smiles ruefully. She is kept abreast of every detail of the complicated relationship I have with my mom, and she knows that anything emotional or sticky is bound to be a battle with her. My mom is so closed off to her feelings, and in turn, I am an emotional hurricane. It's bound to be complicated between us at times. She just does not see life the way I do.

"Okay, we're gonna be late. Time for work." Mia taps her watch.

"I don't want to go," I say, groaning. I roll my eyes. Mia actually likes her job as a graphic designer for a cool creative agency, so she stands and makes a show of pulling me up. We start walking toward our offices. It's bright and warm outside, and both of us quickly throw sunglasses on as if the sun is burning our retinas.

"Margot told me to quit my job," I say, looking ahead at the squat office building coming into view.

"Maybe you should? You hate it."

"It would be very irresponsible. And it's the last bit of writing I'm doing. I hate that I want to hold on to that still."

"Thought Buzz did not turn out the way you expected. I think you can find something better."

"Can I?"

"Yeah, and sometimes being irresponsible is exactly what you need to do, to find what makes you happy," Mia replies. *Happy?* I'd settle for feeling just okay at this point.

"Yeah, maybe," I say, as we hug and split off toward our respective buildings. We wave to each other, knowing the rest of this conversation will continue at some point in the day, either by text or over lunch. Mia goes to her private office, and I find a hot desk in the middle of the fray, annoyed and irritable before I even sit down, as I brush off someone's crumbs from the only spot that's open. Whoever invented the open-concept office layout needs to be psychologically tested.

A Slack chime pierces my train of thought. It's from my boss, Gareth.

"Come to my office. Now, please," he writes.

I look down at my computer and type "sure, on my way" and roll my eyes.

Being called into Gareth's office is the worst part of my job. He's my boss, and he's nearly ten years younger than me. Most times he calls me in for the most inane requests. I'm betting today is no different. I have even less patience for it than I usually do, which is saying a lot.

I sit across from him, set my notebook down, and take him in. He's a clean-cut white man with cropped brown hair and blue eyes, like he should work in finance but ended up in editorial somehow. Gareth is always in a suit and tie, regardless of how casual everyone else dresses in the office, including me. It's a hot day, and I'm wearing a short floral skirt with a square-neck black T-shirt, and white tennis shoes.

"Poppy, I need to talk to you about something," Gareth says, smiling to show his perfectly straight, bright white teeth.

I smile back, my jaw clenching with it. Nausea from both my emotional hangover and my disgust of Gareth starts boiling around in my stomach.

"What is it?" I ask, as upbeat as I can muster.

"Your page views are dipping. You need more clicks, something viral."

I grind my teeth. "Okay," I say. This is the job. Generating clicks. But damn, I hate this job so much. And yet, I need this job. I need the money, even if it's not a lot of money. My stomach roils again, anxiety taking hold. I feel trapped.

"I need you to write for the hate-click, you know? We're not here to write fluff or happy stuff. We need to be edgy," Gareth says, so excitable it makes me cringe. "No political correctness. You know our ethos is free speech. I'm so tired of woke culture. Start coming up with topics that will piss people off. Push the envelope."

"But I don't want to put more hate out onto the internet," I whisper, blinking rapidly. "I want to write things I'm proud of, not things that will just upset people." My words come out slowly. My pulse quickens. I want to leap across Gareth's desk and rip that grin off his face. Another thing I've been going along with for years—writing under a pen name, generating hate-clicks for ad dollars. No wonder I don't even respect myself.

"That's your job," Gareth says, completely unaware that I am seething. "Thought Buzz isn't here to change public opinion. We want to give space for all sides. And you know the hate-click is a moneymaker." He rubs his fingers together.

"But giving a voice to topics that harm people isn't right," I say. I know I'm being pedantic, but I am in shock. Does he not hear himself?

"Who's to say what is right? Not us. We will publish any opinion, you know that." Gareth leans back in his chair and puts his hands behind his neck, taking up as much space as he pleases. He's right. Thought Buzz will publish any trash or drivel, or will literally make up fake stories to generate clicks. Free speech, *right*. That's what people like Gareth tell themselves, as if giving voice to harm and hatred is somehow noble.

You're in the warning zone here, Poppy.

My eyes sting, thinking of Margot.

I inhale quickly.

I stiffen and take a deep breath. My hands curl into fists. My head throbs. I can't take it anymore. I suddenly feel the overwhelming urge to get out of here. Margot's last words to me. My mom's admonishments. Jackson's success. What Gareth is asking me to do. I don't even care that I have nothing in emergency savings or that this might be the worst idea I've ever had or that it's irresponsible. There are hundreds of less horrible ways to make a paycheck. And I think, at this point, I might be happier doing anything else. Thought Buzz is making me miserable. And it's time to find something different. Even if I have to give up the last tiny bit of writing I was still doing. Not worth it.

I look down at the ground and say quietly, almost a whisper, "I quit."

Gareth snaps up and says, "You, what?"

I get my footing and this time I say it clearly, without hesitation, because it feels good. A surge of power travels through me.

"Gareth," I say, looking at him directly, "I fucking quit."

"You can't quit!" Gareth's face is red.

"Of course, I can quit, and I do." I cross my arms. "I'm done."

"I—" Gareth's voice cracks.

"This place is vile and toxic," I say, incapable of stopping what's about to happen. I've been bottling this up for a while. "You exploit young people, making them promises of big writing careers, but most of them end up floundering. You exploit the promise of inclusivity by writing about watered-down feminism and hot-button topics that don't encourage progress at all. All you care about are clicks, and you'll take *anyone* down to get them. Screw this place. I'm ashamed I've worked here as long as I have." I feel an electric bolt move through me.

Gareth stands up, towering over me, and I straighten. He's not going to intimidate me. Not today. Not any day.

"You'll regret this," he growls out. "You know, you women always say you want more responsibility, and then, look at you, not even meeting the bare minimum. A man would never do this. A man would never be this unprofessional."

"Maybe not," I say, looking at him directly, my voice even and not betraying the swirl of emotions happening below the surface. "Men also don't have to suffer indignities just to do a job, so I guess we're even." I smirk at him and he breathes out loudly, his ears going red now.

Before Gareth can speak again, I turn on my heel and walk through the door, letting it close loudly, and forty heads pop up from their desks to watch me. I stifle a giddy, manic giggle. That felt...*good*. Really good.

I drop my staff badge down on the check-in desk with a loud bang, and the receptionist jumps. That's what he gets for having his face in his phone all day, every day. I will not miss this place for one second.

I gulp in the air once I'm outside, like it's the first taste of freedom I've had in years.

I drive home in the middle of a bright August day, admiring the towering palm trees and cloudless sky. I listen to my music loud, with the windows rolled down, my hair whipping around in the dry heat.

I feel terrified and uncertain and ecstatic and anxious; my mind is running with thousands of things at once, but the most pervasive thought, the one that matters the most is this: Aunt Margot would be proud of me.

Realizing this, I feel a broad smile spread across my face.

FOUR

Pasadena, California

Purposefully, I arrive late for family lunch the following Sunday, timing it so that I sneak in the moment food is on the table. Jackson is here, with his wife Phoebe, and their two young daughters—Marigold and Sophia, who run toward me and scream, "Auntie Pop Pop!" I smile widely, even as I see my mom's scrunched eyebrows at the head of the table, frustrated with me for being late. Dad is sitting next to her, checked out as always. His "famous" barbecue chicken is in the center of the table, the one thing he cooks, acting as though it's a great personal sacrifice to do so, despite my mom cooking three meals a day nearly every day, without thanks from him. My younger brother, Liam, taps the chair next to him, and when I sit, he throws his arm around me.

"You're in *trouble*," he whispers, and smiles. I smile back at my ally.

"Sorry I'm late," I say to everyone. "Let's eat before it gets cold."

We all start piling food on our plates, passing around dishes, asking for more, and where are the napkins, and does anyone want something from the kitchen? It's ritualistic and familiar. This is why my family is complicated. Because I love them too much to hate them. I even really like them sometimes, too.

"What a success your book-release party was, Jack," Mom says, starting off the conversation once we've all begun eating. "Sorry you missed it, Poppy."

"Daddy let us wear our fanciest dresses, Pop Pop," Marigold says in her precocious way. She's five, going on sixteen. Little Sophia nods next to her, her little shadow. She's three, and her big brown eyes look at Marigold as if she hangs the moon.

"We had cake," Sophia says, her face aglow. "I love cake."

"I *love* cake, too," I say to Soph. "*And* dresses." To Mari. They both beam at me, and the lump in my throat lessens for a moment.

"I debuted at number one on the *New York Times* list again," Jackson says. "That was cool. We missed you, Pop."

My stomach drops, and I set my fork down.

"I wasn't feeling well," I say. "Congratulations, Jackson. That's a huge achievement. I'm sorry I missed your book-release party." The words burn coming out of my throat. "Genuinely, I am sorry. I was having a bad day."

Jackson's eyes narrow. "Seems like you've been having a lot of those lately."

"It won't happen again," I say, in a voice that's more compliant than I mean. When do they show up for me? I am just expected to show up for everything, no matter how I'm feeling.

"I mean, are you jealous or upset with me or something? I would be happy for you, if you were doing well. I wouldn't make you feel bad about it." Jackson eyes me. "Poppy, is everything alright with you?" He seems concerned, but I'm stuck on something else. If *you were doing well*. That *if* says a lot.

"I'm not jealous of you," I say, trying to regain my composure.

"Then what do you call it when you can't be happy for someone's success because it's not yours?"

"It wasn't about you, Jackson."

"It seemed pretty well directed at me," Jackson says, giving a tired smile and running his hands through his full head of brown hair. I don't know why he cares this much about whether I was at his event, but I'm exhausted by these guilt trips. I'm allowed to have my own life. Does my family not realize this?

"Not everything is about the golden child, Jackson Banks," I say, a little more forcefully than I intend it. Jackson's eyes shoot up and widen.

"Wow, Poppy!" I startle at my mom's voice. "I see you're not in any kind of better spirits from the other night."

"Hey, I thought we were going to have a nice lunch, not a Poppy pile on," Liam says, ever the peacekeeper. "Can we take it down a few notches?"

"I quit my job," I blurt.

"Finally!" Liam exclaims.

"What, *why?*" Mom and Jackson both ask, disappointment and judgment on both syllables.

"What are you going to do now?" my mom screeches out. "Who quits their job out of the blue like that? What's going on with you, Poppy? What's wrong with you?" She shakes her head emphatically. My fists curl tightly under the table, and I clench my jaw. How is this my mom's reaction to me quitting my job? It's so thoughtless. I feel a bad combination of both incredible loneliness and striking anger.

"I couldn't stand that place a minute longer," I say, folding my arms across my chest. "I outgrew it."

"You…outgrew a steady paycheck?" Jackson asks.

"I want to do something else," I say, in a small voice. "I don't know what, but something other than *that* job." I have no conviction in these words, and they come out sounding immature and weightless. I don't feel nearly as powerful as I did the day I quit. I hate that their judgments can deflate me so quickly like this.

"Well, everyone settles, Poppy. That's life," Mom says. "You settle for what you get. You young people, and your high expectations. Not everyone gets to make money with their passion, living some easy, breezy life." Her ears go pink, and the first thought that hits me is: that's an astonishingly sad way to look at life. And yet I'm very familiar with settling.

"Jackson doesn't have to settle," I say, shooting him a look.

"Yeah, well, Poppy, I don't quit," Jackson chastises. "I've worked hard for my career."

"Oh, and I guess I haven't worked hard enough for mine?"

"Well, have you written a book of your own? Because that's a good place to start," Jackson says, not exactly unkindly. He's not wrong, but does he have to spell it out like that?

"Just get a normal job, Poppy," Mom says, as if this were the easiest thing in the world. "And stop comparing yourself to your brother." She shakes her head and starts cutting into a piece of chicken vigorously. As if she isn't the one who constantly compares me to him. *Jackson is so fit, why don't you start exercising, Poppy? If you want all the choices in life, you need to be more like your brother.* Dragging me to every football game, every single Jackson activity, like I didn't have my own life. Like I was always second best.

I shake my head back, feeling exasperated.

A tense silence breaks out over the table. Phoebe, Marigold, and Sophia have been watching this conversation play out as if it's a ping-pong match. Dad has sat there stony and silent, as always. Liam is vibrating with anxiety because he can't keep the peace.

"Maybe it's time to find something else, then," Jackson says. "Figure out what else you like to do apart from writing."

That's what I'm doing, but it stings when Jackson suggests it.

"Yeah, it's different for people like you," Mom says. "Not everyone gets exactly what they want all the time."

"People...like...me? What does that mean, Mom? What are you trying to say?" I swallow hard, the air heavy with tension. But I know exactly what she means: for women with your body. I've heard this before. It's her coded language.

"I just mean, it's okay to let go of dreams when you see they're not happening. I'd say the same to Jackson if he weren't already doing so well." My mom shrugs and takes a sip of water. My appetite is gone.

"Would you?"

"I would."

"But people like me? You mean, women? Or women who aren't thin? Or who? Why me?"

"I just think it's harder to get ahead for you, Poppy. For different reasons. And I don't want to see you get disappointed."

"Okay—" I start to say, clearly angry.

Jackson jumps in. "Pop, calm down. You know what she's saying."

"No, actually I don't," I say, my voice gathering steam. "Or maybe, I know *exactly* what she's saying. She's saying I'm not good enough. I'm not good-looking enough, not thin enough, not talented enough. If I were, she'd tell me to keep going, to never give up.

"I've spent years trying to convince myself to keep going, and I'm realizing that the voice that keeps telling me to give up isn't even just my own. It's yours, Mom. And that is awful to realize." I slump down. The silence in the air is tense. I don't look at anyone else out of fear of what their expressions will tell me.

I bury my face in my hands, uncomfortable in the way vulnerability feels when you finally air it out. The table is frozen, as if we're on pause. Eyes on me that feel like daggers. Maybe it's pity.

My mom tells me to come into the kitchen so we can talk

privately. I get up to follow her, and the moment I leave, conversation resumes at the table, as if the play button has been pressed on the movie.

"Poppy, my goodness, what's going on?" She looks distressed.

"I'm just tired of this. I've been hearing you say the same thing to me for years, and you know what? I've started to believe you. I gave up writing, okay? Fine. There. Happy? Isn't that what you want from me?"

"I want what's best for you," she says, with a shrug. "Why are you fooling yourself? You need to lose weight. All these issues, this jealousy toward Jackson, you being alone, your life not working out the way you want it to—it would be solved if you'd just lose weight. You're being stubborn. Your life would be so much better without…weight issues. Why are you making excuses? I'm worried about you."

I hold back a rush of frustrated, exhausted tears. "I know you think you're protecting me or whatever, but all you're doing is making me doubt myself. Like I have to *wait* for my life to start. That I can't have the life I want unless I'm thin. Do you have any idea how hurtful that is?"

"I'm just being realistic, Poppy," she says, sharply. "I'm your mom. I can't sugarcoat the world for you. And well, I'm sorry, but I do think it's harder to have the life you want if you're not thin. That's how the world works, not me." She holds her hands up in defense.

"But that's the world's problem, not mine, right?" I soften toward her, thinking we're having a minor breakthrough.

She shrugs. "I don't like to see you struggle so much, Poppy. Most people are happy to just have a normal life. You expect way too much."

My mom starts cleaning the countertops with a spray bottle, expelling her frenetic energy.

I gape at her. "Expect too much? It's *my* life. Why are you always trying to make me accept less?"

"Because you can't always get what you want, Poppy! And you're wasting your life! God, I've done the best I can."

"Wow," I say on a rush of breath. "This is you doing your best? Maybe you could have taught me to be more confident in who I am right now."

She looks at me hard then, and I can see her fighting back defiant tears.

"Maybe I didn't know how to teach you something I didn't have myself," she says, in a small, faraway voice. Her eyes go down to her hands. I feel my chest tighten at the admission.

I breathe out loudly. "Okay, well, I can't keep having this conversation with you. For years, it's the same thing. I'm done. I don't want to discuss my body with you any longer."

"Fine," she says, resuming wiping down the counters. "You think I'm being cruel when all I'm trying to do is help you."

I don't know how to make her understand. I'm so tired of this battle.

I go to change the subject, hoping we can get into less fraught territory, but the one question I'd been holding inside finally wants to come out. A deeper reason I feel such anger and confusion and resentment toward her.

"Mom, can I ask you something?"

She looks at me and draws out an "okay."

I drop my voice low and ask her, "Are you okay about Margot?"

She reacts harshly. "God, Poppy, why are you bringing this up right now? Of course I'm fine."

"Whoa," I say, taken aback by the sudden change in her demeanor. "Mom, your sister died last week, and you haven't even mentioned it since you told me. Have you talked to anyone?" I know they weren't close, but surely Margot's death means something to her.

"I hadn't talked to my sister in over thirty years," she says. "As far as I'm concerned, she's a stranger. Her dying doesn't change that." She crosses her arms in front of her. Her face is red. I don't buy it. She can't be this cold.

She goes to the sink, starts scrubbing at a large pot with vigor. This is the mom I know—homemaker extraordinaire, never stops, never relaxes, never talks about herself.

Never expresses emotion.

"Why did you and Margot stop speaking all those years ago?"

"Poppy, I don't want to talk about this right now," she says, under her breath. I think that's the end of it, but she starts up again. "Margot was an incredibly selfish woman, okay? She was opinionated and hurtful. That is not the kind of person I choose to mourn."

"But—" I stop, because this isn't the Margot I knew. In fact, it sounds more like my mom than it does like Margot. But I don't say that.

"You know, you remind me of her," she says, spiteful. I feel like I've been slapped. "Maybe that's why you and I don't see eye to eye much anymore."

I double back.

"We...do see eye to eye, Mom," I say, voice shaky.

"No, you're too much like her," she says, scouring at a stubborn stain on a casserole dish. "It's all about *your* dreams, your art, how urgent it is. What about a husband? What about your family? What about your health, your body? What about kids? What about building a home?"

"Maybe I don't want those things. You would never say the same thing to Jackson."

"You *should* want all of that. And I didn't have to say it to Jackson," she says, turning to look at me. "He built it all already, without flailing." That word again. *Flailing.*

She makes me feel like I'm a disappointment to her.

I start getting hot, anger clouding my hearing. I am tired of this narrative, of this story, of these roles we fill in this fam-

ily. I am the screwup. Jackson, the golden child. Liam, the beloved youngest.

I sigh loudly. There's a beat of silence between us, our eyes
locked on each other. The doubt she has instilled in me feels
like quicksand. I can never quite escape it.

"Okay, Mom," I finally say. "I think we need some space."

"Yeah, maybe we do," she says, her words clipped, face stony
and closed off.

"Okay."

"Okay," she says, nodding, not looking at me.

I hug her quickly from the back, because despite everything,
I can't hate her. And I leave through the backyard without saying goodbye to anyone, wiping at my face as I go.

FIVE

North Hollywood, California

It's later that evening, and after lunch with my family earlier, I need a quiet night. I'm still reeling over Margot's sudden passing. It's been nine days since I found out and six since I quit my job. I haven't regretted it, but I'm also hoping I figure out what I'm going to do next, soon. I've spent all week looking online for a new job, sending out my résumé for positions that have nothing to do with writing. I feel a strange weightlessness. Calm. Like I'm leaving behind a life I've been trying to force for years. It feels nice to not have the crush of dread lying on my chest any longer.

I make myself a hot cup of peppermint tea and carry it over to the couch. I light a candle, and I set a speaker to play instrumental music. I pick up the latest mystery novel that I'm halfway through.

But tonight I can't focus on reading. Instead, I scroll Instagram. I check Twitter. I get sucked into TikTok for way too long. I read a news story about politics that makes my anxiety soar. I see an announcement that an old colleague from work got a six-figure book deal for her novel. I take another deep,

shaky breath. I lock my phone and throw it on the couch behind me. I close my eyes and let the sour feeling of jealousy
crawl through me.

My intercom buzzes. I step up to it tentatively and hold my
finger on the button.

"Yes?" I ask, in a croaky voice.

"I have a package for Poppy Banks." A male voice booms
out of the speaker.

"Okay, I'll buzz you in." A package? On a Sunday night?

There's a light knock on the door and I open it to a young
white man with an average build, wearing a red bicycle helmet
with light reflectors on it. He's holding a heavy high-quality
matte black envelope, a little larger than the size of a standard
piece of paper.

"I'm from a messenger service, and I've been instructed to
deliver this by hand to Poppy Banks," he says. "Please sign here
to confirm you have received this package."

He hands me an electronic device, and I sign with my finger.
He looks at it and nods, then hands over the black envelope.

"Thank you," he says over his shoulder.

"You're welcome," I say under my breath, fingering the
package.

On the front, the only writing is my name in gold lettering, ornately written with what looks like a paint pen. On the
back, at the envelope flap, is one of those old wax seals with
the initials *MB* embossed on it in gold.

I gasp, almost dropping the envelope on the ground.

MB.

Margot Bisset.

Aunt Margot.

I set the envelope down on the kitchen counter, steadying
myself for a moment. I walk a couple laps around my apartment,
breathing in through my nose and out through my mouth, a

meditation technique I learned years ago to help manage my anxiety.

After I've calmed myself down just enough, I break open the seal of the envelope carefully, so the wax stays intact. My heart is beating wildly in my chest. It's almost like I can hear it pounding in my quiet apartment.

There are three separate things inside the package. Another sealed, smaller white envelope, and two pieces of paper. One paper is typed, and I don't read that yet because the other is a handwritten note on thick stationary. A note in the same ornate cursive from the front of the envelope.

Swooping, elegant letters.

I take in a sharp breath.

I sit down at my small dining table and settle myself.

Then, I start reading.

My Dearest Poppy,

I don't have many regrets in my life, except that I didn't get to spend more time with you. Our annual long lunches were among the happiest moments of my life, and I cherished them all year. Life is beautiful and cruel, my darling, but it is imperative that you live it, on your own terms. I see so much of myself in you and that is why I've left behind something that I want you to have and to enjoy. After our last lunch, I knew I had to do this for you.

Enclosed in this envelope is a one-way ticket that leaves for Nice two days from now. It is my dying wish that you take this flight, and you stay in the south of France for six months. Do not overthink it (because I know you will want to). Get on the flight. You have nothing to lose, only so much to gain. You promised me you'd say yes to the next good thing that came your way, and this will be a good thing. Trust me.

At the very least, do it for the plot, my darling girl.

Your itinerary is included.

Start packing. All will be revealed once you get to France.

Love forever and always,

Your Aunt Margot

"What?" I say out loud. "What…is happening right now?"

I look at the typed piece of paper and it's sparse, just flight information. Under that, it says "When you get to Arrivals in Nice, someone will be waiting for you."

I feel a lurch of ten different emotions at once, all of them intense, most of them panicked. This is crazy. Legitimately. I can't just up and leave everything for six months. *Right?*

I open the sealed envelope with shaky hands. There's my name on two tickets for Air France, one from Los Angeles to Paris on Tuesday. The other, a ticket on Air France from Paris to Nice, my connecting flight.

What's waiting for me in France? I've never traveled farther than London. My heart races, breathing shallowed. I wish I knew more about Margot so that I could understand this. I have no idea what I would be getting myself into if I go.

If I go.

No.

I *can't* go. I need a job. I have negative amounts of money. I don't speak French. I need to pay down my student loans, get out of debt, start a savings account. I need to get my shit together. The last possible thing I should be doing right now is taking a plane to France for who knows what reason! I shake my head and walk over to the fridge. I pull out a bottle of white wine and pour myself a generous glass.

I can't do this. I can't just *go to France*. This is eccentric, even for Margot. What would my mom think? This is nuts. Who just packs up and goes to France for six months?

But. I stop, the glass of wine halfway to my mouth.

I remember that I promised Margot I'd take the next good thing that came my way. She put that promise in the letter. And this was her dying wish. Her *dying wish*.

I feel guilt slice through my stomach. And then a wave of fresh grief crests over me, nearly toppling me over. I take some deep breaths and steady myself again.

Okay, I need to call Mia. She'll know exactly what to do.

"Hi, Pop—perfect timing," Mia says, breathing out tiredly. "I just got Jordan to bed."

"How's my favorite little guy?" I ask. I love Mia's six-year-old. He's the product of a wayward one-night stand that Mia had with a guy who adamantly wanted nothing to do with her pregnancy or his child. Mia took it in stride, though, and is a loving, engaged single mom. I think of Jordan as my bonus nephew.

"He's good, but he keeps wondering when his Auntie P is coming over to bake with him," Mia says, chuckling. "This kid can't get enough of it. I've got half a bakery in my freezer."

I laugh, because I've baked cookies, cakes, and brownies with JoJo many times over the last couple of years.

"Sorry, you called for a reason," Mia says. "What's up, love?"

"No, no, it's okay," I say. "The thing is, I got a strange package tonight."

"Okay? That's ominous."

"It's from Margot."

"No."

"I know."

"Oh my god. Well, what is it?"

I tell her about the letter and plane tickets, hearing her gasp on the other end of the line.

"You let me go on about Jo's baking skills while you're sitting on a plane ticket to France? Poppy!"

I laugh, feeling lighter already. "Well, I don't know if I'm going to *actually* go."

"Oh, you're going," Mia commands, in the same stern voice she uses at Jordan's bedtime. "You wanted a sign? Well, Poppy, this is your huge fucking sign. I'd say a plane ticket that lands on your doorstep is the biggest sign you could ever ask for."

"Really? You think I should go? Where is my pragmatic friend Mia? Who is this wild woman? I called you to talk me out of this! I need a job. I can't just go to *France* out of nowhere."

"Why not? Let's see here. You conveniently just quit your job. You and your family are…not really speaking right now. You have no relationship holding you here. No dog. No plants, even. No job offers. What's your reason to stay?"

"Gee, thanks for the rundown of my pathetic life," I say, laughing dryly. But she's right, *technically*. Nothing is holding me here. I take my glass of wine to the couch and throw myself down on it dramatically.

"You know what I mean," Mia says in a softer voice. "Only *you* would overthink about whether to take a free trip to the French Riviera. You need to go."

"Well," I say, my voice low, my heart racing. "I'm kinda scared?" Scared of failing. Scared of the south of France. Land of models and "French women don't gain weight." I don't belong in a place like that.

"Of course you're scared. I would be weirded out if you weren't scared. But that doesn't mean you shouldn't go. In fact, it probably means you *have* to go. And, plus, I know you, Poppy. You'll regret it if you don't."

"Hmm," I murmur.

"And, Pop," Mia says. "I don't mean this to diminish your very real feelings, but wouldn't you rather be the kind of person who does things, even if they're afraid?"

I breathe out sharply. I don't know when I became so risk averse, but I am hit suddenly with the realization that I haven't felt a sense of possibility in a very long time. Not like this, not with fear and excitement all rolled into one.

"I'd like to think I'm that person," I say, fidgeting with my hands. "At one point, I was."

"Well, be that person now," Mia says. "I don't doubt you for a second."

"Ha," I breathe out. "That makes one of us, then."

"You need to do *something*. And this is your something to do."

A tear trickles down my cheek and I wipe it away quickly.

"You're right, Mi," I say. "Worst-case scenario, I go, and I hate it so much I can't wait to come home. Plus, I have to find out why Margot wanted me to go to France." This is the main reason. I have to see this all the way through. I wouldn't be able to live with myself if I didn't at least try to fulfill her dying wish.

Something blossoms in my chest the tiniest bit. Possibility. A sign. A teeny sense of magic. I smile.

"Well, *merde*, I guess I'm going to France," I tell Mia, and she bursts out laughing.

"*Oui*, Poppy." Mia says. "*Oui!*"

SIX

On Tuesday, I get to the airport four hours early because I am wracked with nerves. I'm on the plane, sitting in my window seat, tapping my fingers on the tray table.

As I try to calm down, I get a notification from my phone of a memory from this day last year. It's a screenshot quote from a rare print interview with author PJ Latisse, published one year ago today.

My love of thrillers and mysteries started with Goosebumps as a kid, then Agatha Christie, then Tana French. Then in my midtwenties, my obsession with PJ Latisse began. An author whose identity is just as much a mystery as her books. Nobody knows who PJ Latisse is. She simply publishes one book a year that shoots up the bestseller lists, hardly ever conducts interviews, then returns a year later to drop another incredible thriller. It's delicious. I love her.

I read the quote over and it hits me like a shock, goose bumps popping up on my arms. It's like I saved this quote for future me.

Be the main character of your life. If you do not actively curate the life that you want, you are relegated to the supporting role in everyone else's. If you are stuck, take a risk. If you are lost, start asking questions. If you don't know what to do, take the next bold move. Your life is happening now. Don't you dare waste it.

I sit back in my chair, reading the quote five times over, tears threatening to fall. When's the last time I felt like the main character in my own life? I have been Jackson's little sister. My mom's daughter. Not even my byline at Thought Buzz was mine.

The main character of my own life. What would *that* be like?

"Oh, this is me," a woman in her late sixties stops at the aisle seat next to mine and throws down a heap of flight accessories, a nylon bag, and a paperback book I can't see the title of. I am always nosy about what other people are reading, so I crane my neck to look, just as I make eye contact with the woman. Everything on her person is flowy—scarf and long cardigan and wide-legged pants—and her light blue eyes are offset by pale skin and curly, wild, gray-streaked hair. There are laugh lines on her face, and when we meet eyes, she smiles widely.

"Looks like we're going to France together," she says.

"Looks like it," I say, trying to match her enthusiasm. Well, at least I'm not next to a douchebag who will spread his legs during the whole flight and push me into a ball by the window.

"I'm Joan," the woman says, jutting out her hand.

"Poppy," I say, shaking it back. "Nice to meet you."

"Likewise," Joan says. She moves her possessions out of the way of her seat and starts arranging them in the netting below the tray table, stuffing everything in there, so it bulges out. "I always overpack." She shrugs.

"I think I *under*packed," I say. "I was so nervous that I blacked out. I only brought a book for the whole twelve-hour flight." I hold up the novel.

Joan looks at the cover and her eyes light up. She grabs her book out from under the blanket she brought.

"PJ!" She holds up her book and it's an earlier PJ novel, *The Dark Room.* One of PJ's most popular books.

"That's one of my absolute favorite books."

"Mine, too," Joan says, and finally sits down in her seat, our arms tightly next to each other, but comfortable. "My favorite author of all time, besides maybe Agatha."

"Yes, Agatha and PJ—both are unparalleled. The best mysteries ever," I say, feeling calmer already. I'm not normally a chatty person on planes, but if Joan wants to talk books, then I'm game. Plus, I could use a distraction right now. I'm on a flight to France. I don't think the reality of it has hit me yet. I didn't tell my family where exactly I was going, only that I was going out of town for a while. This is either the greatest thing I've ever done or an adventure that is going to end terribly.

"Did you hear that the one you're reading, *The October Flood,* will be PJ's last book ever?" Joan asks, her eyebrows creased with concern.

"I did hear that," I say, swiping my hand across the cover of the book. "But I don't want to believe it."

Joan laughs. "I don't either," she says, clutching her hand to her heart. "I guess I'll just have to start from the beginning and read them all through again if that's the case."

"Same." I smile widely.

The pilot comes on over the intercom, alerting us to get ready for takeoff. Seatbelts start snapping loudly and I grasp the armrests, my jaw clenched.

"Are you scared of flying?" Joan looks concerned. "You've gone a bit pale, hon."

"Just a bit," I say, taking a deep breath in. "Once we're in the air, I'll be fine."

"Give my hand a squeeze," Joan says. "I used to be a flight attendant. Nothing can scare me here. The sky feels like home."

I grab her hand and hold it all through the ascent to cruising altitude, feeling relaxed by her presence. Her hand is soft, and mine is clammy, but Joan doesn't seem to mind. Once the seatbelt sign dings off, I let go and look over at her.

"Thank you for that," I say, feeling a bit embarrassed.

"Not at all, honey," Joan says. "Thirty years of flying should be good for something." She gives a hearty, full-throated laugh. "So, Poppy, why are you off to France?"

"It's sort of a long story," I say, unsure of whether I want to spill everything to a stranger, but Joan's eyes are curious and welcoming.

"It's a long flight," Joan says, chuckling warmly, turning her body toward mine even more. "Once they start serving drinks, I'm ready for a glass of wine and a nice chat." She pats my arm. I don't know what she sees when looking at me, but maybe she can tell I need some kindness right now.

I tell Joan everything, from my first lunch with Margot all the way to receiving the black envelope on Sunday night. It feels good to say it all out loud, to someone other than Mia, who, by virtue of being my best friend, is obligated to support me.

I am not prepared for Joan's effusive reaction.

"Oh my god, this is so exciting," she cries out. "I thought you were going to say you were off for some study-abroad thing, but you're on a genuine hero's journey!"

"Huh," I say, feeling a fizzy sense of excitement.

"This sounds like the beginning of a movie," Joan says, clapping her hands together. "Or a novel!"

"I hadn't thought of it that way," I say. The sense of dread that had been sitting on my chest seems to lighten. "I've just been so nervous and anxious about it that I haven't really thought about what will happen when I actually get to France."

Joan nods. "What do you think she left you?"

"I have no idea, actually. I wish I had asked my aunt more questions when I saw her once a year, but she was always so focused on my life. We'd catch up on me, and then suddenly, the visit would be over."

"Sounds like an aunt to me," Joan says, giving that good-natured chuckle again. "Do you know anything about where you're going to stay?"

"Nothing," I say. "I'm supposed to just show up at the airport. The letter said arrangements have been made."

Joan stares at me, a long, lingering look. She narrows her eyes. It's a look that someone who knows you very well would give you when you've been missing the point entirely.

"Damn," Joan says with a hint of awe in her voice. "You're one brave cookie."

I laugh. "I don't feel very brave, to be honest."

Joan's mouth falls open. "You hadn't considered that jumping on a plane to France, without even knowing where you'll sleep tonight, is not a brave thing to do? Do you think just anyone would do that?"

"I, well… I guess not." I did have to move pretty fast to make this trip happen. I spent all of Monday looking for a subletter for my apartment since I couldn't break my lease early, and thankfully, a friend of a friend needed a place and I didn't have to rent it out to a stranger. I also made sure the subletter paid a bit extra per month to cover minimum payments on my credit cards, along with the utilities. I deferred my student loan payments yet again. And the rest of the time was spent packing and procuring one of those European outlet adapters, which was surprisingly difficult to find.

The money stress was the hardest part, and I almost talked myself out of going multiple times. The "responsible" thing to do would be to stay in LA, to get a good, stable job, and start paying off my debt. It makes me feel ashamed that at thirty-two, I'm still not in a better place financially. I feel like I should be further along at my age. But, looking back on the last forty-eight hours, it's astonishing I was able to pull everything together so quickly. Maybe I need to give myself a little more credit.

I shake off the way my face is burning from that money shame and focus back on Joan, who is so enthusiastic I can't help but be swept up in her words.

"Right now, your life sounds like the start of a grand adventure," Joan says. "I'm so excited for you."

"You know what, Joan?" I tip my chin up. "I'm starting to feel excited for me, too." Maybe this is a fresh start. Maybe I can let just a little bit of hope in. Maybe, right now, I can trust in Aunt Margot's good intentions for me.

"There we go," Joan says. "Although I will say, your story makes my trip sound a lot less exciting." She laughs loudly. "I'm just going on a wine tour with a bunch of other sixty-something singles. Maybe I'll buy a villa like *Under the Tuscan Sun*." Her eyebrows wiggle up and down.

"Just from knowing you this little bit, Joan, I wouldn't put it past you."

"No, honey, you shouldn't," she says. "I'm wild like that." She winks at me, and we both surrender to a fit of laughter, heads of passengers near us perking up to see what's the ruckus.

The flight attendant comes by with drinks and we both order two small bottles of the white wine. "Just ask for two, us flight attendants don't mind boozing you up during the flight," Joan says, with another cheeky wink. And as we both ride a mid-flight buzz, we discuss books, PJ Latisse, and the hottest European men according to Joan.

By the time we land in Paris, I feel tentatively bold. Just as Joan and I part ways to our separate connecting flights, she hugs me tightly.

"Don't forget to email me," Joan says into my ear, still holding me in a hug. "But if you don't, I'll assume you're having the most ridiculously fabulous time. And that you've fallen in love with some sexy man, and that you'll forever remember your old seatmate who thinks you're a brave cookie." I laugh deeply, and I'm reminded of what happens when you put yourself in situations where life can surprise you. I forgot what that felt like.

Joan pulls away from the hug, just as I hold back tears. Her kindness, her warmth—I will never forget her.

"Enjoy your wine tour," I tell her, through a croaky voice. "Send me a postcard from the villa you end up buying."

Joan laughs that big laugh again, and I can still hear it as I walk away, toward my connecting flight to Nice, toward adventure. A soft smile spreads on my face, thinking of what might await me.

SEVEN

The French Riviera

I'm sweating and disoriented by the time I get to customs, thrusting my forms and passport into the hands of a Frenchman. It's late morning in Nice, the two flights swallowing a full day.

"Bonjour," I rasp out in a small voice. The man says nothing, holds up my passport picture to my face, and nods.

He stamps a page with a loud clang, hands me my passport, and says, not unkindly, "Welcome to France," in a strong French accent. For some reason, this is what makes it all finally feel real. A jolt of excitement moves through me. I am in France. France!

I walk quickly to baggage claim, following closely behind a spritely group of retirees from England talking excitedly about the hotel they've booked right on the water in a place called Antibes. The English retirees and I get to Arrivals at the same time, and they disperse toward a sign with their group name on it. I turn in circles, searching for whatever or whomever I'm supposed to be looking for. Among the crowded groups of signs, I don't see my name. I shrug and walk over to the flight's baggage carousel while being harangued by ten different taxi drivers asking if I need a ride and promising the best rates. I ignore them.

It seems like I wait an eternity for my suitcases to show up. The long flight and the jet lag threaten to catch up to me. Once I finally see my two very large suitcases, I haul them off the belt in a rush of breath, grab a cart, and layer them on top.

My leather jacket starts to feel warm, so I take it off, leaving only a white T-shirt and black jeans with black Doc Martens. Feeling the hot air come in from the outside, I'm glad I packed an abundance of sundresses. I can't wait to peel off these jeans.

I turn around to face the arrivals again, wondering who I'm supposed to be waiting for. I stop suddenly. There's a man coming in through the doors from outside, and I hear myself take a sharp inhale, a ding of electricity moving up my spine. He's hot, sure, but it's something else. Something unplaceable. Like recognition. Like I'm a magnet being drawn to him.

He's about six feet, with messy brown hair that looks to be lightly curly, tendrils dropping over his forehead, a sharp jawline, and a lean but not overly muscular or built body. His skin is a perfect tanned olive. He's wearing a loose cream T-shirt and faded jeans—casual, in that sexy way clothes hang off tall men. One arm is a sleeve full of old school–style tattoos, all in black, and I can physically feel myself lick my lips. *Get a grip*, I tell myself. Except I can't. And my eyes will not move away from him.

Once inside the airport, he looks visibly agitated, darting his eyes back and forth. Probably looking for his beautiful French girlfriend. He's about thirty feet from me, and I can't stop watching him. All the activity of the bustling airport falls away.

We lock eyes and a shiver breaks out on my skin. Something is happening in my body that has not happened before—I feel a little weak-kneed and dizzy. He squints, looks down at his phone, nods, and then starts heading straight for me, a serious look on his face. I stiffen. I look left and right, start to panic a little.

He arrives in front of me quickly, close enough for me to see his green eyes flecked with gold. His features are at once soft and, somehow also sharp. He's so pretty. Androgynous almost. I shake my head to myself, and force my eyes to stop traveling down to his full lips.

"There you are," he says forcefully, in an unplaceable accent that is not quite English and not quite American, either. My stomach is in my throat. The roughness of his stubble makes my breath hitch. I notice his long fingers, a tattoo wrapped around his wrist. There's a spicy, citrusy smell drifting toward me.

I finally find my voice, after what was a too-long, awkward pause as I took my time cataloguing every detail of his face.

"I think you have the wrong person?" My voice goes a little high-pitched. I was tired before, but now I am alert. He's not looking at me directly. He just sighs heavily.

"No, I don't," he says, in a tone that is perhaps a bit too harsh to use on a stranger in an airport. "Aren't you Poppy Banks? Margot's niece?"

My eyes widen. I nod imperceptibly. This gorgeous and yet surly man is here…for me? He scans my face, and when our eyes finally meet, there's a noticeable electricity. I haven't taken an inhale in what feels like hours.

We hold that eye contact for one, two, three seconds longer and I watch him take a deep breath. It's a potent collection of seconds, a tense silence stretching between us. I don't know what to say or what to do, but I know for sure I've never felt this kind of pull toward a stranger before.

But then, quickly, his face contorts back to annoyance. He shakes his head, like he's trying to get his wits about him again, like he needs to steady himself.

Before I can say anything, he says, "Did you not know I was

coming to get you? I've been circling the airport for an hour waiting for you."

I wince. "You have? I'm sorry. All I got was my flight information and that the rest was taken care of. I didn't even know what to be looking for when I got here." I cross my arms in front of my chest. Not the warmest welcome I've ever had.

"Alright, well, let's go, then," he says. "Is this your luggage?" He eyes the tower of both of my large suitcases, along with my carry-on and backpack. "This is *a lot* of stuff." He starts pushing the cart and walking without me.

"Well, I'm here for six months," I say, feeling defensive when I finally reach him and my cart.

"Yeah, well, we'll see about *that*," he spits out. I balk.

"Who are you?" I ask, in a way that it sounds like both a question and an admonishment. He whips his head around to look at me, just as we get through the doors and into the oppressive humid heat of Nice. Immediately, I get a huge whiff of cigarette smoke as I look over to a group of six people huddled near an ashtray.

"I'm Oliver Hayes," my rude companion says. He begrudgingly sticks his hand out to shake mine. "Nice to meet you."

I grab his hand and shake it. "Oh yes, *such* a pleasure," I say. Oliver turns his head away from me and back to the cart, and I see a small, nearly imperceptible lift on the right corner of his mouth.

After a strained but short walk, we arrive in the parking lot and stop at a small red Clio hatchback that looks relatively new and recently washed. Upon opening the hatchback, a tiny, yet high-pitched bark escapes. And in the car, I see two figures, one human in the passenger seat and one adorably tiny dog in the backseat. A small fluff of a light brown Pomeranian is jumping up and down, barking every time it gets high enough to see over the seat. The other figure turns around, and I see it's an older man in his seventies with salt-and-pepper hair, a casual lavender linen suit over a crisp white shirt. His eyes are exceedingly kind as they land on mine.

"That's Sebastian in the front," Oliver says. "My uncle. And the dog is Beau."

"Hi, Poppy, it's an unbelievable pleasure to finally meet you," Sebastian says, in such a friendly way compared to Oliver's frosty demeanor that I breathe out an audible sigh of relief. Sebastian feels more like a Margot person already. "I knew your aunt very well, one of my favorite people in the world. She was my absolute best friend for most of my life." There's a strong hint of emotion in his geniality.

"It's so great to meet you too, Sebastian," I say, smiling widely, almost too wide as a point of contrast to my unsmiling in Oliver's direction. A little pettiness among new friends. "And you, too, Beau." Beau starts jumping up and down even more rapidly, spinning around on the seat, and yipping the air.

Oliver loads up my suitcases, which fit only just in the trunk, and I bring my carry-on and backpack into the back seat with me. Beau immediately sits on my lap and starts licking my hand. I giggle and pet him, already smitten.

"How was your flight?" Sebastian cranes around to talk to me. I sat on the left side of the car, so I wouldn't have to look at Oliver—or wouldn't be tempted to, at any rate.

"Not bad, I made a friend and we talked for most of the flight, so it went by quickly." I think of Joan. *You're one brave cookie.* I savor her words, take a deep breath in.

"That's good, but I bet you're exhausted. That's a long journey," Sebastian says. "And I bet you're wondering why your aunt has brought you here under such a veil of secrecy." He chuckles.

"It's the only thing I've been able think about for the last two days, so yeah, just a little curious what's going on here." I give him a wry grin.

"We have strict instructions from Margot, so nothing can

be revealed until we arrive," Sebastian says, doing a lock-and-key motion on his mouth.

"You can't even tell me where we're going?"

"Nope," Sebastian replies. "What fun would that be?"

"Fine," I say, sticking my lip out into a pout. Sebastian smiles and I find that I already like him quite a bit. Oliver has remained silent, focused on driving through the frantic streets of Nice, but I can feel his energy. He's not nearly as happy to be in a car with me as Sebastian is. I don't know why, but I suppose, at some point, I'll figure it out. For now, I'm too tired and woozy from the beginnings of jet lag to keep wondering.

"Don't mind Olly," Sebastian says, intuiting my thoughts and laying a hand on Oliver's shoulder. "He's an Aquarius. Takes a while to warm up. Aquarians. *Very* dramatic." Sebastian turns back to me. "I bet you're a Gemini."

"I *am* a Gemini!"

Oliver juts in and says, "By the way, Uncle Seb is the *only* person who's allowed to call me Olly." He's so serious I almost laugh out loud. Sebastian looks at me and he rolls his eyes in a mocking but playful manner. I stifle a giggle.

"See? So dramatic," Sebastian says, turning his face into a comical frown. "I'm a Libra, so nothing gets to me, and I get along with everyone." He shrugs and I can practically *hear* Oliver rolling his eyes.

Well, already this is an adventure.

The rest of the car ride passes in small talk between Sebastian and me, my face turned toward the window at the unbelievably picturesque drive from Nice to my unknown destination. Once we get off the highway, we take a long and curvy road through the middle of a mountain, towering rocks on one side and the wide expanse of the Mediterranean Sea on the other. Every once in a while, a small village pops up, with a quaint grocery store and ancient buildings set in terracotta, beige, and pastel green with white shutters.

It's like coasting through a movie set. I'm used to the beach in Los Angeles, but it's nothing like this. The water is always tinged with brown, for one, and the sky is normally a hazy blue from smog and pollution.

This place is like going from black-and-white to Technicolor.

I must have fallen asleep while zoning out on the scenery, because I'm shocked awake by Oliver and Sebastian. "We're here," they both say, one quiet, the other loud and excited. I open my eyes slowly, adjusting back to the sunlight.

When I finally see where we are, my jaw actually drops.

I stagger out of the car without speaking and stand before a large villa, painted light pastel pink with mint green shutters on the windows. The villa is surrounded by greenery, large looming trees of different varieties, mostly towering palms and wide oaks, providing a comfortable shade across the property. There's a long driveway, set away from other neighboring homes, and it smells like the brininess of the ocean. I walk toward what would be considered the back of the villa. I see a swimming pool with six yellow-and-white-striped lounge chairs overlooking a broad view of the water and sky, vibrant blue on vibrant aquamarine.

It's beyond stunning.

It's a dream.

A paradise.

I sway on my feet.

"What...is this place?" I finally ask Sebastian and Oliver, who have let me wander in silence while they've removed my luggage from the car and let Beau out.

They exchange a knowing look. And then Oliver gives a nod of okay to Sebastian who clears his throat.

"This was Margot's home," Sebastian says slowly.

I reel instantly.

"What?" I say, for lack of a better, more coherent reaction. This was Aunt Margot's...home? Back in Los Angeles, my family and I live modestly, middle class right down the road, save for Jackson's successes. My mom and Margot grew up just as humbly, so I can't imagine this villa being part of Margot's everyday life.

"How?" I say. "What? And how?" I take another full look around and it's unbelievable. "How could this be Margot's home?"

"It's a lot to take in," Sebastian says. "Let's go inside." He takes my arm softly and ushers me into the villa, which Oliver unlocks. Each of us carry a piece of my luggage and we drop it together in a heap. The inside is all warm colors with a big, white, worn-in linen couch in the expansive living room off the foyer.

We go through to the dining area, where there's a rough-edged wood table with cozy chairs, enough space for ten people, at least. The kitchen is relatively modern compared to the rest of the villa. It has a six-burner stove and a stainless-steel refrigerator, marble countertops with a large island in the middle, and a row of stools at the breakfast bar.

"This is incredible," I say, staring with wonder at every space we walk through. "This is just…unbelievable. This is every good adjective I can think of." I mean it, too. It's a dream house. It's stunning, like a villa you'd see in a movie and yearn to live in, to wake up in that kind of beauty.

I look out the kitchen window, to the greenery of the backyard, and the stretch of sea in the distance.

My breath hitches.

Margot lived here? I'm so shocked I momentarily forget that I'm here for a reason.

I whip around to Sebastian, who has a delighted smile on his face.

"Wait," I say. "What am I doing here?"

He gives me a crinkly smirk and says, "Well, that's where it gets interesting…"

EIGHT

Cap Ferrat, France

"Have a seat," Sebastian says, gesturing to a stool and smiling. "Let me make you a coffee and then I'll explain everything, kiddo." He grabs a Nespresso pod, pops it into an espresso maker, and the smell of coffee fills the kitchen. Somewhere in the villa, I hear Oliver taking my luggage upstairs.

Sebastian places a small glass cup in front of me along with a container of sugar that has the word *sucre* written on it. He stands on the other side of the island and puts a generous amount of sugar in his own espresso. Beau barks and Sebastian goes around the island, picks him up, and then perches him on the stool next to me.

"Here in France, we drink strong espresso with lots of sugar," he says cheerily, walking back to the other side of the island. I take the tiny metal spoon placed next to the cup and ladle in sugar, finally sitting back and perking my head up to give Sebastian my full attention.

"Ready?" he asks.

"Ready as I'll ever be," I say, my nerves ringing through me.

Sebastian pauses, and a small smile lifts the corner of his mouth.

"This villa is yours, if you want it," he says, speaking slowly as to convey the gravity of his words. "Margot left it to you."

I gasp. My eyes widen and then I gulp audibly. I go to speak, then close my mouth, then start to speak again, but I can't. I have no words. I blink. I put my palms on the kitchen island just to feel something solid.

Sebastian nods at me in a knowing way, letting my twenty different reactions play out as if I'm his entertainment for the day.

"She left it to…me? But, why?"

"She adored you, Poppy," Sebastian says, his eyes watering with emotion. "But there's a catch. Well, a few catches actually."

"Of course, there are. This felt too good to be true." I smile at Sebastian while taking a sip of my sweet and strong espresso.

"The first catch is that you have to stay here for six months before the deed is passed to you. This was nonnegotiable for Margot."

I nod, not quite understanding Margot's logic.

"Okay," I say, drawing out the word.

Sebastian nods, clearly taking some pleasure in watching this well-plotted scheme come to life. He continues, "And the other is—"

"—quite a big catch, if you ask me," Oliver says, entering the kitchen behind me and making me jump. "I don't know if she's up for it, Uncle Seb." He looks at Sebastian. Oliver goes over to the coffee machine, pops his own pod in, and the gurgling of water and the spit of the espresso hitting the cup is the only sound for a few tense beats.

"Excuse me, but shouldn't I be the judge of what I can or cannot handle?" I am pretty sure I won't be able to handle anything they're about to tell me, but I don't want Oliver to know that. "Just tell me, *Olly*." I offer a small, menacing smile.

Oliver narrows his eyes at me. "Don't call me that," he says, so stoically I try to stifle a laugh. "I'm serious."

But of course, Sebastian and I are both cracking up.

"Okay, okay, I'm done," I say, through one last laugh. Sebastian and I exchange a look and we both set our mouths in a straight, severe line. "I'm listening now."

Oliver sighs and rolls his eyes dramatically. My mouth threatens to break into a smile, but I tamp it down. Oliver watches me sternly to make sure I'm listening.

"Well, this isn't just a villa," Oliver finally says. "It's also one of the most competitive writing residencies in the world. Every year, there are two semesters, with four people, each who come here to write and finish a novel. It's called The Colony, and the application process is intense, and nobody knows where the residency is until they've been accepted. It's been this secretive since Margot started it ten years ago. Whoever goes through the residency can't divulge the details of it, so it's a precious resource for budding literary talent, all by Margot's design. Our residents are typically women, but we have had a few nonbinary folks come through, as well. Everything is paid for by the residency once someone is accepted." He gestures his arms up and around. "This, right here, is Margot's legacy."

"Wow," I say on an outtake of breath. My head is spinning. For years I sat with Margot at our lunches, and she never told me about this. Not a whisper of it. It doesn't make me feel angry—I just feel sad. I would have loved to know this part of Margot's life.

"Margot had a few stipulations," Sebastian says, continuing after giving me a moment to process. "Oliver knows the ins and outs of The Colony, so he can help run it with you. After six months, you can stay or you can sell the villa. But," he pauses, looks at me severely, "the only way you can sell it or keep it is if you finish a manuscript of a novel while you're here." He holds up his hands. "These are Margot's wacky rules, not mine. But she was *specific*."

Oliver stares at me, waiting for my response. I am speechless. I have so many questions, but I don't know where to start. *What the hell do I know about running a writer's residency? A manuscript?* I haven't written a book in years. And I'm done with writing. I *promised* myself I'd be done.

"I can't do this" are the only words that seem to come out. I could walk away right now. Panic pulses through me. I *should* walk away right now.

Oliver purses his lips and shakes his head.

"I told you this was a bad idea, Uncle Seb." Oliver looks over at Sebastian who is in thoughtful repose. "I don't know what Margot was thinking."

"Wait just a minute here," Sebastian says, in a tone more forceful than I'm expecting. "Give her a minute, Olly. She just got here."

"Except, as I told Margot, the fact that *this person* doesn't even know about the residency, or that Margot lived here, is everything we need to know."

He's doing that thing again, talking about me as if I'm not sitting right here. But I let him, because I am in shock and he's probably right; I can't do this. I can't believe this was Margot's life and that she's passing this all to me. The weight of that, along with my jet lag, hits me so suddenly. I feel like I could put my head in my hands and fall asleep right here at the breakfast bar.

I don't want to run some business I know nothing about, with a person who so obviously hates me. I don't want to write a book. I don't want to hope again. I don't want the responsibility that would come with owning this villa.

And more so, I don't think I deserve it.

"I..." I trail off. My voice sounds like it's beyond me, under water somewhere. "I need to lie down." I can't be upright any longer. The pressure is bearing down on me.

Oliver sighs again, another long, loud sigh that takes up all the space in the room. Sebastian shoots him a reproachful look.

Sebastian comes to my side and grabs my arm to lead me upstairs to what looks like the master bedroom. I find a large canopy bed, with white linen sheets and an array of fluffy pillows, that looks so inviting I crawl onto it with my shoes and clothes on.

"This was Margot's room—and it's yours now," Sebastian says. "Sleep well, kiddo." He closes the door and I let out a big exhale.

I'm bone-tired, and yet the moment my head hits the pillows, I'm wired. The kitchen felt suffocating with Oliver's sighs and rebukes. Maybe I can't do this, but did he have to be so quick jumping to that conclusion?

What am I even doing here?

How could Margot not have told me about all of this? I feel a deep sense of shame that I never asked her more questions, that I basically took her for granted. I loved our visits, but I also know that I lapped them up for myself, like she was the mom I never had. The mom that believes in me and cheers me on. It hits me now that our interactions must have been so one-sided, and yet here is Margot's gift to me—her legacy and home.

More than ever, I wish I could have just one more of our lunches, where I'd really press her for answers. Who are you, Margot? What do you do? What are you like? Can I come visit you? What is this creative life you've built without me, without your sister, without your nephews? What happened, really, between you and my mom?

And can we fix it all?

I can't deal with this reality right now. It's too much. I bet Margot expected me to be excited about this, but it feels like she's trying to insert her own will on my life when I was clear that I wanted to give up. That I wanted to do *anything* else. I can't tell if it's exhaustion or what, but my response is a surprising hot and bubbling anger alongside the sadness and regret. It feels irrational, but I don't want to do this. I don't want to deal with any of this. And then, just as quickly, a wave of fresh grief hits me. I wish she was here. The emotion is pummeling me now, and the jet lag is starting to take me under, and I let it, burrowing into the same comfortable bed my aunt must have slept in hundreds of times in her life.

It feels like being close to her is the last thought I have before I pass out.

NINE

Cap Ferrat, France

I wake up the next day groggy and disoriented, like I've been transported to a different world entirely, which is close enough to the truth. All night, I thrashed across the bed, in a sort of half sleep, running through everything Oliver and Sebastian told me. I have a *life* in Los Angeles. I can't just move to France and run a writer's residency. Where does the money come from? How would I pay off my student loans and credit card debt? This is madness. Do I even want to do this? How do I help people write their books if I haven't even been able to sell a book of my own? And in order to do anything with this place, I need to write a book? When I haven't been able to write in years? Potentially waste six months of my life with writer's block, empty-handed by the end of it?

What was Margot *thinking*?

I have the strongest urge to get to the nearest airport and pretend this whole trip never happened.

My eyes burn, thinking of all the conversations I'll never be able to have with Margot, all the questions she'll never be able to answer, all the things I missed out on. Oliver seems to

know her better than I did, and I can't help but feel a stinging
sense of jealousy toward him. He had more time with my aunt
than I did—and I'll never be able to undo that.

I groan. I run my tongue across my teeth and they're fuzzy.
I need to find my toothbrush and take a long hot shower.

After I do, I feel mildly human again, and a little more ratio-
nal. My suitcases are on the carpet near the window and I can't
bring myself to unpack them yet. I go to the large walk-in closet
and am assaulted by an array of Margot's possessions, tears form-
ing in my eyes. I finger my way across her colorful wardrobe of
soft and silky fabrics. On a shelf, there's a collection of jewelry,
notably a delicate gold necklace with a hummingbird on it, an *M*
engraved on the back. I unclasp it and fasten it around my neck,
holding the charm between my fingertips. It gives me strength
for a moment, wearing something of Margot's.

I pull down a loose and flowy cream button-down shirt-
dress from the rack above the jewelry and slip it on. It smells
like how I remember Margot smells—cherries and vanilla. I
pair the dress with my thick-soled Doc Marten Chelsea boots,
and for a moment, it feels like armor.

There's a knock at the bedroom door a few minutes later, and
when I open it, I see a young woman. She's wearing no makeup
save for cherry red lipstick. Her dirty blond hair is messy and
long, drawing out her angular face and prominent nose. She's
thin, and her casual clothes hang off her in just the right places.
She looks like a quintessential Frenchwoman, straight from the
pages of a how-to-be-effortless guide.

"Bonjour, Poppy?" She has a thick, charming French accent.
"*Je suis Caroline*. I am the villa caretaker, receptionist, assistant,
and chef." She laughs. "I do a lot here."

"It's nice to meet you," I say, holding my hand out.

She ignores my outstretched hand and comes in for a hug,
then air-kisses me on each cheek.

"Poppy, you are in France now. It's two air-kisses to say hello." She laughs. "*Mon dieu!* You look so much like Margot."

"Shit, I raided her closet. Is that okay?"

"Of course it is." Caroline's eyes are shiny, and she wipes at her cheek. "Sorry. We miss her—well, I miss her."

I grab her hand and look at her soft brown eyes. "I do, too."

We stand there in the doorway just like that, a moment of tenderness, and I feel Margot's presence everywhere. She is alive here, in this house, in the people who loved her.

"Are you settling in okay? Do you need anything?"

"I am. Just a little...overwhelmed by it all."

"I understand. *D'accord*, if you need anything, anything at all, you let me know." She places her hand on my shoulder, and I can feel her sincerity. The jet lag must be making me emotional, because my eyes pinprick with emotion again.

"Thank you so much," I finally say.

"It would be my pleasure," she says, then claps her hands. "Are you ready? Because you have some visitors here to see you."

"Visitors?" I scrunch my nose up. I haven't been here for twenty-four hours, and I already have...*visitors*?

Caroline smiles. "Yes, two very confident American guys. They say Margot arranged the meeting? Is this something you know of?"

"I have no idea," I say. "I'm in the dark here."

Caroline nods. "Margot was mysterious, but she never told me about arranging any meetings with Americans." She shrugs. "Come now, you'll have to see what they want."

I grab my phone and walk out with her, seeing the villa through fresher eyes. It's still astonishing. The bedrooms are upstairs, and I sneak a look in a few of them as I walk past toward the staircase. They are all furnished beautifully, with French linen sheets and ornate white wood side-table lamps. Each bedroom has a writing desk that looks out a window facing greenery and a slip of blue water. There couldn't be a better setting for a writing residency.

"The fall semester residents arrive tonight," Caroline says, as we descend the stairs. "We're going to have a welcome dinner for you and them here at the villa, so don't go too far today. You're here at the perfect time, because tonight is like an orientation. You can learn a lot about how the whole residency works." Caroline turns back toward me and gives me another smile. My stomach bubbles up with nerves. But I just nod and follow Caroline.

She gestures toward the backyard when we arrive at the dining area. "The Americans are in the back. Go on and I'll bring some coffee and croissants for you."

I walk out into a luscious late morning, the heat already rising up, the sun shining brightly, the colors so vibrant my eyes almost hurt to look at them. To my right, I see two conventionally good-looking men sitting at the long outdoor table next to each other, talking in whispers. They both look up when I approach. They have sharp jawlines, and the easy confidence of white men who know their place in the world—and don't question what they deserve or not. One of them has messy black hair and hazel eyes and the kind of body only hours at the gym can get you. The other has dirty blond hair and blue eyes, the look of a surfer wearing grown-up clothes. Both of them seem to be in their early thirties, maybe late twenties.

They stand to greet me and the one with black hair, who is quite tall, puts out his hand. "Hi, I'm Brent," he says, as we shake hands. "And this is Cody," he adds, nodding to the blond man. I shake Cody's hand. "We're the founders of a startup called Booksmart based in Venice, and we'd like to talk to you about a business opportunity, if that's okay?" They are both beaming, the very picture of smooth confidence.

"Uh, sure?" I say, feeling out of my element, just as Caroline arrives with a platter of pastries and a tray of coffees.

"*Et voilà,*" she says and sets everything down gingerly. "*Café crème, pain au chocolat, et croissant. Bon appetit.*" She squeezes my shoulder, then heads back inside. I catch Cody watching her leave, and when he notices me, he shakes his head awkwardly and clears his throat.

We're all quiet for a moment as we take a pastry and doctor up our coffees with sugar, the tinny sound of small metal spoons stirring. I take a hearty bite of my *pain au chocolat* and it's so buttery, so flaky, so delicately sweet that it melts in my mouth. It involuntarily elicits a little moan. Both Brent and Cody snap up to glance at me and I look down at my plate, embarrassed.

"Sorry, this is just so good," I say through a mouthful. Then, to break the tension I ask, "So, a business opportunity?"

Brent claps his hands together. "Yes! Let me tell you a little bit about us first," he says. "Like we said, we're the founders of Booksmart. Our mission is to totally disrupt the publishing game and become like Simon & Schuster meets Amazon. We publish and distribute books, without agents, without booksellers. So, basically self-publishing, but on crack." Brent smiles a satisfied smile.

Cody takes the conversational baton and dives in, "Yeah, so we're looking for incubators for literary talent and this is one of the most successful residencies out there. Over the past decade, you all have produced an impressive amount of bestselling authors. Plus, we really want to capitalize on this whole inclusivity trend. And where is it more inclusive than The Colony?"

I nod, as if I know this already, but he's telling me all new information. Clearly, I had no idea this place existed, never mind that it's wildly successful. I gulp, somehow more intimidated and daunted by it all than I was before.

But also, *this whole inclusivity trend*—are these guys for real?

Brent winds up now, as if they've practiced this pitch several times, which I'm sure they have. "A smart woman like you will recognize a great opportunity like this, so…" Brent says, laying the compliment on heavy with his flirty, breathy voice. "Our proposal to you, then, is we'd like to buy it from you," he adds, casually, as he takes a sip of his coffee.

"I'm sorry, but buy what from me?" I ask, feeling like I'm in a daze. Or a dream. Or maybe, a nightmare.

"Everything," Cody says, swooping his arms in the air. "We want to buy the villa, the rights to the residency, everything."

"And, get this," Brent says, his voice low, his eyes hooded. "We want to turn it into a literary 'spa.'" He mimics air quotes around the word *spa*. "Women would pay thousands to come here to this villa, write their book, be pampered. And we would make it worth your while if you sold it to us."

Cody jumps in, his voice excited now, too. "Margot was leaving so much money on the table, making this place scholarship-based." He shakes his head, like Margot was a foolish woman. I narrow my eyes at him, not loving him rebuking the person who built the very thing he wants to buy so fervently. He takes notice and course corrects.

"We see a lot of potential here, is what I mean. Plus, we had a few conversations with, uh, Margot about it and she seemed interested in selling, if that helps." Cody smiles affably. I'm not sure I trust these guys, but I can't say I'm against the idea of selling outright. Money would give me the freedom to stop worrying. I'd only have to stay here six months to wait it out.

And, shit, write a book. I forgot about that part. My stomach does a recoil. Just the thought of staring at another blank page for six months with all this pressure—it makes me want to run again. I quit writing for a reason.

The strings attached to this villa feel a lot like chains right about now.

"What's the offer?" I ask, my voice rough, uncertain.

"Seven hundred," Brent says coolly.

I choke. Seven hundred? Thousand?

Dollars?

"Wow," is all I can say.

That's change-my-whole-life money.

And suddenly, I'm very alert.

Because the problem is, I think about money a lot. It's like a weight on my shoulders constantly. I have over $75,000 of student loan debt. I have two credit cards that are perilously close to being maxed out and one that actually is maxed out. The amount I'm getting from the subletter at my apartment pays for the rent, and the minimums on my credit cards, but that's it. Writing clickbait did not pay well. But it was only supposed to be a stopover, temporary. Thought Buzz was a long detour that put me in debt while I thought it was an opportunity. Exposure and virality do not pay the bills, regardless of how enticing they are.

A windfall of money like this is so tantalizing to me that I nearly forget all reason. In six months, I could have money. *Real* money.

I can't make this decision right now, though. I would have to complete Margot's requirements before I could even inherit this place. Would it upset Margot if I sold? Would she want me to do whatever I felt was right for me? And, if so, what *is* right for me? I need to be able to think clearly, and my mind is a jumble of surprises and the fuzzy edges of jet lag.

There's a bit of a pause, not uncomfortable, but certainly a tight tension in the air. Both of them are looking at me expectantly, but I have no answers for them. I don't even have questions. I still feel disoriented, like my brain hasn't fully turned on for the day.

"I have to think about it," I say, finally. My voice is shaky, and my head is throbbing now. "And I'm not able to sell for at least six months anyway. It's Margot's stipulation."

"Hmm, okay," Brent says. "Well, whenever you have a decision, we can start making plans on our side and then when the six months are up, we'll make it official."

"But don't take too long to decide," Cody adds, a hint of sharpness in his otherwise genial tone. "We'd need the final answer by December fifteenth, but ideally before then. We'll make other plans, but this is our first choice. That's a hard date, too, because we have a launch plan with some other services that need to stagger with the spa."

"I can't make this big of a decision right now," I say.

"We get it," Brent says, throwing Cody a chastising look. "Let us know if you have any questions."

"Yeah, always here for questions," Cody says. "Well, we better head out." They both stand up. Cody hands me a card with the Booksmart logo on the front and his contact information on the back.

"Don't hesitate to call or email us for anything," Brent says, smiling.

They leave out the side door, and once I hear their steps on the gravel of the long driveway, I deeply exhale, which lasts only a half a second before Oliver bursts outside.

"What was *that* about?" He looks so angry I can see the tips of his ears going pink. "And yes, I overheard almost all of it."

"You were spying on me?"

"The kitchen window was open. It's not like I planned on listening in, but I'm glad I did," he says, crossing his arms over his chest. He walks toward me and closes the space between us. "You cannot sell this place. Especially not to *those* assholes."

I scoff. I've known this man a little over twenty-four hours, and he is already proving to be the most exasperating person I've ever met—and I used to work for Gareth Hartford for god's sake.

"I'm sorry, but is this your decision to make?" I ask, annoyance dripping off every syllable. I sit down at the outdoor table I was just at with Brent and Cody, dropping onto the chair with a thud.

Oliver sits across from me, and his expression softens. "Okay, sorry. I know I'm acting unhinged, but you have to understand something," he says, his voice cracking, an unexpected display of emotion that makes me sit up straight. "It was Margot's *dying* wish that you would fall in love with this place." His words are pleading, but it doesn't make sense. How could this be her dying wish if she never told me about it when she was...alive?

"But, Brent and Cody said they talked to Margot about selling and that she was interested."

"There's no possible way that's true." His lips are set, and his eyebrows are scrunched.

"How would *you* know?" I ask sharply. Oliver winces. My chest constricts knowing that he had enough of a relationship with Margot that he would be privy to her dying wishes, as well as her everyday thoughts.

"Because, I knew her," he says, voice strangled.

"Why would those guys say they talked to her if they didn't, then?"

"I don't know, but I am like 99 percent sure that Margot would never entertain selling this place, especially to two dudes who want to make money off of it," Oliver cries, shaking his head.

"I don't get it."

"The whole mission of this place is to provide a luxury workshop experience without it being exorbitantly expensive," Oliver explains, his eyes lighting up. "Margot was all about making things more equitable. She knew that if she charged thousands of dollars for people to come here, she would only get the most privileged into the residency. By making it completely free, she could accept people on talent alone, and it would make the playing field more equal. That was her philosophy. So having The Colony sold off to two guys who want to just make money off it, it would go against her wishes on a fundamental level."

I mull this over and Oliver lets me, not trying to fill the silence with anything but his low-key fidgeting.

"Where does the money come from, then?" I ask. "How could this whole thing be free for eight women per year? It doesn't make sense."

"Truthfully, I don't know," Oliver says, shrugging. "It's a mystery even to me. And believe me, I asked. Margot would always just tell me not to worry about it."

"It doesn't add up," I say, trying to look for an out. "Sebastian said after six months I could sell it. They offered a lot of money. Money I could *use*. And if Margot didn't want me to consider selling it, why would she give that as an option?" This whole thing is so cryptic.

The mood immediately changes, and Oliver's face clouds over. I lean back as if to distance myself from his wrath.

"You're considering their offer, then?" he asks, sneering, hardened. "Wow, Margot was wrong about you." It feels like I've been punched. I go on the defensive.

"And you would turn down that kind of money? *Please*."

"I would and I will." He scoffs derisively. "Not everything and everyone has a price."

"Well, it's not your decision to make, is it?" I feel petulant and…hurt. And confused.

He makes a whimpering sound that snaps my eyes to his. "Thanks for the reminder," he breathes out.

"Money or not, I have no idea how to do any of this!" I feel fire in my voice. "This is too much!"

"I'll help you," he says, low, nearly tender. "You don't have to do it all by yourself."

"No, you're right," I say, feeling defeated. "Margot *was* wrong about me. I'm not up to filling her shoes here."

Running a business in a foreign country is the last thing I need right now. This is exactly the kind of complication, the kind of ambitious undertaking that I'm trying to avoid. I'm supposed to be giving up. Settling. Making sure I never have to be vulnerable to disappointment, or failure, or rejection ever again. Whatever Margot was trying to do here, it's not going to work.

Oliver has the decency to look guilty. "I'm sorr—" he starts to say, but I cut him off.

"No, it's fine," I say, standing up.

I wave him off, and just as I'm going inside, he says, "Tonight is the welcome dinner, don't forget."

I nod wordlessly, go in the villa, walk silently past the kitchen, hoping not to run into Caroline—I can't face anyone right now.

I just need a moment to rest.

Like yesterday, I enter the bedroom, still darkened by heavy curtains, and I fall face-first onto the bed.

TEN

Cap Ferrat, France

Descending the stairs later after my nap, I take a deep breath, listening to the clattering of glasses and dishes, a jumble of voices, Beau's little paws on hardwood floors. I'm nervous to meet the new residents, apprehensive to see Oliver, and overall uncertain about what I'm even doing here.

I think of the fight I had with my mom and the fact that my family is probably still angry with me. It hits me that there's not much back in Los Angeles that's warm and welcoming, either. I've really made a mess of things on not just one, but two continents. *Great.*

Beau greets me excitedly at the bottom of the stairs and I pick him up, his warm body softening the edges of my nerves. I step into the large dining area with that beautiful rough-edged wood table. It's filled with buffet-style platters of food, from arugula salad to silky mashed potatoes, bookended by cut pieces of a fresh baguette. It all smells delectable. My stomach rumbles, reminding me it's been a while since I last ate. My mouth waters, but I go where the commotion is, which is in the backyard, white twinkling lights set out among the perimeter, a high quarter full moon resting just above the tree line.

Sebastian, Oliver, Caroline, and a group of women I assume are the new residents go silent when I walk into the night air, all their eyes on me. Sebastian steps forward and puts his arm around my shoulders, squeezing them tightly, ruffling the top of Beau's head who's still perched in my arms.

"It's my pleasure to introduce you all to Poppy Banks, Margot's niece," Sebastian says in a friendly, yet commanding voice. "Margot has passed the villa down to Poppy, and I think she's still a little shocked from finding that out just yesterday." Sebastian's eyes crinkle in the corners as he smiles.

I set Beau down gingerly and he pops off in Caroline's direction for a snuggle. I wave to everyone limply, not feeling at all the way I expect Margot would want me to feel. Did she want me to be excited about this inheritance? Ready to dive in? Whatever she wanted, I'm sure I'm not doing it and that I'm letting her down.

"Nice to meet you all," I say, in a small voice. They probably have no idea the uncertainty I feel, considering their eager smiles. I feel awful that instead of getting Margot for their residency, they just get sad, doubtful me.

"Let me introduce you to everyone and then we'll sit down to eat," Sebastian says and leads me to the women standing expectantly. I feel like a fraud, knowing I can't offer them everything they expected from Margot. I look around and notice Oliver has disappeared. Well, good riddance. I don't need his unkind judgment on top of my own.

The first woman I meet is in her early thirties, with dark skin, light brown eyes, and her natural hair pulled back by a colorful scarf. "This is Kerry Yates. She's working on a wonderful queer novel about two married women who reconnect and fall in love after being childhood best friends." Kerry smiles and we shake hands.

"So nice to meet you, Poppy," she says, and I smile back.

"Nice to meet you, too," I say. "That book sounds amazing. Can't wait to hear more about it."

"Thank you," Kerry says warmly. "Still outlining it, but I'm thrilled to be here. It's a dream come true."

"Yeah," I say, wishing I could match her enthusiasm.

Kerry smiles as Sebastian begins introducing me to the three other people.

I meet Jasmyn George, a twenty-seven-year-old light-skinned curvy Black woman who is writing a romantic comedy with the same vibe as the show *Insecure*. She's a social media phenomenon, with vignettes of her writing amassing thousands of likes each. "I'm pretty sure I've both read and shared many of your posts on Instagram," I tell her.

She smiles confidently and nods, and I make a mental note to learn how to accept a compliment like her.

Then I'm introduced to Evie Lake, a white woman in her midforties who is newly divorced and newly motivated to write her first novel, about a woman who gets divorced and sets off on a European sojourn to meet as many lovers as she pleases. "Is this autobiographical, Evie?" I ask her, grinning.

The last woman I meet is Janelle Raye who is the long-standing facilitator of the residency. She hugs me warmly and says in my ear in a soft whisper, "You look *just* like Margot when I met her, thirty or so years ago. She'd be so happy to see you here." When I pull away from the hug, her eyes are misty. "At dinner, I'm going to explain how this all works to you and the residents." I feel instantly relieved that someone is here to facilitate this, and it isn't all going to fall on me.

"Wait, I'm here," a woman with long, swishy blond hair in an impeccable outfit of tailored cream pants paired with a deep blue tank top, comes out from the kitchen. "I got caught up talking to Oliver, sorry."

She walks over to me and holds out her hand. "I'm Stella

Clarke. It's so nice to meet you." I shake her hand and look into her almond-shaped hazel eyes and stunning face. She looks like she stepped off the pages of a fashion magazine.

I hate that I do, but I deflate instantly.

There are certain women who seem to effortlessly embody what a woman is "supposed" to be. Lithe, elegant limbs. Shiny, long, perfectly tousled hair. Charming, but not overbearing or loud. Polite, soft voice. Coy, sexy, but not overt. Thin. Always thin.

And you start to feel like if you don't fit that ideal—if you age out of it or if your body puts you on the fringe of it, or your face does not have the exact symmetry—then you'll never have the exact life you want. And then you start to accept less, because you can't become *the ideal*.

Stella belongs here. In this beautiful place, atop a throne overlooking the Mediterranean. I'm not the sort of woman that gets to have this. I am too much, too doubtful, too eager, too big.

I don't fit.

And maybe that's the heart of it.

It's a familiar thought pattern that I've had a hundred times before. Living in LA does that to you. And all of this bubbles up in my mind before I've even shaken her hand.

This is the kind of woman I would never be—effortless and stunning. Stella would never have to settle or give up on her dreams. The world unfurls easily for a woman like her. *I got caught up talking to Oliver.* Of course, this is who Oliver would be interested in, too.

I stick out my hand as my stomach lurches. "Nice to meet you," I say.

Her hand is soft, elegant, and long in mine. It sits atop my palm delicately.

"You, too," she says so kindly I feel bad for being envious

of her. "Wait, you're not related to Jackson Banks, are you?" Stella's eyes widen. "*The* Jackson Banks?"

I blush with frustration. I can't go anywhere without being reminded of *the* Jackson Banks.

"Jackson's my older brother," I say, in a low, bitter voice, and the residents start tittering with activity. Of course they know who Jackson is—he's a literary darling and success story. Any aspiring novelist would kill for his career.

"No way!" Stella claps her hands over her mouth. "That's so amazing. He's major writer goals."

The rest of the women nod, matching Stella's excitement, their whispered voices a chorus over this salacious piece of news. Thankfully, Janelle calls us all to attention at the door and tells us to come inside so she can begin the orientation.

Sebastian, to my right, jumps in and says first, "This is our final resident for the semester—Stella. She writes romance."

"Not just romance," Stella says, jutting in. "Erotic, sex-positive, LGBTQ+ friendly romance. I've written novellas, but this is my first full-length novel." She smiles proudly.

"Yes, only residents who haven't yet published a book traditionally are eligible for a spot at The Colony. Margot wanted only first-time authors, no matter their age, to get their leg up." Sebastian smiles fondly. "She believed all good art just needed space and time to breathe, which is how she started this residency. It's a magical place. You'll see."

Sebastian puts his arm around my shoulders again and gives them full squeeze. I feel yet another wave of guilt that I'm fighting this so much. The more I learn about this place, the more special it seems.

Once inside, I grab a plate and put some food on it, then find an open chair just as Janelle starts to speak.

"Welcome to The Colony," she begins, her voice a calm yet commanding presence. "I'm so happy you're all here. The structure of this residency is relatively loose, because what we all want is for you to get as much writing done as you can, without distractions. There's a reason we're up here, at the top of a bluff, in a beautiful villa where food, accommodation, and scenery are all taken care of for you. Margot deeply believed that without the distraction of obligation and the external pressure to be domestic, women would be able to contribute so much more to this world in the form of art, and especially with the craft of writing." Janelle is at the head of the table, standing up, while the rest of us are sitting, listening attentively, and nibbling on the delicious food.

"So, how that works is, you have two writing blocks each day. One in the morning, and one in the late afternoon. We fully expect you to utilize those blocks either in your room or anywhere else you want in the villa. Do not overwork, though. Take a siesta. Take a long lunch. Go for a walk on the beach, or a swim. Drink a glass or two of wine. Enjoy yourself. Then come back to write for another few hours, ending the day around six, in time for dinner. Meals will be prepared here, but you can go out, too, on your own dime, of course. This is the Monday through Thursday schedule.

"On Fridays, we workshop together. You can bring pages, your outline, an idea you're stuck on, and all of us will help you. You may not know, but I have written twenty novels myself, with a few of them adapted to movies. I haven't met a plot I couldn't solve. Utilize that. Don't keep all your ideas to yourself. We're here to help you. And you're here to help each other. You should have a finished novel manuscript by the end of your stay here, like all of our residents have in the past."

Janelle stops and takes a long, drawn-out drink of her red wine. My heart starts beating nervously. This sounds like a dream, as if I've walked directly into the best-case scenario for myself. But…a swell of anxiety is piercing through me, too. What if, even with perfect circumstances like this, I can't write? And also, do I even deserve to be here? All of these women earned their spot at The Colony, and it makes me feel like an imposter who snuck in.

"Relaxation is not optional here," Janelle says, continuing her speech. "You must go out into the world and find inspiration. Swimming in the ocean, for example, is as important as writing when you're working on a novel. Having idle time to think through plot points, and to give your brain a break, is vital. Do not overdo it. That's not a suggestion. It's a Margot Rule. This residency is about the infusion of both work and play, about writing, but also the enjoyment of life, which is the whole point. Your life's work is not just to be a successful, stressed-out author, but to know how to *enjoy* life and success. That's a Margot tenet through and through. There was nobody who could enjoy life more than Margot. That was one of her many gifts."

All of us sit in silence, processing this. It's a weighted soliloquy, given with Janelle's exuberance, but still, it's a way of writing and living that I've never really considered. All I've ever known is stressed-out, panicked writing. A sharp, stinging sense of grief stabs at me, thinking of all the Margot wisdom I won't ever get from her directly again.

"Lastly, to be the kind of writers I know you are capable of, here's the secret Margot always shared with residents: you must believe you have something worth saying," Janelle says with reverence in her tone. "Creating art is a meditation on self-belief. Do you feel worthy to be seen? To be heard? The task of writing is incredibly daunting if you do not."

My throat clenches. She's addressing everyone, but it feels like she's speaking to me directly. Do I believe I have anything worth saying? I used to, but as of late…

I suddenly notice that Janelle *is* speaking to me directly and I've been zoning out. I look up at her and she repeats herself.

"Poppy, you're a writer, too, right?"

"Well, yes and no," I say. "I used to be. Or I guess I still am.

Can you be a writer if you haven't written much in years?" I laugh, feeling uncomfortable.

"If not, then I can't call myself a writer either," Kerry, who is sitting across from me, says. "This will be my first book. But before that, I didn't write for almost a decade."

I smile at her. "I used to write listicles and clickbait for Thought Buzz, but in a past life, I wanted to be an author. To write twisty, dark thrillers." I shrug. "But I haven't written anything in a long time, so I feel like a fraud calling myself a 'writer.' Jackson is the real writer in the family now, I guess." I feel myself deflate under everyone's gaze, that familiar sense of shame trickling up and down my spine.

"Nonsense," Evie says, through a mouthful of bread. "Maybe this is perfect timing for you, then. Write your book here, either with us or on your own. I'm forty-six and I thought it was too late for me, but here I am." She smiles and reaches for her glass of white wine, condensation dripping onto her plate from the humidity.

"Seriously," Jasmyn says, cutting in. "Who here hasn't been in the trenches of self-doubt when it comes to our own writing? And who here still wants to do the damn thing even though it's difficult as hell?"

All the residents and Janelle put their hands up, smiling at me. I can't help but feel a sense of relief that I'm not the only one who has found writing to be daunting and terrifying.

"Exactly right," Janelle says. "And there's no time to begin like now." She gives me an encouraging smile. I look down at my plate, warmed by this entire interaction. When I look up, I find Oliver's eyes on me from across the table, his eyebrows stitched together. I catch his gaze and my breath hitches.

His eyes search over me, and I feel like we're both in a trance, the noise of the bustling table is but a faint whisper in the background. We hold eye contact for five, six, seven drawn-out seconds, until he shifts his head away, shaking me off the same way he did at the airport. I watch him pick up a conversation with Stella who's at his right, her hand on his forearm, head tipped back in laughter. I shake him off, too, and the noise around the table rushes back in.

Janelle sits down and eats a plate of food, the orientation part of the evening over. The rest of the dinner passes in a blur of conversation, swapping "war" stories with the residents about paralyzing writer's block, talking about our favorite authors and what our dreams are for our future books. It's so lovely to be surrounded by ambitious, creative women.

I can already tell this place is something unique. A sanctuary. A refuge. And I can feel the heaviness I've been carrying around for a long time start to loosen, just a little bit.

Hours later, we all finally retreat to our rooms, full and tipsy from the many bottles of excellent French wine we cracked open.

I sit down at the armchair by the window. I look out into the backyard, the string lights still twinkling. Could I write here? Could this work out? Maybe this is exactly what I need. I suddenly feel the tiniest bloom of possibility open before me.

ELEVEN

Cap Ferrat, France

The next afternoon, I'm in my room thinking about the night before, all the precious Margot wisdom that Janelle dispensed, and the way The Colony works. I finally have a day to slow down and process it all.

Last night, Janelle said, *there was nobody who could enjoy life more than Margot.* I remember my mom saying something like that once, too, on a rare moment when she talked about Margot, except she said it like an insult. "Nobody *enjoyed* life more than my sister," she spit out, like it was poison. "When I was overwhelmed with responsibility, she was out gallivanting, doing god knows what."

My mom was so angry that day. I was in my early twenties, still trying to write. My mom and I were having another one of our battles, where I mistakenly asked her for some advice about what I should do next. I was working a temp job at a talent agency in Century City.

"I want to enjoy my life," I had told my mom, when she kept suggesting I just get whatever job paid the most and that offered the best benefits.

"You sound just like my sister," she had said spitefully. I remember being shocked because she never talked about Margot. My first lunch with my aunt had been the year before.

"What's wrong with wanting to go after your dreams and not settle?" I had asked my mom, who sighed at me.

"So, you think I've settled for my life?" she countered, suddenly defensive.

"Mom, I don't think that." She waved me off.

"Margot was the one that got to be the *dreamer*. But I grew up. And that woman judged me my entire life because of it." My mom was fuming, and I was confused, because the Margot I had met for lunch was nothing like the person my mom was describing. I couldn't reconcile the two of them together.

"Maybe she wasn't judging you," I said, thinking this was neutral territory, but my mom just narrowed her eyes at me and gave me a haunting look. I shivered.

"Oh, she judged me," she said sounding exhausted by it all. "Judged me for being realistic. 'Why aren't you painting, June?' she'd ask me. You know we grew up with a single mom. Never knew our dad. And when Mom died, I was eighteen and had to grow up fast. Margot didn't do the same. She went wild. Sixteen years old and no care for responsibilities. And she was always critical of me. Like I never did anything right for *Margot*."

"Why did you stop painting though, Mom?" I asked carefully.

"Because, painting wasn't going to put food on the table, Poppy! I had no time for childish hobbies like doing art. I was on my own! I was living in the real world and Margot was living in a fantasy." She crossed her arms and set her mouth in a straight line. "That's enough, Poppy," she finally said when I couldn't think of a response that wasn't going to offend or sound naïve.

I thought of the Margot I learned so much about last night at the welcome dinner and how she was a devoted champion of women. I didn't know which version was the real one. The one my mom may have invented in her defensiveness, or the one I'm learning more about here. Maybe both, somehow.

I finally have Wi-Fi on my phone, so once it hits 4:00 p.m. here in France, I FaceTime Mia when I know she'll be at home getting ready to leave for work.

I breathe out a sigh of relief when I see her face.

"Bonjour!" Mia butchers the word, but it makes me laugh. "Tell me everything."

"Okay, first, how are you?"

"Oh, fine, you know me. Jordan is chaos and work is busy, but I'm not in France, so who cares how I am?" Mia grins and props the phone up in her kitchen as she starts putting away dishes from breakfast. "Now, spill."

"The short version is that Margot has left me a whole villa, which is also a secret yet wildly popular writer's residency that I can inherit if I write a novel and stay here for six months. And also, there's a guy here, Oliver, who basically already hates me." I sigh and throw myself down on the bed, propping my phone up on a pillow. "It's a lot."

"Got it, okay, processing. A villa. A writer's residency. Novel. Lots of questions, but tabling them because answer me this: how hot is this Oliver guy?" She purses her lips at me while stifling a smile. "Because, even across continents, I can see you blushing talking about him."

"I am not!" My voice is so loud it echoes in the bedroom.

"Oh, listen to you protesting," Mia says, a glint in her eye. "He must be *delicious*."

"I'm sorry, but you're failing the Bechdel test here. I just told you I'm inheriting a villa in the south of France, and all you want to talk about is some hot guy?"

Mia narrows her eyes and says, "So, you admit he's hot?" She gives out a roaring laugh, and I shake my head, waiting for her to finish.

Once Mia's laughter winds down, I look at her with a dramatically serious face and say, "Yes, he's hot. Happy now? Are you done?" I smile. "Because villa? Residency? Hello?"

"Yes, yes, I'm done," Mia says, making her face go blank. "Very serious now." I shake my head again and Mia continues, "Wait, is there some kind of problem?"

"Yes," I say. "Obviously."

"What it is?" Mia says, not unkindly. "All you've ever wanted is space and time to write your book, and here you have it, in the form of an actual French villa. You can literally just be there and write. A free writing vacation."

She's not wrong, but it *feels* so much more complicated than that. But, actually—is it?

"It isn't just a villa to write," I say, more to myself than to Mia. "It's a whole lot of responsibility. Plus, I have a life in LA. I have no money and a ton of debt. What will my mom think? I'm supposed to be settling down and getting a normal job, not pursuing some foolish writing dream, remember?"

"But this is a once-in-a-lifetime opportunity," Mia says calmly. "It sounds like you're self-sabotaging a bit. Do you have to decide right now if you want to take it all on?"

I shake my head.

"No, I have to stay here six months to officially inherit the villa. And then after that, I'll have to decide what to do with it. But in order to inherit the villa, I have to write a novel. Can you believe she made that a requirement?"

"I absolutely believe Margot would make that a requirement," Mia says, chuckling. "Take the six months. Enjoy France. Write your book. And then decide when you have to decide." Mia shrugs.

"That sounds suspiciously easy," I say, noticing a nervous and excited fluttering in my stomach.

"And that's...scary?"

"Yeah, because things tend to not work out for me, Mi," I

say. "And I don't want to let down all the people depending on the writing residency. I could sell the villa." I tell Mia about the Booksmart guys and what they've offered me.

"That's a super tempting offer, Pop, but don't make any big decisions yet," Mia says. "How about this? Okay, it's August now. Six months from now will be February. These tech bros need your answer by mid-December, right? If you have nothing to show for your time, and you hate it there, then on December fifteenth, you can totally and completely give up without regrets. Sell the villa or don't. Do whatever with your life. But until then, write your book. And if nothing happens, if it all goes to shit, then you come back, you get some boring job doing boring things, and you never write a single word again. Or you write anything and stay there until February just to get the deed. Margot never said the book had to be good, right? Just done? So why not complete a manuscript, even if it's the worst story ever, then you can sell that place for a ton of money, pay off your debt, go travel and…never write a single word again."

I stare at Mia. Her arms are crossed, and I see a slight smile playing on her lips. She might not be totally serious, but I am. That's the deal. I'll wait it out until December fifteenth. I set the date in my mind. This is going to be my *last* risky move. When it eventually goes to hell like everything else has in the past—when the rejections pile up, and the disappointments start overwhelming me—I have full permission to give it all up.

December fifteenth, I say to myself, fingering it like a precious talisman. I feel a sense of steadying calm, now that I have a plan. Like the air is hissing out of a very tight balloon—release.

"Deal," I say, looking at Mia directly with a curt nod.

There's a knock at my bedroom door, and I hear Oliver's voice asking if he can come in. Mia's face freezes and she mouths, "That's Oliver?" I nod at her, and tell him to come in. I put Mia on the bed, not quite ready to disconnect.

"Yes, Oliver?"

"Sebastian wanted me to check on you," he says. He's in a mood I can't interpret. Sort of sullen, but I'm not sure if it's directed at me. There's a tenseness between us that makes me feel nervous. "Are you good?" His eyes search me, and his voice drops an octave.

"Yeah, I'm good," I say, my voice cracking.

"Do you need anything?"

I shake my head and say, "Nope, I'm okay. Thank you." The whole room feels charged, intense. I am suddenly extremely aware that we are in my bedroom, that a bed is right next to us; that despite his sour attitude toward me and his outright disappointment in everything I've done thus far, I still look at his lips and sway a bit on my feet. He gives a small, sideways smile, and I catch it just before he can take it away. It makes my heart pound, that little smile. I've been here in France only a couple days and already the landscape of my relationship with Oliver is complex.

"Well, I also wanted to say sorry," he says, putting his hands in his pockets and fidgeting. "Anything you need or want to know about The Colony, just ask." He stops for a beat, considering something. "Have you thought about if you want to keep it or not?"

All the sexual tension drains from me, and I just feel white-hot anger. "I've only had a day to think about it!" I feel like I'm boiling over. "Why can't you just give me a second to process all of this?" All the softness has left me.

He looks stunned for a second, but then puffs his chest up. "Because I guess my feeling is that if you don't immediately want this place, then maybe it shouldn't be yours to have."

"And whose should it be?" I ask, combatively. "*Yours*?"

Oliver's weight shifts and he looks uncomfortable. I don't let him answer.

"So, is that it, then? You want to take this place over and the quicker you get me out of the way, the quicker you can do that, huh?" I feel like I'm spinning out of control, but I can't stop myself. My anger is like a third presence in the room.

"No… I, uh…" Oliver hesitates.

"I don't know what your deal is, Oliver, but I need more than a couple jet-lagged days to decide if I'm going to totally uproot my life and take on something huge and unexpected like this. What I *have* decided is that I'm going to stay here for the next six months, so you'll just have to put up with me for that long," I clap back, letting the words seethe out of me.

"The Poppy I expected to come here, the Poppy that Margot told me all about, would have never taken this long to decide," Oliver says, in a tone that is both sad and rebuking. "She wouldn't even think to sell this place because of what it meant to Margot. She would have said yes to this offer without even considering it." My eyes widen. My cheeks flush. Margot told Oliver about me? "Have a good evening," he adds. He turns on his heel before I can respond and closes the door.

I pick up the phone to find Mia still on FaceTime, her mouth in an O shape. I feel tears prickle at my eyes.

"I gotta go, Mi," I say, my voice a whisper.

"Are you okay, Pop? That was—"

"I'm fine, Mia. December fifteenth and then I can give up?"

She nods slowly, like she wants to say more, but I don't let her.

"December," I say, like a prayer. "Love you, Mi. Talk to you later."

We hang up, and I take a deep breath in, willing myself to not cry. I will not let Oliver get to me. I shove all my feelings aside. I reflect on what Mia said, before Oliver interrupted our conversation. She's right. I need to take advantage of this opportunity. This is all I've ever said I wanted—time and space to write. Not just a one-hour window carved into a hectic day with money anxiety pounding through me. If I can't write under these circumstances, then I guess that will be my answer. Then I'll know for sure that writing is not for me.

This is a potentially *good* situation, great even, and somehow, I need to shift my perspective to see it that way, to remember that sense of possibility I felt last night. How quickly those moments of self-belief pass.

But I can do this. At least until December fifteenth. And then I am free to take the escape hatch.

TWELVE

Cap Ferrat, France

It's late morning and I'm out in the backyard with a coffee, willing myself to write ideas in my notebook, but staring at a blank page. I'm listening to the residents typing away furtively at the dining room table, trying not to look in their direction or think too much about the book I'm still not writing.

I woke up this morning plagued about my fight with Oliver yesterday, and all the doubts descended on me in a panic. My fear is so potent, it feels like an entity that follows me around.

You just sit down and write, Poppy. It's not that hard. The chastisement I've been carrying around with me for years rings through me. My jaw is clenched, my brow intensely scrunched, when Sebastian and Beau approach. Beau jumps on my lap and starts licking my hand, and I am warmed by it for a moment.

"Beau demanded we come see you," Sebastian says, the crinkle around his eyes even more pronounced in the morning sun.

"I'm glad," I say, my voice clearly emotional. Sebastian cocks his head at me.

"A little overwhelmed?" he asks kindly, and I admire that his intuition is so tuned-in.

"Just a bit." I give a small, tight laugh.

"I think you need to see some of the magic of this place," he says. "Come on, kiddo, let's go for a little drive." He angles his head toward the water. "You haven't even seen the beach yet."

All I want to do is wallow and overthink, but I know that's not good for me.

"Okay," I say. "Some fresh air wouldn't hurt."

"There we go," he says, smiling. "Let's hit the road."

After a short drive down winding mountain roads, Sebastian parks on the street of a residential area. The little village at the bottom of the road has squat, light beige buildings with vibrant pink bougainvillea snaking its way up the exterior, and tiny streets for tiny cars that zip around with ease. There is no other word to describe it except: stunning. Utterly stunning.

We walk toward the water and away from the village at a slow, wandering pace. I crane my neck back to see where Margot's villa might be, tucked away in the face of a looming mountain that overlooks the water. Terracotta, mint green, light pink, the villas appear as though they've been stuck inside crevasses in the mountain and create a stunning and colorful view. I turn my head back and my eyes meet the Mediterranean. I squint. The aquamarine of the water is so beautiful my heart aches just to look at it.

There's a train track before the beach, so we walk through an underground tunnel, and I hear the train rumbling above us. Over the noise, Sebastian says, "You can take this train from here to Monaco and all the way to Ventimiglia in Italy within just an hour. And if you go the other direction, you can get to Marseilles in four hours. The most beautiful train ride you'll ever take in your life." Sebastian continues, walking beside me, along with Beau on a black leash, "It's paradise down here in the south."

I just nod in agreement, rendered wordless by awe.

When we emerge from the tunnel, we are greeted by the beach.

We take off our sandals and hold them in our hands, and start walking on the velvety, warm sand. The beach is filled with sunbathers, shaded by colorful umbrellas, outstretched on beach towels. There are even more people in the waveless, calm water.

"I wish I had brought my swimsuit now," I tell Sebastian, who nods knowingly.

"You'll have plenty of time for that," he says. "It's the clearest, warmest water."

Beau continues to trot between us, seemingly content to be on the plush sand.

"I feel like I've been transported to a different world."

"You basically have," he says. "Most Americans go to Paris but don't come here as often. It's a shame. This is the jewel of France in my opinion. Paris is nice, but it's not *this*." He gestures toward the water, and I can't help but agree.

We pass by a beach club with people on lounge beds shaded by blue-and-white-striped umbrellas, servers with bottles of rosé perched on trays, and a restaurant with plastic chairs stuck directly in the sand. The air smells of grilled fish and garlic and the brininess of the ocean. It's so achingly charming and picturesque.

We clear the beach club and are back at open sand, water lapping at our feet now. The water is temperate and transparent enough I can see my toes through it.

Our walk is an easy silence punctuated by small conversation, but I suddenly let slip, "I feel over my head here, Sebastian. There's still so much I don't understand. I don't want to disappoint any of you, but I honestly don't know what to do." I lower my head. I may be able to write a book here, but it seems impossible to me that I'd keep the villa or The Colony. The money is so tempting. But would selling it actually disappoint Margot? I honestly don't know what she was thinking, giving me this impossible task, without talking to me about it beforehand.

Sebastian stops walking and faces me.

"Let's sit," he says. "I want to tell you a few things." We find a small patch of sand and settle ourselves in, Beau insistent on being right between us. This dog is a treasure. I lay my hand on the top of his head and pet him, his head lolling in pleasure.

"Margot and I met many years ago on her first visit here and we immediately became friends," Sebastian says, his eyes toward the horizon. "It was a long and enduring friendship that I cherish. I helped her set up the residency. I watched her relationship with your mother deteriorate, and she was so upset. It gutted her." My heart seizes, thinking of what was lost between them, and what will remain lost.

"My brother and his wife died in a freak house fire when Olly was only twelve and he came here to live with me. Poor Oliver was at a sleepover when the fire happened. His whole life, his home, his parents, gone, just like—" he snaps his fingers "—that." Sebastian takes a deep breath in, continuing, "It felt like Margot and I raised him together. Nothing was ever romantic between Margot and me, but we were a partnership in many ways. And Olly and Margot? They were thick as thieves. I don't think Olly would have recovered or become the person he is now without Margot. She brought him back to life." Sebastian's eyes are shining now, and I reach my hand over to touch his arm. I know how much effort it's taking for him to talk about Margot, with her death so fresh. I feel honored that I get to witness the enduring and unconventional relationship they had.

"Margot was like a mother to Olly, is what I'm trying to say." He pats Beau on the head, eyes still cast out toward the water. "He loves The Colony. He's been here since the beginning. I think there was a part of him that thought she was going to leave the villa to him."

Suddenly it all makes sense. All of Oliver's impatience and frustration with me. I take a deep, unsteady breath.

"Margot *should* have left it to him," I say, my voice hardly audible over the sound of children's laughter in the distance. From his perspective, I've come in out of nowhere and have been offered the very thing he may have wanted, and I don't seem appreciative at all. I don't know how to tell him that it's not because I'm ungrateful. It's because I agree with him: I don't think I deserve it and can live up to Margot's idea of me, either.

"No, she shouldn't have," Sebastian says, resolutely. He turns toward me and looks me directly in the eye, Beau shifting into my lap to give him space. "You should have seen Margot when she got back from seeing you for the first time. You may think those annual visits weren't much compared with all the time Oliver got, but you're wrong. They were just as special to Margot, and she thought you were the most amazing human being. She saw herself in you and thought that you may want to follow in her footsteps. That you'd be able to carry her legacy on. She told me every detail of your lunches, regaled us both with your brilliance." Sebastian starts crying, and he pulls a handkerchief from his pocket to dab at his eyes.

"I...didn't know any of that."

"Margot saw something in you, and I do, too," Sebastian says after a long pause. "But, if I can be candid with you?"

I feel queasy, but I nod.

"I think you're being stubborn. You think you don't deserve this, and you think maybe you can't follow through, but all Margot wanted was for you to try. That's it. Not be perfect at it right away. But to *try*."

I feel tears tingling in my eyes, a sour taste in the back of my throat.

I nod. "Along the way, I've lost faith in myself." He puts a gentle hand on my shoulder blade.

"Don't be unkind to yourself, kiddo," he says. "Life is hard enough without you being an asshole to yourself on top of it. Margot believed in fresh starts. She told me that you weren't writing. She told me about your last lunch. She said you needed a direction, that all your talent turned against you. She didn't want you to give up on yourself. She never gave up on you, Poppy."

Tears start streaming down my cheeks.

"I didn't know I needed to hear that," I say, roughly. "Thank you." He nods again in that wise and knowing way of his. I can see exactly why he and Margot were so close.

"Oliver will come around," Sebastian adds. "But also, it's your decision, not his. Margot could have just handed this over to Oliver and he would appreciate it. He would. But not in the same way you might, since you're also a writer. And that's why you're here. You have the ambition for it. At least Margot thought you did. And you could carry this on and make it your own."

I nod, mulling it over. Sebastian is right. I need to be kinder to Oliver, and to myself. I have time here. Whether I want to sell the villa or not, I have Margot's wishes to honor. I can spend that time begrudgingly, waiting to give up, waiting for everything to fall apart—and *expecting* it to. Or I can genuinely try. I can write. I can let myself be excited. I can be hopeful. I feel vulnerable and exposed just at the idea of it, but maybe, for Margot, that's okay. Maybe for Margot, and for myself, I can put a moratorium on my expectations of failure. I can give myself that.

Breaking up the heaviness of the moment, I bump Sebastian with my shoulder and ask, "So, there was nothing romantic between you and Margot?"

"Never," he says, cracking a small smile. "Well, I'm gay."

"That'd do it, then," I say, smiling widely back at him.

"Yep!"

We both erupt into glittery laughter.

"And your aunt was something of a player," Sebastian says. "Hated commitment. That woman had a new lover every other week, it seemed like."

"Stop," I say, laughing.

"Margot left a trail of broken hearts, you have no idea."

"Why do I love that?"

"It was her charm. She wanted to take a bite out of everything. And I genuinely think a lot of people, even if they weren't lovers, were just happy to have her attention for a week or a month or however long Margot gave it."

"I know I loved all her attention when I got it," I say, eyes burning.

"Me too. She had a magic to her, no doubt."

"I also love that she never let her body get in the way. I wish I had her confidence."

"Get in the way? Margot celebrated her body, and I think, because of that, people flocked to her and were so attracted to her confidence." Sebastian wipes at a tear, shaking his head. "Her confidence didn't come easy, Poppy."

"No?"

"She worked at it. She put herself out there. She said confidence was in the action. You had to show up as if you had all the nerve in the world."

"Huh."

"That's why she always said 'do it for the plot.' She meant it. She meant, go live your life and never hold back. Don't wait for permission or to look a certain way. Just show up and try."

"God, I miss her," I say.

"Me too, kiddo," Sebastian replies. "Come on." He gestures upward. "There's something I want to show you back at the villa."

Sebastian and I stand up. We brush off the sand from our clothes, and walk back to the car, the sun warm on our limbs, the beauty of this place starting to permeate through me.

★ ★ ★

When we arrive at the villa, Sebastian steers me to a locked room to the right of the foyer. Beau quickly rushes off toward the smell of Caroline cooking in the kitchen. Sebastian retrieves a key from his keychain and unlocks the door.

"This was Margot's office and library," he says, opening the door with ceremony.

When I step inside, it's wall-to-wall books. And not any of those stuffy books from decades before with gilded edges and unbroken spines. These are all bright colors, pinks and greens and yellows, and cracked spines with modern lettering on them. Books I've read and loved. Ones I've recommended to Margot and she to me.

There's a wide oak desk in the middle of the room, and it overlooks the side of the property, a view of bright flowers and towering palm trees with just a hint of the clear water in the corner. There's an ornate box on the top of the desk with a little light pink sticky note that says "For my darling girl."

I feel emotion rising in my throat as I slowly approach the box, letting my fingertips brush against it reverentially.

"Margot wanted you to have this," Sebastian says, his voice low, fitting for a moment that feels heavy with meaning. "And for you to use this office as your own. It was Margot's little sanctuary. I have a key for you. I know you might be tempted to snoop through the drawers, but unfortunately, everything is cleared out. Margot liked her secrets."

I laugh and then turn to the box. "What's in it?" I whisper.

"Take a look," he says, gesturing toward it.

I pry the lid off and look, to find a stack of books inside. I pick one up and notice it's a full set of first-edition PJ Latisse novels in pristine condition.

"How did Margot get these?" I ask, whipping around to Sebastian who has an amused smile on his face.

"She knew you were a fan," Sebastian replies.

"These are incredible," I whisper, awestruck. I don't even want to touch the books. The spines aren't cracked. They have the original covers. These are so rare and precious.

"All Margot wants from you is to try, Poppy," Sebastian says kindly. "I'll leave you with that." He goes out the door and closes it softly.

I feel suddenly contemplative, surrounded by Margot's beautiful life, this whole world she created for herself. How did she build all this?

And why am I so reticent to even try? Why is it terrifying me to consider the possibility? Because just when I think I can try, I feel locked up and incapable.

Self-doubt does not appear from nowhere, and mine is no exception. The difference, I've realized, is that most people deal with doubt, sure. But they don't have this *extra* layer of doubt. That my weight might determine the extent of my possibilities. All because of a belief that I deserve less than a woman who is thinner than me. So, not only must I wade through normal self-doubt, but I also deal with this constant feeling of unworthiness. It's hard enough to be a woman in a world made for and by men.

But, as a plus-size woman?

Do I even deserve to have everything I want? Never mind whether I am talented or not. I wish I could blame it all on my mom. She'd be an easy target. Beyond the anger I feel toward her is a sort of sad knowledge that the only reason she tried to protect me is because it's what she believes. Society has convinced her that *her* body is unworthy unless it's thin, and she passed that belief on to me, like an ugly heirloom handed down from generation to generation. And then that belief was confirmed thousands of times over in small and often subtle ways from magazines to TV shows to a quick scroll on Instagram.

That my body is a hindrance.

That I need to know my place. Lower my expectations.

Settle into playing a supportive role in other people's lives. That's what I see in TV and movies all the time—the plus-size character is always either the comedic relief or plays the supporting role to the main character. Since I'm not thin, that's what I deserve, right?

Women like me don't get to be the main character.

And I've internalized that belief my entire life.

In the past, I've let this belief drown me. I've bought into it, felt shame because of it, and let it dictate the edges of what felt possible for me. But Margot was one of the few people who saw more for herself and more for me.

Don't I owe it to myself to try, to not give up, to keep reaching? Don't I owe it to Margot? Maybe confidence doesn't come from being the best or thinnest or prettiest or most perfect, but just from showing up for yourself over and over. At least, that's what Margot believed and she had the kind of bold and adventurous life I want for myself.

As I sit here surrounded by not just Margot's things but her presence—I realize that I'm out of excuses.

I don't want to escape anymore. Or hide. Or cower.

I don't want to try just for Margot, but for myself, too.

THIRTEEN

Cap Ferrat, France

Regardless of my fierce commitment to try, I spend the next few days agonizingly staring at a blank page. It's happening again. It's an involuntary response that I shut down at the mere thought of writing. It's Friday and I can hear Janelle speaking to the residents. I'm in the kitchen and I help myself to a fresh croissant and make an espresso, my laptop and notepad in the crux of my arm. Outside the large window, the sky is a clear and bright blue. I can already feel the budding heat of the day.

"A first draft is supposed to be bad," Janelle says. I listen in from the doorway, hiding myself. "All you're doing with a first draft is telling yourself the story. Once you have words on a page, you can shape them. But you can't do a single thing with the words you haven't written. Every good book started as a shitty first draft. Let it suck. And let that be freeing."

Huh, I think. *Let it suck.* That is something I've never tried. I've always had this pressure to get it right. And then when Jackson started publishing number-one *New York Times* bestsellers, that pressure became a noose around my neck. Every sentence was scrutinized. Is this going to beat Jackson? Will I even get a book deal? And if I get a book deal, will it be a bestseller? I had to catch up. Nothing else would be worth it. Anger, embarrassment, judgment—all of it clouding me when I would face a blank document.

But, maybe I've been wrong. Because the only thing I've done is keep myself from doing the thing I love most.

I leave the kitchen, passing by the four residents and Janelle. The five of them nod toward me and say hello but then go back to their furtive typing. Just the sound of those keys, words filling up blank pages, makes my stomach flutter. To be prolific! There's no better sound than keys clacking.

I head into Margot's office, and I set my things down, but I don't sit right away, still feeling the nerves building up around me. My focus is scattered. I pace the living room. *It's just a novel*, I tell myself. *Let it suck.* I finger the spines of the books in Margot's library. All of these novels have started as 'shitty first drafts,' right? I can't compare the beginning of mine with someone's final product. And Margot never said I had to write a good book. Or publish anything. Or beat or catch up to Jackson.

She said I just had to finish *a* book.

I sit down at the wide desk and pull out my notebook. There's a Montblanc pen atop the desk that I assume was Margot's, and I hold it in my hand like it's precious. Like maybe some of her magic will seep into me by osmosis.

I take a deep, steadying breath.

I use the pen to scribble Outline at the top of the blank page. I tap the pen, look outside toward the trees, smell the fresh bouquet of flowers that Caroline must have put in here. I clear my mind. I breathe in and out. I tell myself it can suck. I can suck. I don't have to keep up with Jackson or write a bestselling book right now. I just need to write *anything*.

And then, it happens unexpectedly.

My heart speeds up.

I feel a distinct rush.

A burst of an…

…idea!

It appears fully formed, like it's been dropped in my head from the Universe.

In my notebook, I frantically write:

> The year's It Girl, whose dazzling debut film is set to premiere to rave reviews at Cannes Film Festival, goes missing the day before the festival begins. Nobody knows where Florence James is, and as detectives try to piece together her last week in the south of France, more questions unfold about who Florence really is, who she used to be, where she might have gone, and the secrets from her past she's trying to outrun.

I get chills as I write it down. It feels like the kind of book I'd want to read immediately, with a glass of wine, at one of those beach clubs by the water. I start writing the outline, a running list of scenes that I can organize later. I don't want to cut off the flow of getting my ideas down.

Hours pass in a blur of note-taking, my hand cramping from writing so much. I feel like I'm coming to from a trance.

I check my phone, and it's lunchtime. I haven't been that immersed in a while. I filled five pages with ideas, lighter than I've felt in years.

I go into the kitchen to look for food, and I find Caroline preparing some ham and *comté* sandwiches for us. There's a knife in a squat glass bottle of French mustard in front of her.

"Poppy!" Her face lights up when she sees me. "How are you?"

"Caroline! I'm doing really good, actually."

"No jet lag now?"

"I guess not," I say, smiling, noticing that I have almost fully acclimated to the time here in France. I haven't thought about LA once today.

"Were you just doing some writing?"

"A little bit," I tell her. "Mostly jotting down some ideas for a book."

"Oooooh," Caroline says, genuinely excited. "This place is special, I tell you. Cures writer's block."

"God, I hope so," I say, crossing my fingers together and lifting them up to show Caroline. I grab a piece of cheese off the cutting board and put it in my mouth, letting out a little moan.

"*Très bien*, no?" Caroline smiles.

"It's heaven. I feel like I've never had cheese, butter, pastries, or bread before. Not like here. I have no idea what I've been eating in America."

Caroline laughs. "*Oui*, we take great pride in our carbs and dairy. If you ask for a gluten-free croissant at a *boulangerie*, they will throw you out."

"As they should! That is a crime against bread."

Caroline nods solemnly. "*Oui. Exactement.*" She holds up the jar of mustard and grabs a tiny spoon. "Taste this. It was Margot's favorite."

I dip the spoon into the mustard. It's somehow both sweet and sour.

"That's so good," I tell Caroline.

"Margot had good taste in everything," she replies dreamily. "You're wearing her necklace."

I finger the hummingbird at my neck. "I love it."

"She wore that one all the time. Hardly ever took it off. I think it was really special to her."

"Do you know why?"

"Nope," Caroline says, returning to prepare the sandwiches. "You know Margot had her secrets."

"So many," I tell her. "A mysterious, magical woman."

"Truth." She laughs and then adds, "Oh, I think Oliver is looking for you, by the way."

"Oh?"

I haven't seen Oliver since Sebastian told me about his parents, and I have vowed to be more accommodating when I do. If I hadn't arrived in such a sour state, Oliver and I could be friends by now. We could be on the same side.

"Speak of the devil," Caroline says, nodding in the direction of the doorway where Oliver has now appeared. I am not prepared for my involuntary reaction to him, especially because he's shirtless right now and...wet...and wrapped in a pool towel. My jaw falls open. Not only does he have a sleeve of tattoos, but now I see he has old-school birds on his chest and the phases of the moon across his sternum, along with stars peppering across his body in specific spots. Shit. My eyes travel much too far downward, and I shiver.

Oliver is using a dish towel to dry his hair. It's unclear whether he just saw me gaping at him. I am suddenly very warm. The kitchen seems impossibly small. Is there a window open?

When Oliver finally speaks, having dried his hair to his satisfaction, I exhale. He walks closer toward me, and he smells like salt water and the remnants of a coconut shampoo.

"Do you have plans tomorrow night, Poppy?" He asks the question casually, now walking past me toward the refrigerator, where he procures one of Caroline's sandwiches. She's at the sink, washing off the cutting board.

"*Merci*, Caro," he says, smiling warmly at her.

Oh, to be the subject of such Oliver warmth, I think longingly.

When he turns back to me, his face is impatient. I still haven't answered, and he looks at me searchingly.

"So, tomorrow night?" He sounds a bit tetchy. "There's a dinner being organized in Cannes with a few of Margot's friends. They've invited you along."

I clear my throat. "Yes, I'm free and that sounds great," I say, finding my voice and my sudden commitment to cheer and friendliness. "Thank you so much for inviting me. I can't wait to meet friends of Margot."

Oliver stops chewing and turns his head toward me curiously. The tense look on his face drains away.

"Oh, okay. Well, great. They're excited to meet you, too." He's looking at me as if I'm a stranger. "Prepare for a late night. This crowd can be rowdy." He lets out a loose laugh.

"You're coming, too, right?"

"Of course," he says. "Unless you don't want me to…?"

"No, I…" I say, feeling a flash of guilt. "I'd like you to be there."

"Oh." The room seems to be devoid of air. "I'll see you then…then," he adds, looking at me one last time.

"Wait," I call out and he turns around, his eyes on mine. I take a sharp inhale. "Are you busy later?"

"No," he says, a tiny uptick on his lips that is almost a grin. "Why?"

"Well, if you have time," I tell him. "I'd like to hear more about The Colony. How it works. What I'd do if I stayed. Get all the details."

His eyebrows shoot up and his face softens. "Really?"

"Yeah," I say. "I'd really like to know."

"Okay," he says. "Great, yeah. I'll meet you back here in a couple hours?"

"Perfect."

Before I can say anything more, he's left the kitchen.

I watch his broad back as he goes, and I hear Stella flag him down in the dining room.

"Whoa," Caroline says, laughing. "You two have some *intense* energy."

"We do?" I hadn't realized it was palpable to onlookers. What is it? Mutual irritation? Hatred? Something else I can't even think about without my heart beating a little too wildly?

"Uh, yeah," Caroline says. "Enjoy your little chat later." She throws me a knowing grin and I laugh.

I go outside to the backyard, my mind trying to analyze the small snippets of conversation with Oliver; the way it feels like the world falls away when we're in the same room. But I tell myself to stop thinking about him. Even if there was a tiny chance that we're attracted to each other, it's a bad idea. I may be willing to give my writing another shot, but romance? No. I'm not here to get my heart shattered. That's not the risk I'm willing to take. I'm feeling vulnerable enough. And the very *last* thing I need is a romance with the person I'm supposed to be running this whole residency with. That would be just the type of complication that would make my life anything but simple. I need to be able to make this decision with a clear head.

I've just started the outline of a book I'm excited about. I've made more progress on a novel in one morning than I've made in a combined five years or more. There's a bud of something happening here, and I, for one, am not going to let a man like Oliver Hayes distract me.

I've got a damn book to write.

"I'm really glad you decided to keep the villa," Oliver says softly, taking a sip of rosé. We're out in the backyard a few hours later, sharing a bottle of wine. It's a temperate night and the sound of crickets pepper the air.

"Well," I begin tentatively. "I haven't decided for sure." Then add quickly, "But I'm really open to it."

"Okay," he says, nodding in slight relief. "Anything you need, let me know. That's what I'm here for."

I lift the glass to my lips and drink, then set it down and finger the stem. Oliver seems to watch my movements with unmasked curiosity.

"What did Margot do here, exactly? How does it all work?

Hypothetically, if I decided to keep it, what would my life be like?"

"That's the beauty of it, you can fill whatever role you want," Oliver says with excitement, as if he's been waiting for this question. "Margot was the mentor and morale builder. She was the reason people came here, to be in her presence, to get her wisdom, her feedback. She was the magic of The Colony. Janelle handles facilitating and handpicks the residents. Margot had final say on the residents, but trusted Janelle implicitly. You can be involved in that process if you want, but it's not necessary if you aren't into it. There won't be a spring semester of residents, since this is a transition time, but the ones for next fall are already confirmed. Caroline keeps everything working smoothly at the villa. I do the tech behind the scenes, running our website and also helping with whatever Margot would need. I think you'd be good at keeping morale up. Some people get discouraged after the first month. And you make people feel good, encourage them."

"Me?" I ask, surprised. "I feel like I've been nothing but moody and ungrateful since I arrived."

"You have," Oliver says, smiling ruefully. "Well, to me you have been. But I can forgive you for that." He looks down at his wine.

"Hey, it's not like you were super welcoming, either."

"No," he says. "And I'm sorry for that."

"Eh," I say, swatting at the air. "I can forgive you for that."

His eyes lock on to mine and he gives me a real smile. It does something to me, melts my insides into molten lava. I break the eye contact quickly.

I clear my throat. "What about money?" I ask, changing the subject.

"The money is all handled. Margot never shared those details with me except that Sebastian takes care of it. If you take everything over, I don't know what the money situation is, but

I'd assume you'd be paid a nice salary." He points upward like he just remembered something. "Oh! Speaking of, I should have told you earlier that Margot set aside a monthly stipend for your six months here. It's not much, but it's enough that you won't have to rely on Caroline for every meal. If you need it, of course."

"I need it," I say, a little too quick and desperate. I modulate my voice. "I mean, yes, I'd like that." I feel a huge wave of relief that I can stop worrying about money for the time being. The subletter at my apartment was handling most of the bills, but the thought of going into more debt just to survive here for the next six months was pressing on me. I feel my body relax.

"It's yours," he says.

"So, that's it, then? Keep up the morale? Try to tap into some elusive magic that Margot seemed to possess?" I feel my voice drop, the doubt seeping in. This sounds like a big role to fill, and I haven't been feeling positive about *myself* lately, never mind trying to spread that positivity to others. That well has been empty for a while.

"For now, write your book," Oliver says. "Worry about the rest later. You'll get the hang of it. If Margot thought you were up for it, then, well, I trust her."

I nod and it's nice to have found some common ground with Oliver.

"Why do you love this place so much?" I ask after a few beats of comfortable silence.

He shrugs. "I was here when Margot started it. It was important to her, so I wanted to be helpful. And then I fell in love with it. I don't know why. I love living in the Riviera, that's one part of it. It feels meaningful, this work. I always wanted to do something purposeful with my life, add some good to the world. It's a rush to have the residents here and then they leave, and you feel like your life is better because you met them."

I narrow my eyes at him, and he sort of gives an uncomfortable chuckle.

"Too corny?" he asks.

"Was it honest?"

He nods.

"Then, nope, just the right amount of corny."

He beams.

"You'll see," he says. "You'll fall in love here, too."

The way my cheeks burn, you'd think he meant something else entirely.

"I'm sure I will," I whisper, trying to ignore the thundering in my chest.

FOURTEEN

Cannes, France

The next day, Sebastian, Oliver, and I walk from the underground parking lot to the Croisette, the famous boardwalk street in the center of Cannes, lined with lofty palm trees covered in white string lights. It's a lively evening in the middle of summer on the French Riviera. Every restaurant patio seems to be at capacity. The infamous Carlton Hotel looms in the distance, the iconic green spires on each side of the building in full view in the clear night sky. There's a balmy heat, and I'm glad I wore a light and breathable dress.

We stop in front of one of the many beach clubs that line the Croisette. This one, like the others, has elegant lighting and is furnished modernly. The tables and chairs are situated directly on the sand. I see an undisturbed view of the small waves lapping. It's gorgeous, filled with glamorous people clinking glasses of champagne, and I feel that same sense of not belonging that has followed me everywhere since high school. Too big, and yet not enough. This place is one I'd avoid if I could—too much of a reminder of what it's like to be thin and moneyed.

But, as we descend the staircase, Oliver looks back at me

and gives me a soft smile. It calms me. We walk side by side to where Sebastian is leading us, and Oliver puts his hand on the small of my back and whispers, "Don't be nervous. They'll all love you."

I let out a deep breath, and he notices, smiling.

He offers the crook of his arm and I put mine through it, feeling the steadiness of him. We arrive at a table with four other people already seated. It's a prime spot only a few feet from the water's edge.

Sebastian gestures for me to sit down and as he does, he says, "Everyone, I'd like you to meet Margot's niece, Poppy." I smile and wave.

Sebastian goes around the table to introduce me to everyone.

There's Erik Johansson, a tall Swedish man in his midfifties, wearing casual shorts with a captain's hat and sporting a deep tan. A man of leisure who docks his yacht in Monaco. "It's the only one with a Swedish flag—you can't miss it," he says, jovially.

Sat next to Sebastian is Andrew Clapter, an English writer in his sixties who has light brown skin, salt-and-pepper hair, and an exceedingly friendly laugh. "I write epic war novels about twentieth century England. I won't be offended if you've never heard of me," he says, giving a wonderfully charismatic smile.

Then there's Capri Rodriguez, an American painter, a prodigy with a privileged background, who is absolutely stunning. "My mom is actually the actress, Renalda Rodriguez," she says. Renalda Rodriguez is a legend, and I saw billboards in LA promoting her new HBO series before I left for France.

And then, lastly, the woman seated to my right is introduced as Claudia Drake. The name sounds familiar to me, but I'm not sure why. Claudia isn't actually a friend of Margot, but a friend of Andrew's. She's in town for a few days and asked to come along. Claudia is in a light blue satin dress, her tanned arms exposed. She's in her late forties and I notice she has a rim of gold around her brown eyes when she looks at me directly.

"I'm the founder of Drake Literary," she says, as she pours me a glass of the chilled rosé resting in a metal bucket filled with ice next to her.

"*The* Drake Literary?" I croak. Drake Literary is one of the most popular and sought-after literary agencies in New York. I try to tamp down the nerves that start bubbling up.

"The very same," Claudia says, smiling lightly. "Are you a writer?"

The other people at the table are talking among themselves. Andrew and Sebastian are deep in conversation and there's something intense happening between them that I can't quite figure out. Oliver sits across from me, and I catch his eye when I look over at him, and then quickly turn away.

"Yes, I'm a writer," I say, in a tone more confident than I feel. I go for it. "I'm currently working on a thriller set in the south of France, actually."

"Oh, interesting," she says, her eyes lighting up. "Aren't you also Jackson Banks's sister?"

I clench my jaw. I remind myself that if I'm going to be in this industry, I can't avoid Jackson. He's inevitable.

I casually look at a menu. "Yes, he's my older brother." I try not to let the words sound bitter as I say them. I rip off a piece of bread and dip it in an olive-oil-and-balsamic mixture, letting the vinegar lie on my tongue, and savoring the taste of the pillowy baguette.

"Have you ever thought about writing romance, like him?" Claudia is looking at the menu now, too, and her tone is airy. "Because a romance set in the south of France would do very well. Especially from Jackson's sister. I could sell something like that."

I've never thought about writing romance. It feels more like

Jackson's thing. But, at this point, a story is a story. An agent is an agent. And a book deal…is a book deal.

"I could write romance," I tell her. "But I don't really want to rely on Jackson's name to get started."

"It would be silly not to," she replies. "You just need his name to break into the industry and then you prove yourself on talent alone. It's a good strategy."

"Okay," I say, feeling a bit conflicted. Still, she's an agent. And I am not in a position to turn down potential offers.

"I don't represent commercial thrillers, personally, but if you wrote romance, I'd be very interested in reading it," she says, looking at me directly through half-moon reading glasses and taking a sip of her wine.

"You would?" I ask, eagerly.

"Absolutely," she says, and ruffles through her Louis Vuitton tote bag to produce a thick white business card. "Email me a partial draft as soon as you have it, and we can go from there. I look forward to it."

I've never been the sort of person who can play it cool. And, because of that, I let a wide smile spread across my face. I'll write romance for Claudia. I'll do anything for Claudia. An agent. Finally. After over four hundred rejections, I don't even care what she wants from me—I'll do it.

"Alright, enough shop talk, you two, let's finally order," Capri says in a fluttery voice. She waves over the server. "Here in France, they don't hound you like in America. When you're ready to order, you can call them over. They won't hover for tips, either. It's a very civilized restaurant experience." She smiles at me, happily distilling this knowledge.

"Italy and France, the best food in the world," Andrew says, his English accent crisp. He lifts his wineglass. "To good food and new friends." We clink glasses in the middle of the table just as the waiter approaches.

I feel heat blaze through my body as Oliver orders in perfect, singsong French. The roll of his *R* when he orders a bran-zino makes me think of his tongue, and suddenly, I feel like my thoughts are written all over my face. I must have been watching him intently, because his eyes move to mine and I give a slight smile, a tingle rushing through me when he reciprocates it. I shake my head and turn back toward Capri and Erik, hoping the dim lighting has obscured the way my cheeks have reddened. I feel Oliver's eyes all over me.

No distractions, no complications, I tell myself. I force my eyes to stay away from him.

"*Risotto avec crevettes s'il vous plait*," I say, not quite getting the accent but doing my best. My eyes betray me as my gaze snags on Oliver again. I give a small shrug. He shrugs back, flashes a playful nod, and we both grin. He lowers his eyes to his bread plate, still smiling.

I finger Claudia's card in my hand and slip it into my purse.

The rest of the dinner passes in a lovely blur of bottles of wine, delicious seafood, light and witty conversation, and a romance novel being outlined in the back of my head. Maybe the love interest will have dark hair with curly tendrils that fall over green eyes—and olive skin, and a body marked with tattoos. A man who speaks French and whose slight smile can send heat through a woman's body. *Maybe.*

When we finally head back to the car well after midnight, I walk slowly with Oliver, Sebastian taking up the lead at a brisk pace.

Oliver knocks my shoulder and says, "You look happy. What did you and Claudia talk about?"

I knock his shoulder back. "She gave me her card. She wants me to send her a partial draft of my novel when I have it ready." I try to keep from bursting out into a wide smile, but I can't. My face breaks open.

He looks at me and says, "This place is magic, isn't it?"

"I think it might be," I say, turning to look at the white lights on the palm trees one last time before we go into the underground parking lot. I twirl back around to face Oliver, feeling more carefree and fun and excited than I've felt in years.

Oliver stops and watches me for a moment, everything else blurring around us.

"There she is," he says, a smile lighting its way across his face.

"Who?" I ask, laughing.

He stretches out a hand to gesture toward me.

"*There's* the Poppy that Margot told me about. Nice to finally meet you."

My breath hitches. I feel delight spread all over my body.

"Here I am," I say, taking a curt bow, feeling all the wine I had with dinner.

"We've been waiting for you," he says, beaming.

We look at each other, stop, and everything goes still around us. It's just us two here. Neither of us breathe. Oliver opens his mouth to speak and then—

"What are you two kids doing? Let's go," Sebastian shouts, making us both jump. We smile at each other as if there's a secret between us.

When we get to Sebastian's car, Oliver walks quickly ahead and opens the passenger side door for me with a dramatic flourish, and I can't help but grin when I duck in under his arm.

OCTOBER

Two months later

FIFTEEN

Cap Ferrat, France

A timer goes off in the middle of the table. The four residents and I look up from our laptops, dazed. This is a "game" I came up with last month, a spin on the Pomodoro Technique: we set a timer for an hour, challenge ourselves to write as much of a scene as we can, and keep ourselves accountable because we all get distracted and unfocused.

"One thousand five hundred sixty words!" I say, smiling broadly.

"Nine hundred," Evie says, clapping her hands together once. Evie's been a little blocked from a sticky plot point, so nine hundred words is a big accomplishment.

"One thousand two hundred fifty," Kerry says, nodding to herself.

"Two thousand three hundred twenty-two," Jasmyn says, excitedly, looking around at the rest of us as if she's won.

"Two thousand four hundred fifty," Stella says, her cheeks pink. We groan loudly. "Did I win?" She smiles and we all nod with overdramatic glumness.

I put a little check next to her name on the scorecard I've

been keeping. I've won a couple rounds of our game, and every time I do, it feels like an outsize accomplishment. Honestly, writing at all feels like an accomplishment.

So far, this little game has doubled our collective word count. Even Janelle was surprised by how much the residents have been writing and making progress. They told me this after their last Friday workshop day. I still haven't gone to one of those yet. All of this writing feels fragile, and I'm not sure I'm ready to be critiqued.

I close my laptop, stretching my arms over my head. I feel really good. With 1,560 words, I've got another completed scene for my romance novel, so that means I can spend the afternoon's writing block working on my other book. The idea of getting back into the world of my main character, the mysterious and tormented Florence James, gives me a little thrill.

Caroline comes into the living room with a couple bottles of light and chilled white wine, handing out glasses to all of us, along with a few dishes of olives.

"When in France," she says, laughing.

We sit in a contented silence, drinking our wine, scrolling our phones.

Evie pierces the quiet and groans. "A woman I follow on Instagram, who is like twenty-five years old, just announced she got a book deal," she says, staring at her phone as if it might detonate in her hand. "They say she's the 'next' Sally Rooney. I know this shit shouldn't bother me, or get in my head, but it does. I feel like an old fart trying to keep up with the cool kids." She sets her phone down and puts her hands on her face.

This has become a ritual of sorts, too. We finish our morning writing time, drink wine, eat snacks, and talk. Something about this environment has given us all a safe space to share and connect—I am starting to understand how special it is to be with other writers like this.

"You know what?" Jasmyn says. "I love social media. Obviously. I'm basically glued to my phone. But I just don't think we need to be exposed to everyone's achievements all the time. It's messing with our heads. I've got something like 150,000 followers on Instagram and sometimes I'm, like, but why does this woman have half a million? What's wrong with *me*? Why don't I have half a million followers?"

"This is why I don't partake in the social media," Kerry says, laughing. "It's a mindfuck of comparison. I'm already dealing with self-doubt. I don't need to see everyone's highlight reel to make myself feel worse."

I jump in. "Right? Everywhere you look, there's some brand new twenty-five-year-old ingenue who's written a novel that's become a TV series, when you still haven't even finished your own book. It feels like a race even when it's not. By a certain point, you start to think if it hasn't happened for me yet, it won't. And then, why did it happen for that person and not me? Does that mean there's something wrong with me?"

"I think that's why I didn't write for so long," Evie says. "I felt like, what's the point? There are millions of books, millions of writers, and do I have anything interesting to add? And if it hasn't happened yet, maybe it never will. Exactly the same for me, Pop."

"Comparison is the thief of joy," Stella says, shaking her head. "I turned thirty this year and I'll never be on a 30-under-30 list. It bugs the hell out of me. And it shouldn't. I'm great. I don't need to be on some stupid list. Why don't they do 30-over-30 lists? Isn't it more impressive to achieve later in life? Where is the late-bloomer love?"

"Exactly," I say. "But also, why is anyone over thirty considered a 'late bloomer'? That's how warped this all is." The four women around the table nod emphatically. "We know that you don't need to be young to be successful, but this world has created an obsession with youthful, prodigal talent. These are the stories that are told. The ones that stick out. The people we celebrate. I still have to remind myself that we celebrate them, because they are rare. *Because* they are the outlier. And if I tell myself that enough, I can go on." I laugh dramatically.

"Well said, and same," Kerry says.

"But it's not easy. It's a lot easier to give up," I say, my voice almost a whisper. It feels like a vulnerable thing to say out loud, but then all four women go quiet and nod to themselves. I feel my heart quicken. Oh, to be understood.

"Also, have you noticed these young literary darlings all look the same?" Jasmyn asks, sucking on the end of her pen. "They're all thin and white and have a sort of conventional beauty about them, as if that's part of the allure. A woman, so pretty, chose to write, and it's *good*. Wow. She's not just a pretty face. She's also…intelligent. As if intelligent women are so few and far between it needs to be called out."

"And it's important to note they're all white," Kerry says. "But you know what bothers me? Everyone wonders if I'll write about race in my book. It's always about race when you're Black. And it is about race. Of course that's in everything I write. How can it not be? But the expectation that I will write about it is so annoying."

"Amen," Jasmyn says. "White women get to write without it being political. Anything I write is inherently political. It's always mentioned that I'm Black. My novel can't just be a love story, it's a 'Black love story.'" She rolls her eyes.

"Yep," Stella says. "Not the exact same, but, you know, I'm bisexual. If I write a romance where the character falls in love with a man, it's a love story. With a woman, it's a queer love story. One is commercial, the other less so. Why is there a difference? Both are love stories, but it has to be qualified."

"These boxes they put everyone in," I say. "It's exhausting."

"It really fucking is," Jasmyn says. "It sucks to be the 'other,' with the qualifications they use. Like there's a norm. White man, white woman. Everything else needs a label."

Evie, Kerry, Stella, and I all "mmm-hmm" to agree.

Stella leans in toward the table and asks in a low whisper, "Can I tell you all something I never say out loud? Is this a safe space?"

We all lean in conspiratorially, and nod, waiting.

"I hate to say this, but I care so much about how I look because I know it gives me privilege. I know it opens doors. I can stun people with my intellect, but my looks are the way in. And while it works, it also makes me so fucking angry that the world is like this. Every time it works, I get angrier. And then I get angrier when I see people's faces when they realize I'm actually smart. The amount of times I've been asked to a meeting, only to find out it was a date in disguise... One is too many, but it hasn't been just one. That's its own brand of awful, let me tell you."

"Wow, Stel, that's fucked-up," Jasmyn says.

"So fucked-up," Evie says.

"Yeah, I feel like, as women, we have to choose between two different directions to make it in this world," I say. "Either we try to split from convention, set ourselves apart, break the rules. Or we accept the rules and play along in order to make sure those doors open. And I can't blame any woman for whatever path she chooses. Stel, that fucking sucks, but I get it."

This makes me think of my mom and Margot. One who chose the traditional path, the other an unconventional one. They were both trying to survive in their own way. I wish they had been able to see that and reconcile their differences.

"On the other hand I know, theoretically, my life wouldn't be better if I looked like you, Stel, but then I go on the internet, or out in the world, and I start to believe..." I say, shrugging.

"You know the most fucked-up part, though, Poppy?" Stella asks, leaning in even more. "They try to draw lines around what we deserve, and make the rules impossible to follow. Maybe you think you don't deserve your dream because your body isn't like mine, but they make me feel like I don't deserve my dream because my body *does* look like mine. It's an unwinnable battle. And instead of practicing and getting better and working on our craft, we waste years of our lives trying to play by their rules. As if we need their permission in order to do what we love to do."

"Yeah," Kerry sighs.

"Uh-huh," Evie adds.

"Women need to have more conversations like this," Jasmyn says, smiling slyly.

"Rage-filled rants with gratuitous use of the word *fuck*?" I ask.

"Yes, Poppy!" Jasmyn cries out and we all descend into laughter.

As the laughs die down, we do a collective sigh, smile to ourselves, then disperse to take a break, content to be with others who understand completely.

I step out into the backyard after lunch and the late afternoon sun feels blinding. Down by the pool, I spot Oliver. I rush over to him.

"Hi," I say. "How's it going?" Oliver and I have been circling each other for a couple months, but I've managed to keep to myself. He joins for group dinners, but I have tried to avoid being alone with him, because when I'm around Oliver, everything gets confusing for me. Instead, I've been focused on writing not one but *two* books. It's thrilling.

"Hi," he says. He seems preoccupied.

"Sorry, do you want to be alone?" I ask.

"No," he replies, looking up at me and giving me a warm smile. "Sorry. Just got an interesting email."

"Do tell."

"It's a little awkward," he replies, his hands going to his hair. "But I got a job offer for an art director position at a digital marketing agency in New York. It would start in the new year. They're setting up a division and want me to head it up. It's a good offer, and I figure if there's a chance you might sell this place, I'll be out of a job soon anyway." He doesn't say this unkindly or angrily, but he sounds more resigned than happy about it.

"Oh," I say. "When do they need an answer?"

"Soon. By mid-December, at the latest," he says. "I don't want to pressure you, though. Promise."

Mid-December. That's when the Booksmart guys need to know, too. I hope I have more clarity by then, because I may be writing, but I'm not certain about anything else.

"Do you want to take it?" I ask.

"Not really," he says. "But if you sell The Colony, I don't want to be here to watch it happen."

I don't know what to say to that. I can't tell him not to take the job, especially if I'm still undecided about what I'll do. I really hate how tempting the Booksmart offer still is to me. It's so much money. It's hard for me to let go. If Margot really didn't want me to consider selling, why did she give me that option?

And now, caught up in making this decision is Oliver's entire life plan? If I sell, I'll lose him to New York, and why does the idea of that make me feel nauseous?

I am so torn about everything, and writing has been a great distraction.

"I'm sorry," I manage to say, and Oliver holds his hand up to stop me.

"I swear I didn't tell you so you would feel guilty," he says. "I understand that it's a hard decision. I really do."

I breathe out a sigh of relief. "Okay," I tell him.

"You know, I worried that the magic of this place would leave when Margot died, but truthfully—" he swallows and pauses, seemingly debating whether he's going to finish his thought, then continues "—you have the same energy as her, when you actually want to be here. The residents seem really happy you're here. Stella says you're the one that's cheering everyone on."

He's been talking to Stella? My face burns. I try to stave off the rush of envy that overcomes me, but it's too quick. Maybe they're dating? My stomach drops at the thought. But why wouldn't he date her? Stella is a "dream woman," and on top of it, she's accomplished and talented. I don't want to be competitive, but damn if I don't feel like an invisible lump next to her. Oliver regards me curiously, as if he can sense I'm spanning ten different emotions at once.

I remember the first part of what he told me and pick up the conversation.

"That means a lot to me," I tell him. "I'm starting to love it here, truthfully."

"Well then, I think it's time I tell you one of Margot's requests, one I've been keeping a secret to let you get settled in and focus on your writing."

"I'm intrigued," I say. "What's the secret?" I sit up straighter and lean in conspiratorially.

"You may not have known, but Margot had been sick for a while. She knew she was running out of time, and she put her affairs in order. About a week before she died, she told me 'when Poppy gets here, I want you to make her fall in love with this place,'" he says, mimicking Margot's playful voice, but with an added stern finger, like a mother chastising her child. "I've done a terrible job so far, but I'd like to try. I didn't think you'd need a tour guide, but now I see, of course, Margot had it right." He shakes his head to himself. "Are you busy this Saturday? I want to take you to one of my favorite places—Villefranche-sur-Mer."

A mix of emotions flood me at once. Knowing more details about Margot's last days, that she was thinking of me, and regret that I wasn't here. I wish I had been. I wish I had known she was sick. I wish she had told me at our last lunch.

"She didn't want you to know," Oliver adds, seemingly reading my mind. "That she was dying. She didn't even want me to know, but it was hard for her to hide it toward the end."

"Why?" I croak out. "I mean, why didn't she want me to know?"

"She was just like that," Oliver says, shrugging. "Secretive. She kept a lot of things to herself. She was the warmest, kindest person ever, but enigmatic. She made me feel understood, but I feel like I never got to fully understand *her*."

"Yes," I say. "I know exactly what you mean."

"I think she didn't want you to be sad. Or, maybe, to see you sad. To make anyone sad because of her."

"And here I am, sad anyway."

"Yeah," he says. "I think Margot had enough tragedy in her life. She wanted to die in peace, leave you with good memories."

I want to bring up Oliver's parents, but it doesn't feel like the right time to open that conversation. He looks a bit fragile. I want to reach out for him, but I don't.

Instead, I tell him, "Sure, I'd love to go to that Villefranche place with you on Saturday. Let's do it."

"Right," he says, remembering his offer. "Great, we'll take the train over instead of a car."

"Just tell me when to be ready," I say, and he nods again.

"I better head out," he says. "I have a client project I need to complete by end of day. See you later."

He walks away, looking back and giving me a small smile, the smell of him on the breeze as he goes.

SIXTEEN

Villefranche-sur-Mer, France

Seeing Villefranche for the first time is like walking directly into a postcard. It's late dusk when we arrive from the short train ride, golden sun reflected off the crystal blue water. There's a slight humidity in the air, and it's a warm October evening. Children and adults are still swimming in the small cove, tiny rocks instead of sand leading them ashore. There is one lone beach club with uniform beige-and-white-striped umbrellas, and a restaurant on a platform behind the sun beds.

I'm wearing a short black dress with small daisies on it. It has a flouncy hemline and a hint of cleavage. I have white sneakers on, and gold hoops in my ears, and my lips are red. I feel good, sexy. Oliver wears shorts a few inches above the knee, black-and-white Vans, and a light, white button-down rolled up to reveal his forearms. He smells like lime, coconut, and sandalwood. I feel an easy joy, walking in a beautiful place with a beautiful man.

Yachts and boats are in the far distance, a mountain to the right with large villas punctuating the peaks, and to my left, water splashing on rocks where the beach ends. There are two or three restaurants serving people on the edge of the water. The buildings are old and painted in bright shades of coral, terracotta, and yellow, with washing hung up to dry—the very picture of charming beach village.

The buildings cascade up a steep hill. People hike the ancient staircases. It's a lively area, small as can be, but there are people everywhere, swimming, zooming off in boats, and clinking glasses of wine.

I let out a big sigh of contentment and Oliver breaks the comfortable silence between us. "Amazing, isn't it?" He looks to the distance in a dreamy way, and I follow his sightline.

"See that pink villa?" He points to an area past the cove, and I squint, searching for it. The sun is sinking quickly into the horizon, and suddenly, there are golden streetlights lit around us, amplifying the charm of it all. The light from the lamps reflects on the rippling surface of the water. I watch the reflection and think this doesn't look real. It doesn't *feel* real, being here.

I squint again in the distance. "I don't see anything," I tell him. He moves closer to me, close enough that I feel his body behind me, the heat of him. I seize up. His chest pushes into my upper back and he's just tall enough to be able to rest his arm on my shoulder to point his finger directly. I follow it, happening upon a bright pink villa with white shutters in the distance.

"I see it," I say, excitedly. I accidentally move backward a bit and fall into Oliver's chest. He grasps my shoulders with both his hands and steadies me. I take a sharp intake of breath as I feel his cheek hovering near mine. I hear him exhale, and feel his breath on my neck. My stomach flutters. I am aware of every inch of my skin.

Oliver stays where he is, his hands still on my shoulders, and says, "That's Villa Ephrussi. It's open to the public. You can tour the house and the gardens. The view from up there is unbelievable. Margot loved it."

When he moves his hands off my shoulders, his fingertips brush bare skin on my neck and my eyes lose focus.

"I want to go there," I say, turning around to face him. We are so close to each other I can see the stubble on his face, smell the mint on his breath.

"I can take you sometime," he says, smiling.

"Yes," I say, quickly, and he responds by beaming back at me, dropping his eyes to my lips, and giving a small, nearly imperceptible shake of his head before walking away, gesturing with a quirk of his shoulder for me to follow.

It takes me a moment to move my legs. My logical mind is telling me to not get caught up in the romance of this place, of the looks and brushes and touches that feel heightened. But when I'm with Oliver, something happens to my mind—I lose all good sense.

"I hope you're up for a bit of a hike, because the restaurant I want to take you to is up quite a few stairs. Can you handle it in that little dress of yours?" he asks, and the way he's looking at me, it's as if I'm wearing nothing at all.

"Yes, I think so," I say, voice raspy.

We walk together in step, dodging weary-looking tourists and darting up a long and steep staircase through a cobblestoned enclave. Both of us are quiet as we climb, the only sound our labored breathing.

Wiping sweat from my upper lip, and trying to catch my breath, I follow as Oliver leads me to an area covered in trees with tables situated outside. The only indication that it's a restaurant is the menu propped up at the entrance. There is no sign, no storefront, just a patch of greenery, a little secret garden perched on an incline.

"This is it," Oliver says, opening the wooden gate for me and letting me pass. "The best Italian food around. Sebastian, Margot, and I used to come here all the time."

"It's adorable," I say, looking back at him. All the tables have flickering white candles on them, and above us, white string lights are hung across the trees. It's…romantic. It feels like a date. And then I think I'm probably imagining that. Insecurities quickly flare up. *He's not into me. I don't belong here. I'm too big. Not enough.* A torrent of thoughts. I take a long swallow as we find a table for two. I sit down, and immediately lift the menu to my face.

"I thought you'd like it here," he says, his face in a menu now, too.

I take a deep inhale, steady myself, let the insecurities move through my body until I can speak again. I hate that. Hate the way the doubts are like an assault. But it passes, and I'm able to find myself again.

"Asparagus risotto," I say. "No question." I close the menu with a flourish.

"Decisive," he says. "I like that." He gives a little smile, and my body feels boneless.

"I love risotto. If it's on a menu, I order it."

"I noticed," he says. "You had it in Cannes, too."

"Observant," I say, pointing my finger to my nose.

He shrugs. "You're an interesting person to observe."

I look at him, and our eyes meet, the air shifting around us.

"Thank y—" I start to say before a squat man in his fifties, wearing a white apron with red stains on it, approaches the table and claps Oliver on the back.

"Oliver!" the man says with infectious jubilation. "It's a pleasure to see you." He speaks English with a heavy Italian accent. Oliver stands up and they kiss on each cheek.

"Mossimo, this is Poppy," Oliver says, gesturing to me. "Poppy, this is Mossimo, he's the owner and head chef."

"Nice to meet you," I say, holding out my hand for him to shake it, but he kisses the top of it lightly instead.

"*Ciao, bella,*" he says, giving me a wide smile. He looks over at Oliver and says, "Finally, you bring a beautiful woman for a date here." Mossimo gives me a jovial smirk, and I feel my shoulders straighten.

"No, no, this isn't a date, Mossimo," Oliver says, reddening quickly. "This is Margot's niece." I give Mossimo a little helpless shrug, but something seizes inside of me. I feel myself construct a wall between Oliver and me. He quickly denied this being a date. Take it at face value. If he was interested, I'd know. I don't want to be a fool by falling for someone that's just being nice and accommodating.

"Oh," Mossimo says, frowning slightly. "I loved Margot. I always tried to get her to fall in love with me, but no luck." I laugh with his convivial nature. "I will bring wine for you both, even if it's not a date."

He gives Oliver a playful stare, hugs him quickly, and whispers something in his ear that I'm sure he doesn't want me to hear, but I do. "It's been a long time since Camille, Oliver. This should be a date." Oliver reacts strangely, by shrugging and looking as downtrodden as I've seen him.

When Oliver sits down, I say, "I heard that." I nod toward where Mossimo stood before he returned to the kitchen. "About Camille."

He shakes his head. "Mossimo is very bad at whispering."

"Who's Camille?"

Oliver groans. "Camille *was* my fiancée," he says, the words coming out like they taste sour. "She, uh... Well, she left me at the altar for someone else. A mutual friend of ours." He hangs his head, as if ashamed.

"She didn't show up to the wedding?" I ask him, aghast.

"No, she did. She got ready, was in her dress and everything, but didn't walk down the aisle." He shrugs. "That was three years ago. She said it didn't 'feel right' with me."

"Wow, what an idiot," I quickly spit out before I can stop myself. Oliver's eyes meet mine, his eyebrow raised, and he pauses, really looks at me, and I stare back, the air between us charged again. He smiles. My throat constricts. Before Oliver can speak again, Mossimo returns with a bottle of red wine.

He regards us staring at each other and says, under his breath but loud enough for both of us to hear, "See? Date!" He shakes his head while pouring the wine into our glasses.

Oliver and I look at each other and give sheepish little grins, both of us not quite sure how to neutralize the awkwardness.

We order our meals—spaghetti bolognese for Oliver and asparagus risotto for me. Mossimo claps and gives me a knowing smile, as if everything about this dinner is transparent to him.

"I'm sorry, Oliver," I say, regaining the conversation. "How do you even recover from that?"

"I did a lot of soul-searching, went to therapy, too," he says. "In the end, I could see where she was coming from. We weren't right for each other. She did us both a favor."

"But how do you trust again after that?"

He looks at me, his eyes studying mine, like I've just revealed something important to him. "If you interpret every difficult experience as a reason to not try, or have hope, or not believe in people and love, that's what life will become. You'll look for evidence for why something isn't working out for you. I choose to stay open. I don't want to spend my life afraid and guarded."

"Damn, that resonates," I say, looking down into my wineglass. "I think I've been spending a lot of time lately being afraid and guarded."

"Life is all about where you focus. I've been through a lot of tragedy and pain, but I can't let it define me. I want to take chances," he says, his eyes finding mine with purpose. My heart speeds up. "Even if the outcome is uncertain or I could get hurt—or left at the damn altar." He gives a warm laugh.

"You're very evolved," I say. "I wish I could approach life like that."

"Okay, I sometimes know better than I act, obviously. I'm saying this is how I *mostly* want to be, but I don't always get it right. Plus, you can approach anything this way. You just have to figure out how you want to live—from your fear, or from your courage."

"I want to live with courage, but every time I try, I go back to my fear."

"Yeah, well, who doesn't?" Oliver smiles and shrugs. "We're all works in progress, aren't we?"

"Yeah," I say, a little lost in my own thoughts.

"Anyway, speaking of bad romances, do you have some jealous boyfriend back in LA? Someone who's going to come to France in three months to try to whisk you away, like some predictable rom-com?"

"Why, should my hypothetical boyfriend be jealous right now?" I ask, unable to stop myself from flirting.

"Well..." Oliver smirks.

I break the eye contact, start rearranging the silverware on the table. "I'm very single, anyway. Nobody will come to whisk me away, thank you very much. I am a single woman with agency, you know?" I meet his eyes again. "And I hope I'm anything but predictable." I curve my lips into a sly grin.

"Hmm," he says. "Well, I'm glad I won't have to fend off an angry boyfriend who thinks we've been in cahoots."

"Cahoots, you say?" I laugh heartily. Mossimo drops off our dishes, and gives us both another appraising look, while shaking his head as he walks away.

"*Cahoots* is a very good word," Oliver says, twirling spaghetti on his fork.

"It is, if you're, like, eighty," I say, taking my first bite of the risotto and moaning in pleasure at the rush of flavor. Oliver's eyes shoot up and he regards me intensely, then just as quickly goes back to his meal.

"It just so happens I'm eighty at heart," he says. "My best friend is my seventy-something uncle, for god's sakes."

We both laugh and out of the the corner of my eye, I catch Mossimo watching us, another quick shake of his head.

The rest of the dinner is punctuated by good conversation, a lot of wine, and that little hint of flirtation, glinting eyes and lingering looks. We walk back to the train station. On the train, despite the protestations to myself, all I want to do is lay my head on his shoulder, let him wrap his arms around me, and feel the warmth of him.

But, instead, I push myself closer to the window, cross my arms across my chest, and wait until the feeling passes, frustrated when it doesn't.

We decide to walk up to the villa from the train station instead of taking a taxi. It's past midnight now, and there's a slight breeze in the air. It's a beautiful, clear night sky, an almost full moon illuminating the pavement in front of us. I look up at the stars and sway as I walk.

"This was a really fun night," Oliver says, speaking into the space ahead of him.

"Yeah, it was," I say, losing my footing a bit. The outside of my hand accidentally grazes the outside of his and it feels like it catches fire.

"You a little drunk over there, Poppy?" Oliver laughs.

"No," I say. "Well, maybe. We didn't need the second bottle of wine." I giggle.

"We definitely did," he says, a bit of a slur on his words. He seems loose.

"Tell me about your parents." I look at his profile, see him wince and then smooth his face into a set smile. His voice is faraway when he speaks.

"Sebastian told you?"

"He did. And I'm so sorry, Oliver. I'm sorry you lost them."

"Me too," he says, heavily. "Thank you."

"Tell me about them?" I ask quietly.

He nods.

"I loved them. I loved them so much," he says. "We were that kind of perfect family. My mom and dad, they were so in love. We did everything together, the three of us. When I lost them, it felt like my whole world had been ripped out from under me. I didn't want to go on without them."

"Oh, Oliver," I say.

"What are your parents like?" he asks quickly.

"My parents?"

"Yeah, you know, the people who raised you," he says, laughing. "It tells a lot about a person, who their parents are."

I sigh. "They are the opposite of in love. My dad didn't want my mom to work. He likes things traditional. He likes dinner on the table. He's not mean or anything. He's just checked out. He's a man of obligation. A provider. So, I've never really seen my parents in love. They cope with each other. I'm surprised my mom is still with him, considering my brothers and I are all older now."

"Maybe there is love there, though?" Oliver asks.

"No, I think it's comfort and routine now. They both seem resigned to life. It always made me sad. I guess that's why I had so many big dreams. I didn't want to end up like them." I stop, clasp my hands over my mouth. "Wow, that's an awful thing to say."

Oliver shrugs. "It's the truth and that's okay. We either want to emulate our parents or we desperately avoid becoming them."

"Huh, I guess that's true."

"So, you don't have much of a relationship with your dad?"

"Not really. When I was living at home, he would get back from work, eat, and then turn on the TV. It's my mom who paid the most attention. But now, she and I don't get along that well."

"Sounds kinda lonely."

I look at him, admiring the ease in which he can traverse emotions without being uncomfortable. "It *was* lonely, actually," I say. "It really was. I had my brothers, but that's complicated, too."

"How so?"

"My older brother was the golden child. Football star. Popular. I lived in his shadow. Now he publishes successful books, so that doesn't feel great. Writing was my thing and then he took it, seems better at it, too." I spit the words out and I wonder when they won't taste bitter to me. I shake it off. "And my younger brother, Liam, is one of my best friends, but for some reason, everything he does is perfect. I was the one that my mom was harsh with. I think it was because I reminded her of Margot."

"Whatever happened between Margot and June defined Margot I think."

"Do you know what happened?"

"No," he says. "Seb does. But Margot never wanted to discuss it."

"I wish I knew," I say, swaying a little. "I wish I had tried to fix it between them. Maybe my mom and I would be closer if I had."

"Maybe. Or maybe it would have made things worse." His hand bumps into mine again and it sends a shock through me. "It's so frustrating that all we want is to be understood and yet it sometimes feels impossible to find the people who do."

"It sounds like you were understood by your parents."

"Yes, and now they're gone."

"And you had Margot."

"And now Margot is gone. I have Uncle Seb. But they weren't my parents."

"Lonely?"

"Very."

We both pause, letting the words hang in the air like confessions.

"But it was Margot who brought me back to life. She was a

force of nature. I always loved Uncle Seb, and had visited many times, so I was close with Margot. But when I moved here after the fire, Margot was determined to be there for me. She made me talk about my feelings all the time. She made me express my anger. She gave me this place to be myself, and she never judged me for anything I ever said. Uncle Seb was a mess, of course. He was close with his brother, my dad. But Margot was there for me. Through it all. She had no reason to be. I mean, she wasn't family or blood. But she wouldn't let me get lost. That's how I think of it. She just wouldn't let me lose myself."

"Wow," I say, my eyes stinging with tears. "I had no idea about any of that. I wish I did. I wish I had visited and met you before and known this whole part of her life. I'm so happy she was there for you, Oliver." I'm surprised to find that I genuinely mean that.

"Me, too," he says. "Even though sometimes she was a little over-the-top." He laughs.

"In what way?" I ask.

"She gave a lot of advice," he says.

"Right? Margot was always dispelling wisdom. Sometimes on our lunches, I'd be like, 'Margot, you don't have to be my life coach. Chill.'" We both laugh and nod.

"Exactly," he says. "She was adamant. She had a way about her. Like she wanted to mold every person she met into someone who could carry out her idealistic version of the world. That's, I'm sure, part of the reason she started The Colony. She wanted to impart little lessons and shape them and then let them go shape others."

I abruptly stop walking and turn toward him. He does the same.

"That's so beautifully said," I tell him. "The Colony is really special."

He smiles widely; I feel my heart tighten.

"It is, I'm glad you're seeing it," Oliver replies. "She also had this whole thing about raising boys to become actual good men, not just 'good men.' She didn't want me to be ashamed of having feelings, or being sad, or feeling anything that might not be deemed 'manly.' Margot didn't really give a shit about conventions. She always said, 'we leave men alone too much!'" He seems like he can't stop talking and I'm entranced by him, his passion, this bond he had with Margot. "It was a bit much at first. I just wanted to go in my room and be alone, to be sad about how much I missed my mom and dad. But she was persistent. And then I talked, and eventually, I felt better. And now, I'm glad that my parents' death, or Camille leaving me, isn't a burning hole inside me, killing off anything good."

"Wow," I say. "I'm exactly the kind of person that lets disappointment kill off anything good."

"You may be that kind of person now, but you don't have to stay that way," Oliver replies gently.

"I wish Margot was still here," I whisper.

The air shifts between us, unsaid emotions and energy swirling.

"Yeah. I know. Me too. It feels like she still is, though. Margot was something special. Like a spiritual being from another world sent to evolve the species."

I laugh. "Really? A spiritual being? Oliver Hayes, who even are you?"

He shrugs, stops walking, and turns to me. "I can get deep."

I shiver at the double meaning.

"Apparently," I say.

His eyes land on mine like an electric charge. My body inches closer to him. Anything happening between Oliver and me would be a bad idea. How can I make this monumental decision about The Colony if Oliver and I are involved? That is just reckless. Oliver's drunk right now. I'm drunk. Nothing about this is a good idea, and yet...

And yet, all I want right now is to step forward and take his face in my hands.

I watch Oliver's eyes go to my lips.

My eyes go to his lips.

I take a sharp inhale. The silence between us feels like a promise. He steps forward, our eyes locked on each other.

I blink and my stupid better judgment wins out.

I break the trance and step back from him.

"It's getting late," I say, too forcefully.

He looks at me as if I've hurt him, but then quickly rearranges his face into something pleasant.

"Yeah, I guess it is," he says, putting his hand through his hair, and then rubbing his stubble. His eyes find mine again, and I lose my resolve for a moment. "Poppy…" he says, strangled, and moves toward me. I step back.

Oliver and I are not a good idea. He's grieving. I'm grieving. There's so much he wants from me with the villa, the residency. And so much I still don't know. And I'm finally writing. It's too precious to mess up.

Writing broke my heart for years and I'm just now finding a way to trust it again. I'm not here to risk getting my heart broken in multiple ways.

This is what I tell myself and hope I believe it.

"I need to go," I say. "I'm sorry." I turn on my heel before he can say anything more and walk up the last stretch of the hill without looking back to see if he's following me or not.

SEVENTEEN

Nice, France

I need a day to think. And breathe. So, I'm going to Nice today to explore on my own, and to find a new journal. The notebook I brought from home is already filled. Shopping for a new journal is one of my absolute favorite things to do. And it's been months since I've spent a moment alone.

I raided Margot's closet again and I'm wearing one of her flowy dresses, a wide-brimmed sunhat, and large sunglasses that make me feel like a film star. I love the idea that Margot walked these same streets, in clothes just like this. Channeling her confidence almost makes me believe I have some of my own.

Disembarking the train, I walk out of the station and up a steep incline. It's sunny, and warm. There doesn't seem to be a touch of autumn in the south of France, just one long continuation of summer.

Nice is bustling, a far different atmosphere than the small villages I've seen so far. I like it immediately, and walk in the direction of the water, through small side streets, dashing around French teenagers on skateboards and women pushing strollers on uneven pavement.

A group of tourists rush by me, and their guide is holding up a German flag, ushering them in the same direction I'm going. I let them pass and walk slowly behind, not in any rush.

I stroll by sidewalk restaurants, small tables and smaller chairs perched perilously close to the street where tiny cars zip by. Nobody sits inside to eat.

I see the water in the distance between buildings, a long strip of ocean. I find the paper goods store I looked up on Google earlier to my left and pop in. It's called a *paperie* and I love it on sight. I buy three new notebooks and conduct the entire transaction in my rudimentary French. I store them in my tote bag, and I carry on to the water.

I've got my swimsuit on under my dress, and a beach towel and a novel from Margot's library in my tote. Stopping off at a small *boulangerie*, I buy a ham and brie sandwich on a baguette, and a Perrier, which I store in my bag. I feel strangely accomplished by maneuvering myself through the streets of Nice on my own.

Once at the beach, I spread out my towel among the throngs of people. I'm already hot from my walk, and I want to strip off my dress quickly, but I hesitate. This is the part where I always turn back around, in fear. I have a swimsuit on, a black one-piece with a deep V neckline. I feel good in it, and yet, I'm suddenly terrified to be on a French beach in my very not-slim body, the assurance I felt only five minutes ago quickly draining from me.

I never go to the beach in LA for this exact reason. How many summer days I missed out on—it's too many to count. I hate that I still care more about how other people *perceive* my body, rather than how I *feel* about my body. I want so desperately to be someone who is unapologetic, who loves herself, who doesn't have to analyze every moment.

I want to be bold, adventurous—to say yes to life.

I finger the bottom of my dress, hesitating, ruminating.

According to Margot's wisdom, you can't *think* your way into loving yourself or feeling confident. So maybe I need to keep making one bold decision after another. Maybe I need to act in loving ways.

What would Margot do right now? Of course she'd rip off her dress and run into the water, head flung back in joy. She'd embody confidence and act on her fear.

So that's exactly what I do.

I throw my dress off in a rush and I walk with my head high to the lip of the water, and I fling myself in and float on my back, letting the salt water fill my ears and silence the world. As I buoy in the water, I smile for so long my cheeks ache.

After an hour, my fingertips are wrinkled, and I emerge from the water, wrapping my towel around me. Just as I'm about to lie down to sunbathe and read my book, a tall man with a muscular build comes into view, blocking the sun. He's shirtless, with blue-and-white-striped bathing suit shorts that cut above the knee. He is deeply olive-skinned, with amber eyes, and a sweep of dark brown hair.

"*Ciao, bella,*" he says, smiling. I squint up at him. He's quite good-looking in an obvious way. I smile back.

"*Ciao,*" I say, softly committing to the conversation he's looking to start.

"Are you American?" he asks, in accented English.

"I am."

"A beautiful American," he says. "I am Mauro."

"Poppy," I say, extending a hand. He shakes it and softly rubs his thumb on the side of my palm in a way that sends a tiny charge through me.

"It's nice to meet you," he says, letting go of my hand. "I saw you coming out of the water, and you looked so happy, so full of life, I had to come say hello." I flush and feel flattered. I guess confidence really is attractive. Another thing Margot was right about.

"It's nice to meet you, too," I say, jutting my chin out. My thoughts veer to Oliver and I shake them off. *This* is harmless for my heart. Oliver is *not*.

"Are you staying here in Nice?" Mauro asks.

"No, I'm staying over in Cap Ferrat." I point in the general direction of the villa.

"Oh, Cap Ferrat, *bella*," he says effusively. "I know a great restaurant over there. Would you have dinner with me tonight?"

I hesitate for a moment. What would Margot do? She'd say yes. No question. This could be fun. Adventurous. Daring. Bold. Wasn't I just saying I wanted to be more of those things?

Plus, I'm writing a romance novel. Do it for the plot, indeed.

So, I say to Mauro with a flirty smile, "I'd love to."

"Va bene!" His eyes light up, and he flashes me a bright smile. The way he's looking at me, it feels like he wants to devour me right here. I stand up straighter, lift my chest, and I watch his eyes rove over me, landing on my lips.

"I can't wait," he finally breathes out and touches my arm, skin to skin, and I feel heat there.

I give him my address and phone number. He tells me he'll pick me up at eight and I spend the next four hours of the afternoon intermittently sunbathing and swimming, unsuccessfully reading my book due to overactive nerves, and cataloging my very small wardrobe trying to decide what to wear.

When I get back from Nice, the mood at the villa is lively. Evie, Jasmyn, Kerry, Caroline, and Beau are seated at the large dining room table. Beau has his own chair, his fluffy head peeking out above the table. When he sees me, he rushes to say hello. I pick him up brightly and carry him over to the table and deposit him back on a chair, then say hi to everyone.

"You look glowy and tan," Jasmyn says. "And smiley. Did something happen in Nice?"

I laugh and spread my hands across my face, remembering the way Mauro looked at me.

"Something did happen!" Evie exclaims with genuine excitement. "Look at her!"

"Tell us!" Caroline trills, smiling.

"Well, I had a great day," I say, being purposefully obtuse. "Got some new journals. Always love the thrill of a new journal." I take a dramatic pause. "And I may have a date tonight with a very sexy Italian man."

"Yesssssss," Evie screams out gutturally.

"Get it," Kerry says, smiling widely.

"It's casual," I say, laughing. "Very casual. Just fun. Good research for my romance novel."

"Right, *research*," Jasmyn says, eyeing me.

"You're my hero, Poppy. I love how you just go for it," Evie says. "You *would* go to Nice for a day and land a hot date with a stranger."

I would? Since when?

Huh. I don't see myself that way at all. This isn't the first time that someone has a perception of me that is wildly different than my own. Before I can respond and tell her I'm flattered, Stella approaches from the backyard with Oliver following behind her.

"Who's going on a hot date with a stranger?" Stella asks. My stomach drops. Oliver and Stella, together again.

"I'm going on a date tonight," I tell her, looking at both of them but focusing on Oliver, whose eyes widen in surprise. He quickly maneuvers his face into a neutral expression. This strengthens my resolve to go out with Mauro. My feelings are too complicated when it comes to Oliver. Just seeing him makes my mind spin. It could never be casual with him. There's way too much between us with the villa, with Margot, with the residency. And if he's dating Stella, then, well, that makes it easier all around.

I just wish I could stop myself from feeling anything for him.

Stop that flood of jealousy when I see them together. Get him out of my head.

"How fun," Stella says, showing sincere excitement, but looking at Oliver with narrowed eyes. I don't understand this dynamic at all.

"Okay, most importantly, what are you going to wear?" Caroline asks me. I watch Stella and Oliver shuffle by together and head into the kitchen.

"I don't know," I say, pretending to be distressed for all their benefit. They laugh.

"I'll help you get ready," Caroline says. "It will be so fun!"

Beau, Caroline, and I head upstairs. When we get to my room, I lower my voice and I ask Caroline, "Not that I care, but do you think Stella and Oliver are like…together now?"

Caroline's eyes narrow at me. "You have feelings for Oliver and you're out there talking about your hot date? Bad girl!" She smiles and I feel my breath rush out of me.

"Okay, say, hypothetically, I had a couple feelings for Oliver. It wouldn't really matter, because I'm not interested in anything serious," I say, crossing my arms over my chest, and sitting down on the bench at the end of the bed. Beau jumps up to snuggle in right next to me, his warm body comforting. "And who knows how Oliver feels about me."

Because isn't that part of it, too? That I'm scared he doesn't feel the same way. That I'm being foolish for thinking a man like Oliver would ever choose someone like me over someone like Stella. That I'm reading into everything when all he's doing is being accommodating and kind. God, it really brings me back to those days in middle and high school when I used to get it wrong all the time. When boys would choose my thin friends over me. When I mistook friendliness as flirting. When nobody ever wanted me. When I expressed interest and a guy would say he only saw me as a friend, when all that time I thought he had been interested. My face burns.

I have done such a good job of healing from those days. Past boyfriends always had to make their feelings overwhelmingly known for me to notice or get involved. The sort of unreadable nature of Oliver scares me. And the thought of being rejected by him, of making this all up in my head—I'd rather not know. It makes me nauseous just thinking about it.

"Poppy?" Caroline asks, breaking me from my overthinking.

"Huh?" I say, coming to. "Sorry. You were saying."

"Well, you would know how he feels if you asked him," Caroline says, walking toward my closet and rifling through it, hangers banging against each other. "But Stella did tell me she was interested in Oliver and the difference between you and her is…she seems open to something happening with him." Caroline smiles, but it's a stern smile.

"Sure, but Stella looks like *that*," I say. "She can have any guy she wants."

"And…you can't?" Caroline scrunches her nose up at me.

I shrug helplessly and she rolls her eyes.

"Poppy, I don't know who convinced you that you're not beautiful, but they were wrong." Caroline crosses the room and sits on the edge of the bed. Beau jumps over to be next to her, and she pets his head.

"Okay, I don't think I'm not beautiful, but I'm not Stella, that's for sure," I say, hating the way my voice has lost its conviction, hating the way my confidence seems to deflate and inflate from moment to moment. I remember my mom saying to me, that I have "such a pretty face." In a way where the "it's a pity" was implied. Like my face was wasted on my body. That's not something you forget quickly.

I wave off Caroline's praise. Caroline is naturally, effortlessly thin. It's easy to dole out compliments when your body isn't something people have to *get over*. When you fit in, you can never understand what it is like to stand out, in ways that aren't always favorable. And plus, you never know when a thin woman, even your own friend, will drop a bomb on you and say she "feels fat" or is terrified of gaining weight, of, essentially, looking like you, even in the same breath that she calls you beautiful. You never know what kind of thin woman you're talking to. But I don't say any of that to Caroline, because she is so earnest and genuine. I wouldn't want her to think I don't appreciate her support.

"Have a shower, Poppy. I'll do your hair and makeup when you're ready." I nod and go into the bathroom, emerging twenty minutes later with freshly shaven legs and my dark brown hair wrapped in a towel.

I sit on a chair next to the expansive bedroom window, Beau on my lap. The last of the natural light is flooding in, casting a golden hue across the room. I let Caroline's soft sweeps of eyeshadow and blush relax me.

"Your eyes are stunning," Caroline says while applying mascara. "The red lipstick I'm going to use will make your green eyes stand out even more." She smiles warmly, and I feel like I'm in good hands.

Caroline blows out my hair and curls it with a rod she retrieved from Evie. She won't let me look in the mirror yet. She pulls out something from the back of my closet, a short red dress with a nipped in waist and a low round neckline. I brought it in a panic, thinking I might need at least one nice dress, but I haven't worn it once. Caroline insists I do. I protest.

"It's too booby!" I tell her, and she laughs.

"It's a sexy dress, and you're wearing it," she says, in a tone that says the conversation is over and the dress is going on. I shake my head and laugh.

I put on the dress, and it feels good, hugging my body in a way that makes me feel bold. I add thick gold hoops that offset the hummingbird necklace and a pair of tan heels that slide on with ease. I turn around and Caroline gasps, her hands covering her mouth, eyes slightly weepy.

"Poppy, you look like a fucking goddess."

When I look in the mirror, I can't help but agree with her. The makeup is smoky and sexy. The red lipstick matches the dress with precision. My skin is luminous and full of color from my day at the beach. The dress highlights every single feature of mine I like, my shapely legs, the curve of my waist, the soft skin of my chest, the just-right amount of cleavage. My hair falls in loose waves below my shoulders, and while I know for sure beauty isn't everything, I notice the way I feel as I walk down the hallway toward the stairs. *Powerful.*

It's five to eight, and I expect Mauro any moment. I thank Caroline profusely and she waves me off like it's nothing. She is such a kind, generous soul. It seems like Margot attracted the best people into her life.

Caroline goes downstairs with Beau, and I rush back to my room for the clutch I forgot. I stuff the red lipstick in it, my phone, and the keys to the villa. My stomach gives a small lurch of nerves. It's just a date. It's research. It's a night out. It's low risk. A harmless adventure with a good-looking man.

I descend the stairs, and down at the foyer, standing stock-still is Oliver, a pained and indecipherable look on his face as he watches me. I lock eyes with him, and I notice him gulping. If I were impartial, I would say he's looking at me as if I am a delectable dessert, and maybe tonight, maybe the way I feel right now, I could believe that.

The entire room stills. That thing is happening again, where there is no noise, no movement, nothing but the blur around us. It's just us, even when it's not. That needs to stop happening.

On the last step, he holds his hand out to help me down, and I take it, feeling my body tingle in response to the slight and soft touch.

"You look...stun—Uh, I mean, you look different," he says, his voice low and intimate. I hear commotion by the dining room table, but here in the foyer, it's private.

"Different bad, or different good?" I ask him, moving closer, unable to stop myself, despite all my better judgments.

He swallows audibly and runs his hands through his thick hair. "Good," he chokes out. "Definitely...good. Very good."

I smile, forgetting where I am, or why I'm dressed like this. I want to step even closer toward Oliver, but I stop myself. I don't think I've breathed for a full minute. His gaze is so intense on me, nerves build up in my stomach.

Oliver starts to speak, but before the words come out, there's a loud knock, and we both come to, jumping slightly. We look at the door, as if we're confused.

Oliver's hands stroke his stubble, and he grimaces. "Well, uh, enjoy your date," he says, in the same resigned tone I've heard from him before. He walks off quickly, and all I'm left with are complications and subtext—exactly what I don't need or want right now.

I open the door to Mauro, and his eyes immediately fall to my chest. He smiles widely and says, *"Bella!"* No obfuscation. There is no confusion here, and it's that conviction which leads me outside, into the warm evening, Mauro's hand at the small of my back, ushering me forward.

As Mauro starts the car, I stare at the closed door of the villa, with a longing that I can't ignore. It takes me a few minutes of pause before I can bring myself back to the present moment, to engage Mauro in a conversation, and to let go of the way Oliver watched me on those stairs. He had a look of such pained yearning. I force myself to forget about it so I won't make Mauro turn the car around.

EIGHTEEN

Nice, France

"Red or white, *bella*?" Mauro holds out two separate bottles of wine in his hands, and I point to the white one. "Good choice," he says, grinning at me over the kitchen island.

It's our third date in four days, a casual yet fun whirlwind. I'm at his apartment for the first time. He's cooking his "famous" puttanesca, and I have been told to sit back, relax, and let him take care of everything.

Mauro is romantic to an almost comical degree. On our first date, he told me he wanted to sweep me off my feet, in those exact words. He's almost too stereotypically Italian, with his lavish compliments and completely transparent desire for me.

"And how was your day, *bella*?" Mauro turns away from the pot on the stove and looks at me. The aromas coming from the kitchen right now are glorious—garlic and tomatoes and fresh olives from a market Mauro told me he went to earlier today.

"Great," I tell him. "I got a lot of writing done." I beam. It feels nice to finally be able to say that. And have it be true.

"Writing?" He shoots me a quizzical look, and I feel a small surge of surprise. Surely I've told him, several times over the last two dates, that I'm writing two books?

"I'm writing a book," I say. "Well, two, actually."

"Oh yes, yes, right," he says, hitting his forehead with his hand. "I forgot for *un momento*."

I wave it off.

"And how was your day?" I ask.

"Good," he says, turning around again to stir the contents of the pot. "I shopped for our dinner, did some work, and thought about you all day." He wheels around and gives me another winning smile, and an exaggerated wink. I blush under his gaze, and he sees the color on my cheeks. "I like when you blush like that."

I give him a coy smile. The air feels charged. We've made out a few times, but haven't slept together yet. I don't even know if I want to. I'm not against casual sex or flings—I've had a few—but I just don't know if I'm that attracted to him. I was thinking this date would determine whether I want to continue seeing him. I don't feel that *spark* yet.

I've finished my glass of wine and Mauro pours me another generous one. He sets down the spoon he's been using to stir his sauce, covers the pot, and walks over to me.

"That needs to simmer for a while," he says, edging closer to me until his face is level with mine, until I can feel the exhale of his breath on my cheek. "Let's go to the couch." He gives me a lingering kiss on my forehead, and I take my glass of wine as he leads me to the living room.

We settle down on the couch and put our wineglasses on the coffee table. Mauro's arm goes around my shoulders, and he slides as close to me as possible.

"You smell so good, Poppy," he says, taking an inhale and trailing his fingers down my neck to my collarbone. Before I can answer, he's pushed me on my back and is on top of me, clawing at my thighs, and kissing my breasts through my dress.

It's fast—too fast.

My breathing picks up.

He grabs my face and kisses me hard. I can feel the outline of him pushing into my leg. I don't feel turned-on. I feel suddenly alarmed. *Very* alarmed.

And it's clear to me that I do not want Mauro. At all.

"Stop," I tell him, in a voice that feels far away from me.

"Oh, come on," he says, placating me. His mouth is on my mouth, his tongue darting in and out, and this is nothing like the soft and gentle kissing of the last two dates. This is forceful.

"Get off me," I yell out, my dress askew, Mauro's pants almost completely off. In the swift movement, my dress nearly rips from his tight grasp. I push his broad chest hard, and he falls back on the couch, a perplexed expression on his face.

"What the hell?" he asks, harshly. That tone tells me everything I need to know about Mauro. A gentleman until he wants what he wants—and can't have it.

"I'm leaving," I command. I stand up quickly. He grabs my arm and yanks me back down, too hard, much too hard.

And then, he softens, his face contorting back into something gentle. What was once charming now looks like a grotesque mask.

"Please, Poppy, just stay. Let's go in the bedroom. We can just cuddle." I shake my head, but he still has me pinned, and I feel like I'm about to explode. He goes in for a kiss, and I dodge under his arm, and dart up from the couch.

My possessions are haphazard around the apartment, and I go around quickly collecting my purse from the chair in the living room, my phone from the kitchen island, my shoes from the entryway. I head to open the front door and Mauro is there, with his hand gripping the handle to stop me from leaving.

"Let me go," I say, through clenched teeth. I'm about to scream. I'm about to scratch the skin off his face. I could kill him, I'm so angry. He is the amalgamation of every man who has ever disappointed me, made me feel small and helpless and foolish. Rage blinds me. I start to shake.

"I thought American girls were supposed to be easy," he says. "Especially fat American girls. You're rejecting *me*?" He laughs sharply and snarls. I look at him closely and see the real Mauro now.

Part of me wants to just walk away, hang my head in shame, let those words take all the confidence from me that I've been building. That's what I would have done in the past. But no. Not anymore. I'm done letting people say whatever they want to me and feeling like I deserve to be cast aside.

"And who are you? Some small man in a cheap suit, thinking women owe you something," I finally spit out. "You're a piece of shit. Let me out. *Now.*"

"Gladly," he says, finally releasing the handle and opening the door for me. I slip out and before the door closes fully, I hear him shout at me, "Bitch." My eyes widen in surprise and the words feel like a slap across my face, but I am sprinting now, down the hallway and to the stairs.

I can't get out of his apartment building fast enough.

When I finally hit the open air, I gulp in huge breaths, my hands on my knees, doubled over. An older woman passes by me on the street and looks at me strangely and then asks, *"Ça va?" Are you okay?*

I nod at her and tell her, *"Oui, ça va, merci." Yes, I'm okay, thank you.* She nods, concerned, and rests her hand on my shoulder for a beat, looking me in the eyes, and then continues on her way. A little moment of humanity. A tiny kindness that emboldens me enough to stand up straight and figure out a way home. I'm in Nice, driven here by Mauro, and I need a taxi stand.

I walk into the cool night air, feeling safer the more space I put between Mauro and me, and the fact that Nice is lively any time of the night. Being around people right now, and not isolated in an apartment with a man I hardly know, is what I need.

Finally, after a few blocks, I find a taxi stand, with three taxis waiting for customers. I climb into the first one, show him the address for the villa on my phone, and let out a gust of breath.

Why did I go to a man's apartment…alone? I hardly knew him. That wasn't smart.

No.

I stop that train of thought.

This isn't my fault. Or my shame to carry. This is *his* shame. Mauro is probably shaking his head right now, angry that some woman he thought was beneath him had the gall to reject him. He should be the one feeling ashamed. He should be the one who analyzes how he got to that place, how he ended up there. I didn't do anything wrong.

And I stood up for myself. Finally.

I refuse to spend this long taxi ride home carrying the shame he should feel.

I'm not going to do it.

I find, to my surprise, that I have too much self-respect to blame myself.

As the taxi driver and I ride in silence, the low hum of the radio coming in through the speakers, all I can think is: thank god I got out of there when I did.

Just. Thank god.

NINETEEN

Cap Ferrat, France

An hour later, I'm outside the front door of the villa, collecting myself before walking in. I feel like I am askew and distracted. I smoothed my hair down as much as I could in the taxi, but mascara is smudged across my face. I just want to get inside the villa without seeing anyone and take a long and scalding hot shower.

I open the door tentatively, but it's an old house, and it creaks in the quiet night. The lights are dim, and when I walk in, the first thing I see is Oliver and Stella, sitting very close together on the large couch with an empty bottle of wine and two glasses on the coffee table. When they look over at the door, they spring apart, like I caught them doing something they shouldn't be doing. I don't even have the energy to be jealous. I just want to go to my room.

Stella stands up, her face downcast, and moves toward me. Her eyes narrowed and concerned, she asks in a soft voice, "Are you okay, Poppy?" Her kindness almost breaks me, and I take a strengthening breath in, and nod my head.

"I'm fine, just tired," I say, biting back emotion. She doesn't believe me, I can tell, because her face is creased with worry.

"How was your date? We thought you'd be spending the night there for sure," she says. *We.* Yeah, I can't deal with this. I just shake my head and rush upstairs, not trusting my own voice, not trusting that I won't break down in front of them. *We.* My throat drops into my chest. No, stop. One crisis at a time.

I finally get to my room, and I rip off my clothes and get in the shower, scrubbing the night off, the faint smell of Mauro's strong cologne that's lingering on my skin.

After, I wrap myself in a large white robe. It has Margot's initials on it, and I am comforted just by knowing it was hers. I sit down on the chair by the window and try to breathe calmly, when I hear a soft knock at my bedroom door. I groan, thinking it's probably Stella. She knows I'm in here, though. I'll just get rid of her. I feel bad, because she's being kind, but she's the last person I'd want to divulge a romance gone bad to. Especially if she and Oliver are dating. I'm trying not to feel mortified, but that emotion is hovering near me, and if I see a look of pity on Stella's face, I might just lose it.

When I open the door, I'm surprised to see that it's Oliver, his face pained, his hand stroking over his stubble.

He speaks first, breaking the tense silence between us.

"Poppy, what happened tonight?" He strokes his stubble again, and his eyes deepen with anxiety the more I look at him and don't say anything. What can I say? It's not something I want to relive right now.

"Nothing," I say, my voice high-pitched, not hiding anything at all. "Don't worry about it." I try to give him a smile, but I know it's forced. It's a tight line, and Oliver is much too intuitive to take it at face value. I can tell he's not going to leave without knowing more and my heart sinks.

"That didn't look like nothing. Something happened. What

did he do?" His hands are balled into fists. "When I saw him earlier this week, I had a feeling something was off about him."

He searches my eyes and I nod. I feel tears threatening. I don't want to cry, but it might be impossible to stop it.

"Turns out, he's not a good guy," I concede.

"What did he do?"

I don't meet Oliver's eyes. I keep them trained on the ground, speaking in almost a whisper. "He got forceful with me. He was so sweet on our first two dates, but then when we were alone, it was like he turned into someone else. Before I knew what was happening, he was on top of me, and so aggressive. All of his charm was gone. He just wanted what he wanted, regardless of me. I should not have gone to his apartment. I don't know what I was thinking." I feel the bubble of shame coming up, and Oliver lays a gentle hand on my forearm.

"Did he…?" Oliver asks, trailing off.

I shake my head. "I got away before that could happen, thankfully. But he was spiteful and mean. So mean." I try not to remember the words he called me, the venom of them.

"Hey," Oliver says tenderly. His voice sounds breakable. "You don't deserve to be treated like that. Ever. I'm sorry this happened."

All the adrenaline leaves me at once, and in its place, a sadness comes rushing in.

Oliver comes toward me with his arms out and looks at me, waiting for permission, and when I give him a slight nod, he wraps himself around me. I start crying then, big tears that fall on the shoulder of his hoodie, my face nuzzled into his neck. He tightens his hold on me and his hand palms my head, strokes my wet hair. I don't even know why I'm crying. I know I did nothing wrong tonight. I'm just… It was a lot.

And I feel this sense of sheer vulnerability pulsing its way through me. I'm in a foreign country, surrounded by people I only just met, all the risk I was trying to avoid now back in my life. This whole thing with Mauro just makes me feel more raw and exposed.

I take a deep breath and pull away from the hug. The spot on his shoulder where my head was is wet with tears. I brush at it and say, "Sorry."

He looks over at it and shrugs. "Better that you cry and let it out, then keep it in and let it consume you. Believe me." I realize that, of course he understands. He's had unspeakable tragedy in his life, some of which I can't ever relate to or be able to comprehend. His compassion is hard-won.

I wipe my eyes dry, feeling cleansed, feeling much better than I expected to feel tonight. "How did you get through it all?" I'm asking about his marriage that never happened, but also his parents.

"I got through it by not going through it alone. I let people help me. Sebastian, Margot, my friends back home when Camille left me. I got myself into therapy. I had no interest in suffering on my own. I guess that was a gift, because a lot of people think they have to. Sebastian and Margot wouldn't let me, honestly."

"Wow, Margot really did do a great job with you," I say, laughing.

"Thank you," he says seriously, not realizing I was making a slight joke. "That means a lot to me. I hope I make her proud." He's so earnest I almost have to look away. I'm not used to men who are as sensitive and open as Oliver.

"I'm sure you did and do make her proud, Oliver," I say. His eyes moisten. How he got me to open up, process what happened, and genuinely smile within the space of half an hour, I do not know. "But really, thank you," I add. "I feel a lot better."

"Do you? Well, good. I mean, I didn't come up here to make you feel better. I just got so worried," he says, looking shy. He clears his throat. "So, do you want to be alone now? Or, I don't know if you want to take your mind off things, but there's a Scrabble board downstairs? If you'd be up for a game?"

I'm surprised to find I'm very up for a game.

"That sounds perfect," I say. "But I have to warn you—I am a truly dangerous Scrabble player." His lips quirk, and he unleashes a blindingly wonderful smile.

"I'm not surprised by that," he replies. "But I'm also dangerous. Two out of three? Winner buys dinner next time we go together?"

"Deal," I tell him. I hold out my hand, and he shakes it. The contact sends a buzz through me.

Over the next few hours, as the night deepens, and the villa is quiet, we play three games of Scrabble at the dining room table, drinking copious amounts of chamomile tea with milk and honey. We laugh, we challenge each other's words, and in the end, as it nears 3:00 a.m. and my eyelids are drooping, I drop a bingo on a triple-word score during our tiebreaker game. Oliver's eyes dart up to mine, his face the picture of admiration.

"Damn," he says, shaking his head. "You were right. Very dangerous." He smiles, that blinding, beautiful smile, and the pain of earlier tonight is not exactly forgotten, but lessened considerably.

"Looks like dinner's on me," he adds, and I expect him to look chastised, but instead, he looks pleased as hell.

As we collect the tiles on the board, I realize something suddenly. It hits me like a lightning bolt of recognition. For the first time ever, something has happened to me, and I haven't made it mean anything. I didn't take on the blame. I didn't make it about me at all, that I'm not good enough, or that I deserve to be treated that way, or I'm a person that attracts bad situations. Instead, I blame Mauro for the way he treated me. I didn't do anything wrong. This experience does not have to define me. How many times in the past have I let the "negative" experiences define me, to tell me what is possible or not for me? Too many to count.

This is such a huge point of growth; I feel almost light-headed to realize it. I have grown into a kind of self-respect and worth I didn't know I needed or would ever be able to access.

It feels good. It feels…strong.

I realize, I haven't thought about the escape hatch of selling the villa in December, giving up, my life back in LA, or my past writer's block in a while.

Hope. This is hope. After a long drought of it, here it is, flooding in.

NOVEMBER

TWENTY

Cap Ferrat, France

The rest of October passes in a blur and suddenly it's November, and the French Riviera is starting to feel like home. I have a month to make my decision to sell the villa and two months after that to complete a book. I'm nearly halfway through both of my novels, so I'm feeling cautiously optimistic I'll finish in time. When it comes to the villa, I'm leaning toward keeping it, but I haven't fully committed. I'm scared to draw a line in the sand. Scared to leap into that unknown. Scared, more than anything, to get my hopes up too high. Everything good right now feels so fragile.

I'm in the backyard of the villa with Sebastian and Oliver at sunset. I've been avoiding being alone with Oliver since the Scrabble night. My feelings are becoming harder to deny, and being around him—desperately not wanting him to leave or take that job in New York—is confusing the situation. I don't want to keep the villa *for* Oliver. But I also don't want to lose him. And whenever he's in the vicinity, I lose all my good sense and seem ready to risk it all. Plus, if it happens that I sell the villa, Oliver will hate me. I just need to keep things simple, and creating distance between him and me helps that. It's the smarter, more measured choice.

I am trying so hard to not take too many risks that I'm out here exposed to disappointment and heartache again.

But it's a Friday evening and Sebastian wanted to have a glass of wine with Oliver and me before they leave for Portugal and Spain for the next few weeks on a trip they apparently take together every November.

We're all sharing a bottle of dry sauvignon blanc in the open air as the sun dips into the horizon, casting the sky in a pink-and-orange gradient.

There's a slight chill as the day blends into evening, but it's still nice enough to sit outside with the electric heaters warming us.

"How's your writing going, Poppy?" Sebastian asks while he tops up my glass of wine. "You think you'll finish by the time the six months are up?"

I beam. "Writing is going amazing," I say. "It's so good to actually say that and mean it. And yeah, I think I will finish. That's the plan, at least." I know I should be deciding on The Colony, but all my time has been spent writing, amazed that it hasn't dried up yet, focused entirely on how good it feels to be prolific.

"So, being here has cured your writer's block, then?" Sebastian asks, chuckling. "You can see why Margot chose this place for The Colony."

"I totally see why," I say, as my eyes travel to Oliver who is watching me with an unguarded smile.

He looks so damn beautiful tonight it reminds me of why I've been keeping my distance. He is, to me, actually irresistible and the only thing that helps is drawing boundaries around how often I'm alone with him.

He's wearing a cream cable-knit sweater, the waves of his hair tousled, with a tendril hanging over his forehead that I keep wanting to twirl on my finger and push off his face. I can't seem to peel my eyes from his, and when I look back at Sebastian, he's giving me a knowing look.

I clear my throat. "Seb, what made Margot want to start The Colony, by the way? Like what's the story behind it?"

"About eleven years ago, she got an idea completely out of nowhere to start a residency program for writers," Sebastian says, a fond smile on his face. "Said it was a dream. Like an actual dream. She saw it all happening, exactly the way she wanted to create it, the camaraderie, supporting artists, all of it. Said it felt like her whole life was leading her to this moment."

"I remember that," Oliver says, looking at Sebastian. "Came into the house one day and said 'this is what I'm starting, do you want to help?'"

"Just like that?" I ask.

"Just like that," Oliver says, snapping his fingers. "She had a whole idea planned out."

"It was exactly the kind of thing Margot would want to do," Sebastian says. "Help people realize their full potential. Give them a space to be themselves. The Colony is about writing, of course, but it's also about community, inclusivity, acceptance. And she felt like the people who came here were *meant* to be here. That the souls meant to be at The Colony would always find their way here. And she has never been wrong about that."

"Was Margot a witch?" I ask, laughing.

"Yes," Sebastian says, a little more serious than I expect. "She kind of was."

"She was definitely witchy," Oliver cuts in. "Always did some sort of ritual for the full moon and solstices. Believed the Universe led you where you were meant to be. A little psychic."

"Plus, she was a Scorpio," Sebastian says, laughing. "The witchiest sign."

Oliver nods.

"I want to trust my intuition like she did," I say, almost a whisper.

"She didn't really come into her gifts until her late thirties," Sebastian says. "You have time." He gives me a soft grin. I smile back.

"She always said that every group of residents left feeling like better versions of themselves," Oliver says, his voice reverential. "And she said every group made *her* a better version of herself, too."

"She really was the most special and unique person," I say, emotion laced in the words.

"Your grandmother, Margot and June's mom—she wasn't very supportive of the girls," Sebastian says. I sit up straight, eager for information. "She was angry their dad left, took it out on them. She wanted the sisters to make sure they had a man to take care of them, so they never ended up like her. That's what she focused on. I think that made your mom choose the traditional route. It was what your grandmother thought was right. But instead, it made Margot want to help women escape domesticity. Margot was fiercely independent as a result of her mom's worldview."

"Wow," I say. "That explains my mom a lot, actually. She never talks about her past. I hardly know anything about my grandmother. My mom is a homemaker. It's her whole identity. And she always seemed disappointed in me that I didn't want the same thing."

"Margot had a feeling June was like that with you," Sebastian says sadly. "That's why she reached out to you. June was like that with her, too. Hated Margot's wild, rebellious side."

"I think she was jealous," I spit out.

"Maybe," Sebastian replies. "Their mom was a hard woman. I think they both had to figure out how to survive it."

"My mom doesn't seem happy. Was Margot happy?" I ask. "Like, really happy?"

"Margot was complicated," Oliver says, cutting in. "She enjoyed life on her own terms, but she wasn't always happy, no. I personally think she didn't let enough people in. She used work to distract her a lot." He looks at Sebastian. "I know she had all her lovers, Seb, but I think she just didn't want to get hurt and that's why she never committed with any of them."

"I would agree with that," Sebastian says. "Over the years, there were a few great loves she could have had, but whenever it got too real, she cut out."

"I can't imagine Margot ever being too afraid for anything," I whisper.

"Poppy," Sebastian says. "Margot gave a lot of advice, but she didn't always take her own. With her career, she always did what scared her and was quite brave. With people, she kept everyone at a distance."

"That's how my mom is," I say. "She never stops moving and it's very hard to get close to her. Whatever happened between them scarred them both it seems." And I wonder if it scarred me, too. Made me afraid of everything, some sort of sick combination of both of their fears manifesting within me. I look at Sebastian. "Do *you* know what happened?"

He nods. "But, it's not my story to tell."

"Except, Margot's not here to tell it," I say.

"I don't think she'd want me to tell you." Sebastian sets his palms down on the table. "You'll have to ask your mom."

"I have. She won't tell me."

"Then, it's not my place to say."

"Okay," I say. "I get it."

"Shall we open another?" Sebastian asks, pointing to the drained bottle of white resting in a bucket of ice. "How about a nice red?"

"Sure," I say, but I feel far away. What happened between them? Why was Margot so closed off? Why is my mom the same way? And...am I that way, too? Have I been doing the same thing, keeping myself from being fully vulnerable with the people I love? Something about it rings true. It sends a wave of recognition through my body.

I love Margot, but I don't want to be closed off like that. I want the good parts of Margot—the boldness to start a business based only on a dream and an intuitive sense. I don't want to be like my mom, stuck and angry. I want to live and be known. I want to risk my heart being broken. I want to write books, even if I get rejected over and over.

As I look out over the backyard, feeling full and at peace and happy for the first time in a long time, it hits me that I could do this. I could live here. This could be my life. My real life. I don't have to keep bracing for the next disappointment, making my life and dreams smaller and smaller so I never have to be let down.

I don't want to go through my life afraid. I don't want to collect broken hearts like Margot or discarded dreams like my mom.

I can be brave. Take chances. That's the kind of person I want to be, at least.

TWENTY-ONE

Cap Ferrat, France

It's the Monday before Thanksgiving, and the month has rushed by at a breakneck pace, full of more writing and more of me thinking about what I want to do and the type of person I want to be. I keep telling myself I want to be bolder, and then I hedge on it. I still haven't made decisions on what I want to do and the December deadline is fast approaching.

Oliver returns today from his trip, and Sebastian flew from Barcelona to London for the week. That stretch of time gave me a moment to breathe, and to work on both my books. Just yesterday, I sent off the partial manuscript of my romance novel—*You Had Me at Bonjour*—to Claudia, who responded immediately, confirmed she received it, and effusively assured me she can't wait to read it. And just like that, it's happening. I'm back in the game again.

The residents are gone for the week, off to their homes for Thanksgiving, and Janelle made sure that every single one of us would not write a word of our books during the break. "Let your ideas marinate," she told us. "Trust that rest brings inspiration." So here I am, alone in the villa for the first time ever, trusting.

I go down the hill to the beach for a walk. It's gray and windy, which is a welcomed change from the constant sunshine of the Côte d'Azur. Walking through the maze of villas, I finally have a calm moment to think and no writing to distract me. I take a deep breath to process and parse out everything that has happened lately.

The tap of my writing has been opened and it's flooding in, finally. I haven't written with this much passion and joy since my early twenties. I sent a book off to an agent. A real agent. Things are happening. Old stories and patterns are being broken.

I'm not just starting to feel a tiny bit of hope; I feel practically flooded with it. And I'm having a very hard time trusting myself because of it. When I hope, I do stupid, reckless things. At least, that's been the story I've told myself in the past.

I need my sounding board, my best friend, and one of the only people I can trust to tell me the truth and have my best interest at heart.

I call Mia, catching her on her drive to work.

"Pop," she says, answering the phone cheerfully. Mia is already up to date on everything since we text nearly every day.

"Mia," I say.

"You're calling and not texting, so something is on your mind. Tell me. I'm stuck in traffic on the 405 so you know I've got some time."

I laugh. "You know me too well. So, yeah, the thing is: Would it be ridiculous for me to stay here? And run The Colony? And like, move my life here? Is that nuts? Because, I think I want to."

"Ridiculous?" Mia asks, laughing. "I think you'd be ridiculous to *not* want to do that."

"But it's a lot of responsibility and my whole life is in LA."

"People move all the time, Pop," she says, kindly. "If it feels right, why would you question it?"

"Because lots of things in the past have felt right and then I end up disappointed," I say through a rush of breath. "The fear that nothing will ever work out for me is so loud."

I pass by an older woman walking her dog.

"*Bonjour,*" she says.

"*Bonjour,*" I say back, waving.

"You love it there," Mia says, bringing me back to the conversation. "I can tell. Stop fighting it."

"But I don't know what's best for me," I say. "Sometimes I feel like I can't trust myself at all."

"I think you do trust yourself," Mia says. "But you're afraid of the risk."

I let that sink in for a moment.

"Maybe," I say. "I mean, I'm trying. I came here because it was Aunt Margot's last wish. But how do I know if I'm supposed to stay? I think I want to. I missed Oliver so much when he was gone. I don't know if I can keep fighting all of this. I think I really want this to be my life, Mia. And that's so scary to admit. I wanted to *stop* wanting things. I hate feeling vulnerable and open to disappointment."

"I'm so glad to hear you finally admit it," she says. "I've been waiting." She chuckles loudly. "Pop, what if the fact that you're writing, that you have feelings for someone, that running The Colony all sounds exciting is the only proof you need to stay? You're more open to good things happening to you, which hasn't been true for a long time."

"Good point," I say, smiling to myself. This is all resonating hard.

"I'll say this one last thing," she says. "Let yourself be loved, let yourself want and desire and have. Challenge yourself. Don't be so afraid. If things don't work out, just try a different direction. I know you don't want a life on the sidelines, Pop. You're the main fucking character of your story, remember? You've got to live it as fully as you can, don't you think?"

I feel my eyes moisten. She's echoing all the same thoughts I've been having.

"Yes," I say, my voice cracking. "I think the only way I'm going to get past this fear is to walk right into it. I've tried to avoid it, but that doesn't work. Obviously. I need to just go straight into the fear." My heart starts racing, but I know this is what I need to do. Make the decision to keep the villa. Go after Oliver. Be bold. What would Margot do? I actually don't know in this situation. But I know what the Poppy I *want* to be would do. She'd be brave as hell, not just about the writing—but about everything.

"You know I'd support you if you wanted to quit everything," Mia says. "But I don't think you're there anymore."

"You're right." I take a deep breath. "Thank you for being my life coach today."

Mia laughs. "I'll send you my invoice."

"Please."

"So you're really going to stay? I'll miss you terribly, but now I have an excuse to come to France."

"And a villa to stay in!"

"Secretly, I've been trying to convince you to stay there just for that reason," Mia quips.

"I love you," I say, laughing.

"I love you too, Pop. Now, go be brave. Channel that main character energy."

I smile. "I'll try."

I walk a bit more and think about that conversation with Mia. The defeat that I was trying to run away from—I realize so much of it is about my body and what the world (and my mom) have told me about what is possible. All those rejections I received about my past writing felt like rejections of me. It felt like my mom was right, that every time my life didn't live up to the expectation I had of it, it was because of my body. And I brought that belief with me to France. That I don't deserve all of this and it's better to sabotage it before it can be taken from me. That someone like Oliver can't possibly have feelings for me. That things never work out for women who look like me. And I've been moving through the world under that belief for way too long.

And I guess what I realized, standing on the edge of possibility, is that I'm really tired of believing those voices. Of not letting myself have exactly what I want.

It's *still* about my body and I'm tired of it.

Don't I get to decide what is possible for me?

So, on that beautiful overcast beach, while the wind picks up and whips my ponytail around my face, I wipe my eyes and realize that the Poppy who loves herself, who is brave, who trusts herself, who is the damn main character in her own life…really wants to accept Margot's gift, take all the risks, enjoy the fact that I'm writing without worrying about the outcome, and finally admit that no matter how hard I try, I can't get Oliver Hayes out of my head.

I want to be bold as hell. Fearless. Take risks. Take what I deserve. And stop being afraid. For real this time.

And I know just where I want to go.

I take a deep, steadying breath and pause outside Sebastian and Oliver's door. Making my intentions known to Oliver feels like saying yes to everything at once. I feel electric, the thrill of finally letting myself have what I want—Oliver, the villa, The Colony, a career as a novelist, all of it.

I ring the doorbell, and when Oliver answers in gray sweatpants and a hoodie, his face lights up when he sees me. Beau peeks his head out quickly and jumps into my arms.

"You're back," I say to Oliver, as Beau settles into me. "How was it?"

"It was great, but I..." He trails off and rubs his stubble. "I missed home," he finally says, and our eyes meet.

"Home missed you," I say boldly, and he smiles that wonderful smile again. There's an intense beat between us. I clear my throat. "So, it's Thanksgiving this week. I was wondering if you had plans?"

"Nope," he says. "Truthfully, I usually try to avoid Thanksgiving altogether. Long story. What were you thinking?"

"At some point, I want to hear that long story," I say. "I don't know, but I thought we should do *something*."

Oliver's lips quirk into a mischievous smile. "I have an idea," he says. "You can say no if it's too much, but..."

"I'm listening." I set Beau down and lean in.

"Let's go to Paris."

"Paris?" My heart starts racing.

"Why not? It's only six hours by train. And you've never been. What else do we have to do, with the residents gone? My friend has an apartment there. He emailed me just the other day saying his place is free. It's right around the corner from Place des Vosges in the 4th. Stunning."

I don't know what any of those terms mean. But considering I just promised myself I'd be brave, there is nothing I would rather do than spend Thanksgiving in Paris with Oliver.

"Okay," I say. "Let's definitely go to Paris."

"*Parfait*," he says. And we both stand in the doorway of his home, grinning madly.

TWENTY-TWO

On a train, somewhere in the middle of France

I'm giddy. After months of trying not to feel anything toward Oliver—I'm positively unleashed. Walking through the train station, my hand keeps landing on his arm, and a shiver of feeling is sent through me. Something unspoken and provocative sits between us like a third wheel. Unsaid words, little touches, the way we keep stealing looks at each other across the table we've sat at inside the train.

Oliver stands up from his side of the booth, gives me a tender smile, and fetches us two sodas and a couple bags of chips from another car.

I take a moment to just…collect myself. I feel feral and transparent. We're going to one of the most romantic cities in the world. Alone. And there's no denying the way I feel about it. Every nerve of my body is attuned to him. I can't remember the last time I've felt this way about anyone, if I ever have, and now that I plan to keep the villa, I don't feel like I need to hold myself back anymore. I can't wait to tell him I'm keeping it.

I want him and I want him to know it. Bold. No more hiding.

Plus, if he didn't feel the same way, why would he have invited me to Paris? He didn't say it was a Margot request. I hope I'm not reading this all wrong, but even if I am, who cares? I am done being afraid. If it all ends badly, at least I *tried*.

"So, what's your plan, Oliver?" I say when he returns with our snacks. "What's the grand vision for your life? What do you want?"

"That's some opening for a conversation," he says, eyebrows raised. "Not much of a small-talk person, Poppy?"

I laugh. "Not particularly, no. The weather is nice. Trains are fun. I have two brothers. Let's get on with it. Let's crack you open, Oliver Hayes." I make a gesture of cracking open a nut and he squints at me, a smile lingering on his mouth. I watch him nod and decide to open up, like a flower beginning to bloom.

"I'm a little afraid to tell you, actually," he says. "About my grand vision."

"Afraid? Why? I don't judge." I hold my hands up in surrender.

"It's just…you have big dreams for your life. I don't. I want simpler, smaller things, on purpose. I want to be with someone I love." That sends a noticeable shiver through me. "I want to have a family. I want to do work that is meaningful, but I'd also be happy staying home with kids. Cooking, teaching them to ride bikes, how to be good people. I've never had really big ambitions. Maybe it's the French in me. Something. But I just want a happy, full life. A simple, uncomplicated life. Surrounded by people I love, doing things that matter." He shrugs. My heart fills to double its size, and I have to look out the window for a moment to shake off the intensity of him.

I look back at him. I don't speak for so long he narrows his eyes, gives a nervous laugh, and asks, "What?"

"You think that's not a big dream?" I playfully scoff at him. "That is a wildly big dream. Loving people is so hard. Why do you think most people find it easier to love a career? That, at least, makes some sense. But love is sacrifice. It makes demands all the time. It forces us to grow. All I'm saying is you have bigger dreams than you think you do. And I mean that as a compliment."

"Hmm," he says, as if he's tasting my words to see how they adjust to his palate. "What about you? Besides the books? What's your vision? What's the grand plan?"

"See, now I'm afraid to tell *you*. After all that."

"Tell me," he says tenderly. "Please?" The pleading in his voice is so sexy, I swear I black out for a moment.

"Well, it's a whole thing," I say, shifting my eyes from his so I can focus. "You know, before I showed up here, I had totally given up on the life I thought I'd have. It's why I arrived in the worst mood ever. I felt like Margot had forced me here against my will, dangling this mystery in front of me, not respecting that I didn't want to write anymore, or have hope anymore. I wanted to be done with it all. But Margot brought me here, forced me to really try, and I was fighting it."

"And now?" he asks, his voice low, tender. "Are you fighting it?"

I look into his eyes. "No, I'm not fighting anything now."

He doesn't look away, just stares right into me. I swallow, feel the world cloud around us.

"Good," he finally says, nodding, breaking the moment. "You have the heart of a writer. And I mean that in the most flattering way possible. Most people don't do any sort of inquiry into their life. They live as if their life is a list of demands, given to them by someone else. I appreciate that you think about all of this. That you go beyond the surface." He stops and looks at me intensely, and I can't turn away. "It's a very attractive quality."

"Wait... Attractive?" I shake my head. "My overthinking and existential crises have been called many things, but never *attractive*."

"Maybe you haven't been sharing them with the right people," he says, his head inclined toward mine. "Because I'm impressed with the way your mind works. You're so curious and thoughtful—" he stops and looks down at his hands "—it actually intimidates me a bit."

"No, it doesn't," I say, shrugging him off.

"It does. I've always been a sucker for strong women. I was raised by two of them. My mom was extraordinarily talented at everything she did and smart as hell. My dad worshipped the ground she walked on. And you know how Margot was." He shrugs. "I like being a little out of my depth, what can I say?"

"What about Camille?" I ask, voice low.

"She was lovely, but she didn't make me nervous. That should have been my first clue. She ended up with my friend, you know? He's some corporate lawyer, who I have on good authority does not treat her all that well. She wanted that big, rich life to brag about on Instagram and I don't really care about image. I just want to be happy. Like, really happy. Not just pretending to be happy, you know?"

"That's...refreshing," I tell him. "But, honestly, to most women, a man being intimidated by her is *not* a compliment. At least in my experience. A lot of men say they want strong, willful women, but they want them in theory, not practice."

He tips his chin up. "Well, it's a compliment from me. Absolutely. Most men are idiots. They're missing out. The intimidating women are the hottest."

I hope that the blush I feel isn't visible.

"Hmm," I say. "Do you really mean that?"

His gaze lands on mine like fire taking spark. "Oh, I mean it."

I try not to show him the way my body floods with longing, but he doesn't look away, and it's as though he knows and can read everything I'm thinking. I slowly smile at him, he smiles back, and we both look out the window, eating the last of our chips in heavy, lust-filled silence.

TWENTY-THREE

Paris

It's night in Paris by the time we arrive. Cold. Remarkably, bracingly cold, compared to the temperate weather in the south. From the train station we get a taxi and I stare out the window as the city whooshes by in a blur of activity. I can't help but do anything except sigh in contentment as I see the towering beige buildings, with their cobalt blue spires, passing by some of the most iconic landmarks in the world. It's a short ride, though, and then we're in Oliver's friend's small apartment, with its one bedroom and pull-out couch.

I swallow nervously, realizing I hadn't exactly thought through the apartment situation. We'll be sharing a bathroom, and only about four hundred square feet of space. We set our luggage down and I go to remove my coat, and Oliver's hand brushes my neck and stops me.

"Before we settle in for the night, there's something you have to see," he says, a glint in his eye. "Are you up for it?"

"Of course," I say.

I wrap a large scarf around my neck and follow Oliver out the door. He's so animated and in his element. He told me on the train he's spent a lot of time in Paris, that it's one of his favorite cities, and when we get out to the street, it's clear that he knows his way around. He expertly maneuvers us toward a metro station, gets us tickets from the kiosk, and navigates us to the correct train through a maze of tunnels and escalators and staircases. I'm completely turned around, but Oliver knows exactly where we're going and deposits us at a busy platform, a train arriving just in time.

I feel a little dazed once we sit down, side by side, on the packed metro car.

"Where are you taking me?"

"It's a surprise." He looks nearly gleeful.

"Okay," I say, drawing out the word.

"We have to change at Grands Boulevard station in a couple stops." I like seeing Oliver this way. Capable, excited.

We make the metro change, walking through long tunnels, barreling into hordes of people. The station goes on for so long. We walk up a few different flights of stairs. My layers start to feel warm. I loosen my scarf, pocket my gloves. The energy in Paris is frenetic, so different from the south. And I love it. I feel invigorated by it.

We settle ourselves onto another train. "Last one," Oliver says, his shoulder bumped up close to mine on the small seats. We sit in comfortable silence, watching every kind of person get in and out of the metro car. A dizzying display of humanity. Five different languages being spoken in our proximity. People of all races and histories holding shopping bags and totes, navigating their way onto the car with bikes and strollers, pushing through each other, saying *"Pardon."* All I hear is *pardon, pardon, pardon.*

When we finally get to our stop—Trocadéro, it says—half the train seems to empty with us. Going through the turnstiles to exit I say *pardon* to everyone. Oliver looks back at me and says, "You're a natural."

We go up a short escalator, and I put my gloves back on as we hit the cold air. Just as I do, Oliver grabs my hand and says, "Come on, it's almost time."

"Time for what?" I ask, but instead of answering he just pulls me with him, our gloved hands together.

There's a large roundabout street surrounded by cafés five tables deep, all brimming with people. I don't know where we are, but it certainly seems popular. We walk away from the cafés and toward a line of food trucks serving crêpes and *chocolat chaud,* and everything smells delicious as we go. But Oliver is determined, his gloved hand still in mine, leading me.

And as we round a corner to an open expanse between two very large structures, I see why.

I stop short, jaw open. "Wow," I gasp lightly. Oliver turns around and watches me, a smile so wide on his face it's almost as beautiful as what I'm staring at.

Before me is the Eiffel Tower, centered in the distance, awash in golden lights, breathtaking and stunning. It's so unexpected and gorgeous and perfect, I can't help but let out a giddy sound.

"Come on," he says, pulling me again. "Let's get closer."

We walk to where dozens of people are gathered. We're quite far from the tower but being up on an incline gives us a breathtaking view. Just as we reach the railing, the tower starts sparkling and the crowd dims to a hush, a chorus of "aaaaaah" rings out. We stand, all of us, a group of total strangers, transfixed at the glittering tower. It shouldn't be this magnificent, this magical. It's so cliché, but it's gorgeous. It's better than I could have imagined. A rush of joy moves through me like lightning.

If I hadn't taken any risks, I wouldn't be here right now, seeing this, feeling this, experiencing this. I feel so present, so rooted in this moment. I simply sway on my feet, sighing.

Oliver stands close behind me, and I drop myself into him. His hands fall on my shoulders, steadying me. He removed his gloves and I feel his bare finger trailing on my neck lightly, almost imperceptibly. I lean into the touch.

"Magic, right?" he whispers in my ear, and I get goose bumps on my arms.

"She's spectacular," I say, looking back at him.

He's not even looking at the glittering tower when he nods and smiles and says, "Yeah, she is."

After staring at the tower for a good long while, we decide to go have some hot chocolate at one of those cafés I saw back by the metro station. We each have a *chocolat chaud*, thick and rich, with a pot of fresh whipped cream on the side. It's decadent and delicious.

"Turns out the Eiffel Tower is a tourist thing that is not overhyped," I say. "Wow. Thank you for taking me here right away."

He looks at me, eyes softening. "I know. I always come here right when I get to Paris. It never gets old. People try to see it too close-up, though. This is the best view by far. My mom took me here the first time when I was, like, six."

"She loved Paris?"

"Loved it," he says. "It was her favorite city in the world."

He looks down at his hot chocolate, stirring it over and over.

"I can see why," I say, laying a hand on his and stroking my thumb across his knuckles.

His eyes go to my thumb, and he seems to shake off the mood he was falling into. "So, it's Thanksgiving tomorrow," he says. "What should we do?"

"Right," I say. "I'd like to do something to celebrate."

"Let's do something nontraditional, then," he says. "I'll cook. We can make our own tradition."

Our *own tradition*. Something dizzying flutters through my body.

"I like that," I say. He nods and looks down as he stirs his hot chocolate much more than he needs to.

"Does the holiday make you miss your family?" he asks.

I give a wry, sharp laugh. "The opposite, actually," I say. "We had a big falling-out before I left, and I think if I were there tomorrow, all we'd do is fight. They are not my biggest fans right now. And vice versa." I don't betray how much this upsets me. It's been this constant, low-level pain since I've arrived in France, but I still don't want to patch things up with them, especially not with my mom.

She has been instrumental in planting seeds of doubt in me, and being away from her for a while has helped me more than it should. I don't think I realized how much influence she was having over my well-being until now. I've emailed her and the family to tell them I'm fine, but this is the longest I've gone since talking to her. I've been attending Sunday dinner for years, feeling smaller and smaller each time. It's no coincidence that my confidence has blossomed, getting out from under her critical eye.

"Are you okay?" he asks.

"Yes. I am. I think this distance has been good for us all." I catch myself. "I'm sorry, I shouldn't even complain." I fidget with my napkin. "I shouldn't go on about not missing my family when you... Well. Did your parents like Thanksgiving? Celebrate it?"

"Please don't apologize. I get it. Families are complicated. But yeah, Thanksgiving was a big thing with my parents," he says, casting his eyes out toward the street. "They were immigrants. So when they had me a year after moving to America, they decided they'd celebrate every holiday to the fullest. They went all out. The Fourth of July was out of this world. And Thanksgiving—it was the best of the best. We had so many traditions. My dad prepared the menu weeks in advance, always trying new side dishes. He was a great cook. He loved it and did all the cooking. I got my love of it from him, helping him in the kitchen for hours, making elaborate dishes. Remind me to make you lamb couscous at some point." I nod, and then, ridiculously, I start to cry. His face falls.

"No, please continue," I say, wiping tears on a napkin. "It's just, they sound so wonderful."

His face is tender as he continues.

"They were," he says, his eyes going glassy, as well. "It feels good to talk about them."

"Tell me more?" I ask. He lights up, and nods.

"We would eat so much on Thanksgiving. My favorite thing, though, was my mom's charcuterie board. She was French, so her specialty was always preparing these elaborate boards of dried fruits, cheeses, and meats. They were so beautiful. She'd shop the day before Thanksgiving, buying everything up from her favorite artisan stores, and then spend all morning artfully arranging it. Then she'd proudly present it to us, and we'd snack on it all day before eating dinner. It was always a running joke between my mom and dad. He would get playfully angry that she was spoiling our dinner that he was painstakingly preparing, and she'd just shrug and say in her French accent, 'It is just *fromage, c'est petite!*' Every year! I loved that.

"But then, when I came to France after the fire, I started ignoring Thanksgiving. Sebastian isn't American, so he didn't care. And Margot—well, no offense at all, but Margot hated Thanksgiving. It reminded her of your mom. She would always get sad and want to be alone. I usually just tried to get through this week any way possible."

"That's..." I trail off, looking for the right word "...heartbreaking." I feel a pinch of my own emotion. All those years I had lunch with Margot, should I have tried to repair what had happened between her and my mom? They were both so closed off that I never considered it. But now I wonder if I should have forced it, told my mom I was seeing Margot, arranged for a reunion. It makes me unbearably sad to know there was so much left unsaid between them.

Oliver shrugs, but I can tell he's stifling a lot of hurt. "Margot, Sebastian, and I had a lot of other great celebrations," he says. "But after the fire, Thanksgiving has never been a good day for me." He looks away from me, resigned to it all. And my heart aches.

I lay my hand on his forearm. "I'm sorry, Oliver," I say. "Thank you for telling me and trusting me with all of that."

He has tears in his eyes, I can see them glittering in the flicker of the dim café light.

He wipes at the tears, shakes his head, and gives me a rueful smile. "I really appreciate you asking," he says. "I think people avoid it. Death scares them. But I like talking about them, even if it's painful. I feel like if I told anybody else, they'd be so uncomfortable and awkward, and then I'd feel like I needed to apologize to *them*. Grief makes people act weird."

"Well, don't get me wrong, I feel terrible for you," I say. "But I'm honored you feel like you can talk to me."

He looks at me, his eyes roving across my face. "It's strange," he says, low and gentle. "Doesn't it feel like we've known each other a lot longer than just a few months?"

We stare at each other for a long moment.

"It does."

After a bit, we take a taxi back to the apartment, since it's even colder now. Oliver offers me the bed, and he takes the pull-out couch. We negotiate the bathroom, taking turns to brush our teeth. And before I fall asleep, I get a flash of inspiration for tomorrow. Something I hope will, at the very least, ease the pain of Thanksgiving for Oliver.

TWENTY-FOUR

Paris

The next morning, Oliver arrives with croissants and makes us espresso in the coffeemaker. He doesn't tell me what he's going to cook tonight. Only that he'll be out shopping for ingredients for our Thanksgiving dinner. I don't offer to go with him, because I have my plan, and I need to be alone to execute it. By early afternoon, we're dressed, and walk off in two different directions from the apartment.

Last night, I googled and found an open-air market close by, so I rush off in that direction.

Shopping basket in hand, I set out to gather up everything I need.

I go to the cheese shop—a *fromagerie*—and the cheesemonger smiles at me, and wraps up a selection of brie, *comté*, camembert, and a special *manchego* he tells me is from Spain. He also sells me on a mustard that I taste on a small espresso spoon, and it's exactly the kind of Dijon you couldn't get anywhere but in France. I load it into my basket.

I head into the *boulangerie*, ordering two baguettes with sesame seeds.

The last shop I go to, before walking through the stalls for the finishing details, is the *bucherie*, to see about a selection of prosciutto and other cured meats. I wait patiently as the butcher wraps up a handful of packages. I grab a few sleeves of crackers, as well.

Making my way through the stalls, I gather up olives of every different variety, sampling them as I go. I get dried fruits from a young woman with an adorable toddler who waves to me as I choose apricots that are flavorful and sweet. Once I've made a lap of the market, my arm is aching from holding my full basket. It's already late afternoon, and Oliver will be back in just a couple hours, which means I need to hurry.

I climb the five flights of stairs, out of breath and sweating as I open the door to the apartment. In one of the cabinets in the kitchen, I find exactly what I need, and start preparing, angling, and displaying everything with precision and detail.

Once I'm done, I put the final product on the table on the wide balcony, hiding it from view. I rush inside to shower, nerves fluttering in my stomach.

When Oliver comes in with bags weighing down his hands, I've just finished getting ready. It's a bright and exceedingly cold day, the sun shining. I'm wearing a long-sleeved hunter green dress that hugs me at the waist and has a low round neck. I've paired it with my Docs, and delicate gold hoops for earrings.

My hair is loose and wavy, air-dried, and I've put on a small amount of makeup. My lips are a soft red. I have a new perfume on, a floral and sweet scent from Fragonard I got in Cannes. I feel good. Sexy. Daring.

"Well, hello and happy Thanksgiving," I say, entering the kitchen. Oliver's eyes meet mine, and we both stand there in tense silence. He's wearing light blue jeans and a black button-up shirt with the sleeves slightly rolled up, a hint of his tattoos on his forearms. I feel heat flush my chest. His hair is waved and tousled, and that curly tendril keeps falling into his eyes, and I still am dying to wrap my finger around it.

In the silence, we both give each other coy grins—and the heat moves from my chest to all over my body.

"Happy Thanksgiving," he says, raspy and low. "You look… Wow." His eyes widen.

"You do, too," I say.

What I really want to say is: Oliver, you look *devastating*.

Instead, I ask him what he's planning on making tonight.

"Well, even though it's not a traditional Thanksgiving meal, I'm going to make a scallop risotto," he says, pulling out a wrapped brown package. "Got the scallops fresh. And I know how much you love risotto."

"My favorite," I say, smiling so big my eyes are half-closed. "But, before you start, will you come out to the balcony with me for a second?"

He cocks his head, intrigued, and follows me toward the door, the slight brush of his fingertips dancing across the small of my back.

I stop him at the double French doors and turn around to face him. He stops, too, and he's close again, so close. I can see the flecks of gold in the irises of his eyes.

"Okay, I hope you like this, but I wanted to do something for you," I say.

"For me?"

"I just wanted to say thank you, for how you helped me through the Mauro situation, for showing me around the Riviera, for being there for me. For being you."

"You really didn't have to do anything," he says, pushing that tendril out of his eyes and rubbing his hands on his stubble.

"I did, and I wanted to," I say. "It might be stupid." I feel a wave of nerves, my heart racing so much I'm certain Oliver can hear it.

"I'm sure it's not," he says, and I lead him outside.

On the big balcony table is a long and large cutting board, painstakingly filled with everything I gathered today from the shops and market. Olives in small bowls, cured meats folded between cut pieces of cheese, with green pistachios and curved cashews, and the dried apricots sandwiched in between. The baguette is cut on the diagonal and the crackers are positioned just so. It took me half an hour to put it together, but it looks picture-perfect.

Oliver walks toward it, silent, and I can't gauge his reaction. His head is down, his back to me, and I step closer toward him. His hands are moving across the board, fingering olives and the rind of the *manchego* cheese.

"It's your Thanksgiving charcuterie board," I say, in a small, nervous voice. "I don't know if it's too much, or—" I trail off, not sure what else to say, feeling more anxious the longer he's silent.

I still can't see his face, and I'm about to start panicking that I did something wrong, and completely misjudged this act of kindness or overstepped on his memories, but then he turns around, and there are tears in his eyes.

He rubs his face, and goes to speak, then closes his mouth.

My heart is beating wildly in my chest.

I'm a few paces away from him, but he closes the space between us quickly, his body close to mine.

"You...did this...for me? You re-created my mom's Thanksgiving charcuterie board?" His eyes are searching mine, and I feel myself go still, very still, as if the moment right now is so fragile just the slightest movement could break it.

"Yes," I say, choking back the word.

"It's..." He stops himself. His hands go to my face, and he gently moves a strand of hair aside. His fingers brush the tops of my ears, and I close my eyes to it. "Poppy," he says, through something strangled.

I open my eyes and see him watching me, intently, a storminess there that catches me off guard. I decide to be brave. I decide to be bold.

"Oliver," I say, and I take my hand and I lift it, and caress the side of his neck. Before I can stop myself, before I can think too much, before I lose this moment forever, I pull him closer to me by grabbing the fabric of his shirt, and he responds instantly.

His hands go into my hair, and then…his lips land on mine, warm and soft and perfect. He kisses me, deeply, urgently. I put my hands under his shirt, caressing the soft space of his stomach. And the lower I get, feeling a patch of hair, he pulls me even closer. His left hand is in my hair still, and his other one is roaming my body, feeling the soft skin of my upper chest. The kiss deepens, and I feel his hands back on my neck, then he moves to kiss where his fingertips are, on my ear, to my neck, all the way down to the space above my bra. My skin is on fire. I lose all sense of time and place. I have never in all my life wanted a man as much as I want him.

"Bedroom," I say, through a strangled breath. "Now." He locks eyes with me, and he looks momentarily uncertain, searching for consent. "Now, Oliver." I'm nearly pleading with him. He doesn't say a word, but he doesn't need to.

He grabs my hand, and we rush through the kitchen, through the small living room, kicking off our shoes, his lips on my neck from behind, and into the bedroom, a frantic rush, like a movie scene, except it's real life. Except it's me. This is happening to *me*.

In the tiny space of the hallway, right before the bedroom, Oliver's hands go into my hair again and he pushes me against the wall, presses himself against me, like he can't wait another second to kiss me again. I don't complain, I simply roll my hips toward him and feel his body respond, his hands on my neck, my shoulders, roving up my dress between my thighs so softly that I take in a sharp inhale. He lifts my leg up by the thigh and I press into him, hearing a soft, high-pitched sound from the back of his throat. His eyes find mine and he slants his lips onto my mouth.

I still us, and watch him intently. I finally get my finger around that tendril and smile.

"I've been wanting to do that for a long time," I tell him. "Bed. Now."

Oliver only nods, and then I loosen myself from him and lead him into the bedroom. Our eyes lock on each other, and I know—completely, totally—that this is real. This is nothing like it was with anyone in the past. This is something entirely new.

Oliver proceeds to undress me, lifting the dress off my body, kissing every space of skin that he uncovers. I unbutton Oliver's shirt and roam my hands across his chest, paying extra attention to the tattoos that have haunted my fantasies for months.

"These," I say. I lightly trail my way from star to star on his torso, my hands tracing outlines on the tattoos on his arms— the anchor, the rope, the tiger, the way his arm looks like a catalog of his life. "My god."

He gives me a satisfied smile.

His hands rove over my chest, to my neck, to my thighs, over the curve of my hips.

"This," he says. "You."

I see goose bumps pop up on his skin. Feel my body flood with heat.

"I can't believe this is happening right now," he says, his voice low, almost a whisper.

"Me either," I whimper, and his mouth finds mine again. And then we are on the bed together, and his body is over mine. We rip off the rest of our clothing, my bra discarded, my panties flung in the direction of the window, his boxer briefs pulled off quickly. Then we are naked, in the dim light of the room, and I feel myself go completely still, and he does, too.

He strokes his fingertips across my cheek.

The golden light of a setting sun streams in through the gauzy curtain, and I see him see me so completely. Just as I am.

"You're so beautiful," he says, his voice raspy, and I lift my hips toward him in response.

"You are too, Oliver," I breathe out.

And then, words are no longer necessary. His lips are everywhere on me, leaving heat wherever he touches. His hands roam every inch of me. I can't get enough of him, pulling him closer to me, devouring his mouth with mine.

And then finally, finally, finally, he sinks into me, and we both gasp. Our eyes trained on each other's, his hands in my hair, my hands in his hair, his breath on my neck, his tongue on mine, his hands on my breasts, my fingers on his back.

When he finishes, his body wracked and shivering, both of us gasping, we regain our breathing. He curls up next to me and asks, "Did you…finish?" I shake my head.

He nods and says, businesslike, "Well, we can't have that now." He reaches his hands down and finds the spot that makes me cry out, sensitive and full of pleasure. He gets close to my ear, his outtake of breath on my neck, and says, "Tell me what feels good." My eyes roll back, and I let a moan escape me, hearing him take in a sharp breath in response to it.

"That," I say, nearly breathless, the word like a gust of air coming out of me. "Don't stop." He smiles into my neck, and I let myself go, in his very capable hands. When I come, his name is on my mouth, and he kisses me hard.

Suddenly, my body is not the enemy anymore.

It's the source of this pleasure.

And I am a fucking goddess.

After doing *that* twice more, we are both famished. It's nearly midnight, and I sit on the stool in the kitchen, both of us munching on the charcuterie board that we brought inside. Oliver starts preparing the risotto, even though it's late.

"We need sustenance," Oliver says, laughing. His cheeks are flushed, and he looks so happy, I have to sidle up next to him and give him a soft kiss on his neck. He turns toward me pliantly and kisses me back.

"You need to sit over there," he says, gesturing to the stool on the other side of the island. "Or I won't be able to concentrate."

I laugh and then sit down, giving him a look of feigned innocence.

As Oliver starts measuring out his ingredients, I ask him, "How did this happen? For a moment there, I thought you were with Stella." I try to sound breezy, but I still remember the way they leaped apart after my horrible date with Mauro.

"With Stella?" He stops what he's doing, and stares at me, holding a bottle of olive oil in his hand.

"Yes, you were dating Stella," I say. "Well, I *thought* you were…"

"I was never with Stella."

"You weren't?"

"Poppy, are you serious?" he asks. "I haven't stopped thinking about you since I saw you in the airport. I have been pining and miserable over you. You didn't know?"

"But…you hated me when I first got here!"

He gives a sheepish look. "Hated? Or just didn't want to admit how much I wanted you?"

I choke out a little laugh.

He shrugs. "Remember Camille? Yeah, she broke my heart. But she never made me nervous the way you make me nervous. It freaked me out."

"What? Wow, I'm…shocked."

"I was also angry that you didn't want The Colony. That was a good cover." He gives a dry laugh. "Sorry."

"I mean, it's okay. I was trying to pretend I didn't have any feelings for you, too, so I guess we're even."

"I almost died the night you went out with that guy. Stella and I spent the whole night talking about you. I was pathetic over it."

"Wait… What…? Really?" That night I found them cozy on the couch they were…talking about…*me?* "I had no idea!"

Oliver rakes his hands through his hair and shrugs. "I may have been overcompensating," he says. "I was interested, but we were fighting. I was supposed to be carrying out Margot's dying wish with you and instead I was harboring a ridiculous crush. Then, everything that happened with Mauro. I couldn't say anything after that. I've wanted to tell you how I feel for a while, but it never felt like the right moment. And truthfully, after what happened with Camille… I was scared to tell you anything." He comes around the kitchen island to be closer to me.

"I thought for sure I was imagining all of that," I say, fidgeting with the hem of my sweatshirt.

"I thought I was being completely transparent," he says and smiles, taking my hands in his. "I thought for sure you knew and weren't interested."

"Nope. I was scared, too. Terrified, actually. Still am, if I'm being honest. But I'm interested."

"How interested?"

He smiles then pulls me up from the chair so we're both standing, and he gently touches the side of my neck, and kisses me softly. After a minute or so, we break apart, both of us out of breath.

"It's going to be difficult for me to cook risotto with you around," he says, laying a soft kiss on my jaw. "It needs attention, but I want to give all of mine to you."

"I'll try to make myself very unappealing for the next hour," I say, as he walks back to the other side of the kitchen island.

"As if that's possible."

"I want to keep the villa," I blurt out. "If that wasn't clear." My heart starts to race, but it feels right. I want this life. I do. I'm all in.

He turns to face me.

"Are you sure?" he asks tentatively.

I nod. "I am."

"Thank god," he says on an exhale. "Because I already turned down that job offer."

"You did?"

"Not just because of The Colony. I didn't want that job. Or to leave France."

Panic laces through me. He's already making plans. Plans that involve me. But aren't I doing that, too? Why am I suddenly anxious? He turned down this job for himself, I tell myself. Not for me. Or for The Colony. For *himself.*

Didn't I just say I was all in?

I even my breathing, because it's just an old pattern. Worry that I'll get disappointed, yet again. But it's different this time. It is.

I look up at him and watch him stirring the risotto. I don't have to brace myself anymore. Life is working out for me now.

"Best Thanksgiving ever, Olly," I say, in a low whisper.

His eyes meet mine, and the spark between us, now expressed, hits me with a force.

"Best Thanksgiving ever," he repeats back to me, and we both lower our heads, smiling to ourselves, heady with the potential of what's to come. "You know? My mom used to call me Olly. It's why I don't like when people use it."

"Do you...? Should I stop?"

"No," he says, quickly. "I like it. I like when you say it."

Later, as we eat scallops and risotto by candlelight, it feels like everything is perfect, almost too perfect. I have to stop myself from spiraling out, stop myself from thinking I don't deserve it, stop myself from rejecting the good before it can reject me. I have to keep yanking myself back into the present moment.

I shake the spiral that's threatening to unravel me. Not tonight. Not here. I'm going to let myself have this. I'm going to let myself enjoy.

TWENTY-FIVE

Cap Ferrat, France

The day after we return from Paris, flushed and blissful, Sebastian invites us out for dinner at the Café de Paris Monte-Carlo. Sebastian is already in Monaco, so Oliver and I take the car and drive out there, zipping in and out of the tunnels along the cliffs, the expanse of water to our right.

The café is touristy, the roundabout near it displaying beautiful and expensive cars, shiny and moneyed. I notice, thankfully, that the pinch of insecurity I used to feel in places like this is gone. It doesn't even occur to me that I don't belong. It feels completely normal for me to wear a nice dress, take Oliver's hand in mine, and walk into a glitzy restaurant in the French Riviera.

The day we got back from Paris, we called Sebastian and told him we're dating. Not only was he ecstatic, but he said, laughing, "I knew there was something between you two, ever since that intense drive from the airport."

Sebastian mentioned that he wanted to share something special with us tonight, and we arrive to find him and Andrew

Clapter, the English writer I met back in Cannes with Claudia, at the table with him.

They both rise, looking happy and glowy. Andrew is dressed in a navy blue sweater, while Sebastian is in one of his signature suits, a brown tweed that offsets his olive skin. And while Sebastian is typically in a good mood, there is something nearly giddy about him tonight.

"What's going on?" Oliver asks, looking at me playfully, picking up on the energy. We all sit down at a circular table outside with heaters blaring above us.

I watch Andrew and Sebastian exchange a look.

"This happened," Sebastian says. He raises his hand and Andrew's is clasped in his. Andrew—this sophisticated and put-together man—breaks into giggles.

"Finally!" Oliver cries out and claps his hands together.

"Finally?" I ask. "Wait, I need details. Fill me in. I'm lost here."

All three of them laugh. Sebastian and Andrew keep gazing lovingly at each other. It's so beautiful to see.

"Well, the story is that I've been in love with this man for the last, *oh*, thirty years, and it took him quite a while to figure out he loved me back," Sebastian replies, shaking his head ruefully and looking so fondly at Andrew.

"It's true," Andrew says in his soft English accent, incapable of taking his eyes off Sebastian. "We met three decades ago and shared a night I never forgot, but I wasn't ready. To come out. To be with a man. I got married, had two wonderful children. But that dinner when I met you, Poppy, it all came flooding back. I had just gotten divorced. I hadn't seen Sebastian in a long time." He looks over at Sebastian tenderly, his face soft and unguarded.

"We reconnected," Sebastian says, with a light shrug. "After Spain, I went to London to visit, and it was like no time had passed."

"Uncle Seb tried to forget you, but he couldn't," Oliver says to Andrew. "I'm happy you found each other again."

"Me too," Andrew says. "It took me a long time to accept myself, but I won't spend another minute without Sebastian." He gives him an adoring look. "I'm moving here. I've already wasted enough time."

"Margot's laughing up there right now," Sebastian says, wiping his own eyes, chuckling through the emotion. "She always told me Andrew was my person, that we'd find each other again. She never lost hope. Before she died, she told me to look him up and reconnect with him, then she just made it happen on her own."

"So that's what the dinner in Cannes was really for, then?" I ask, laughing.

"She orchestrated it all, knowing Andrew wouldn't refuse a last dinner in her honor," Sebastian says, shaking his head.

"You two are the cutest," I say. "You have to hand it to Aunt Margot for trusting her intuition on this one."

Sebastian places his hand on his chest, looks upward, and says an exceedingly sincere "Thank you, Margot."

"Speaking of love stories," Sebastian says, pointing between Oliver and me. "Margot used to tell me, you know who Poppy would really like? Our Olly."

I look over to see Oliver shaking his head and blushing. I squeeze his hand and his eyes find mine.

"Margot was a witch *and* psychic," I say, laughing.

"She was!" Andrew says animatedly. "I remember when I was writing my fifth book. I was quite discouraged. The previous four hadn't sold very well. I called her one day and we spoke for hours about the new book. She gave exceptional writing advice and said with complete certainty that it was going to be the one to break out."

"And it was!" Sebastian says, pride beaming off his face.

"Bestseller and all that. I loved that one. Well, I love all of your books, my dear."

The energy at the table is so cheesy and beautiful, I feel unguarded and joyful. This is my life now. It hits me again. These are the kinds of nights I'll have, double dates with Sebastian and Andrew. Exploring France and Europe. It feels a little fragile, but only because it's so good. Better than I ever expected.

We order a bottle of wine, dinner, and stay there talking and laughing for hours. It's one of those perfect evenings that you know will become a core memory. The love at this table, the feel of Oliver's hand in mine, the way he keeps finding a way to touch me, kiss me, the buzz of Andrew and Sebastian, their obvious love for each other and the reminder that it's never too late to begin again—I feel nostalgic for this moment even before it ends.

As Oliver and I drive back to the villa, hand in hand across the console of the car, I can't remember the last time I've ever felt this happy.

DECEMBER

TWENTY-SIX

At the first of December, the residents return from their break, and activity in the villa resumes at a dizzying pace. It's nearly December fifteenth and the Booksmart guys got in touch to set up a meeting with me in a week to propose a new offer. I can't wait to turn them down, make this official.

All I have to do now is finish one of my two books before February. I feel optimistic that I can pull it off. It feels like things are *finally* working in my favor. I haven't heard back from Claudia about the partial draft of my romance novel yet, but I've been checking my email obsessively, waiting and hoping. I don't know if she wants to sign me, but I am acting as if she does. Manifesting it.

At the last minute, I decide to throw a welcome-back dinner for the residents tonight. A little deviation from Margot's way of doing things, a way to put my own stamp on The Colony, now that I'll be the one running it. I still can't believe this is my life now. All Oliver and I have done over the last few days is make plans for the residency and get the villa ready. It has been thrilling to finally commit to it all.

The four residents, Oliver, Sebastian, Andrew, Janelle, and I sit around the large table that I decorated with wildflowers and long-stem candles in preparation for tonight. The mood is lively and upbeat.

Caroline cooks and I pour wine as the residents share stories about their holiday break. Janelle beams at them like a proud teacher and says, "You all look refreshed. Nobody worked on their books, did they?"

They all shake their heads and Janelle claps. "Good!" She turns toward me and says, "And what about you? Did you work on your books?"

"I didn't. I definitely took some time to relax," I say and throw a sheepish look toward Oliver across the table, who smiles so broadly everyone seems to catch on at once.

"That finally happened?" Stella exclaims. "This man was driving me crazy."

"I knew it," Caroline says, dropping a large platter of pasta in the middle of the table. "You two had such a vibe."

"Yeah, we all knew that was bound to happen," Kerry says, laughing.

"Someone could have told me," I say. "I had no idea."

"And here I thought I couldn't have been more obvious," Oliver says.

"Wait!" Evie screeches out, stands up, and holds up her glass of wine. "Does this mean you're staying? And keeping the villa?"

Multiple pairs of eyes turn to me, and I nod, beaming. "Yes, it means I'm staying."

Cheers ring out all around the table and I blush feverishly.

"Poppy," Jasmyn says, throwing her arm around me. "You're going to kill it. That's incredible."

"Couldn't agree more," Sebastian calls out.

I sit there, beaming with pride, feeling unbelievably lucky that Margot somehow knew exactly what I needed when she sent me here. The happiness I've been feeling all week seems to heighten, and the rest of the dinner passes while I exist in a haze of uncomplicated joy for the first time in a really long time.

Over the next week, during the day, I write almost constantly, freshly determined to finish the romance novel before the February deadline and so when Claudia gets back to me, I'm ready to go.

In the evenings, Oliver sleeps over, and I find myself sneaking out to work on my other book for a couple hours, the mistral winds in the south of France whipping branches across the windows, a creepy atmosphere that makes the thriller I'm also writing come flying out. A few months ago, I had zero books written and had given up on myself entirely. Now I almost have two down. I might have an agent soon. A book deal. It's so close I can almost taste it. I'll be able to call my mom and Jackson and tell them the news. Prove everyone—including myself—wrong. I didn't need their help after all.

Oliver and I are in the kitchen on a lunch break over the weekend, the residents out exploring a nearby village. We're tearing off pieces of a warm baguette and popping fat green olives into our mouths. Beau is on his stool, his tongue flapping, eating pieces of canned tuna we put on a small plate for him. This dog must have been a human in a past life. He won't eat unless he's perched on a chair like a proper gentleman. I shake my head at him, laughing.

"What're you thinking about over there, Poppy?" Oliver asks, grabbing a kalamata olive and throwing it into his mouth.

"You," I say, and his cheeks flush. I don't tell him that I'm also thinking about the upcoming meeting I have scheduled with Brent and Cody. I plan on telling them that I'm not interested in selling or to hear about their "new offer," but I don't mention the meeting to Oliver. He'll be worried that I'm even seeing them.

"I—" Oliver starts to speak, but both of us turn at a loud

knock at the front door of the villa. Beau's head perks up from his tuna and all three of us look at each other, puzzled.

"Who could that be?" I ask, my stomach fluttering like a bad omen.

"I have no idea," he says, and we all three slowly walk toward the foyer, where another loud knock is delivered, making me jump a little. We answer the door, Beau sitting between us at our feet, Oliver's strong arm around me, the picture of domestic bliss.

The person on the other side of the door gives a shocked look when she sees me.

"Mom?" I croak out. I quickly throw Oliver's arm off me. Beau starts yipping nervously, picking up on my energy.

"What...what are you doing here?" I splutter, immediately on the defensive.

She stands there unfazed, her eyes looking to Oliver, dipping down to Beau, and everything in her expression says: *I disapprove completely of whatever is going on here.*

Finally breaking the tense silence, she reaches her hand out to Oliver and says, in a tone that is so friendly it comes out sounding sinister, "I'm June Banks, Poppy's mother. And you are?"

Oliver looks so uncomfortable I feel bad for him. "I'm Oliver Hayes," he says. "I knew your sister, Margot." My mom's eyes narrow at him.

"Pleased to meet you, Oliver," she says, and he looks to me for help. Beau is now jumping on my mom's legs.

"I repeat," I say, in a slow, measured way that I don't feel. "What are you doing here, Mom?"

"I came to see you," she says. *"Obviously."*

"I don't remember inviting you?" I am hostile, but I feel like I might cry. Just when I thought things were going to work out—here's the pin bursting that bubble. Like reality just swept in, and I can already feel my confidence plummeting. My mom will cast doubt on everything I'm tentatively building here.

She will make me feel like I don't deserve it, that I'm foolish for believing this could be my life. I can already feel myself start to believe her, those critical eyes of hers boring into me. I don't think I'm flailing anymore, but she might convince me otherwise—she's done it many times before.

Pushing through to the foyer, she walks into the villa, Oliver and me splitting off on either side of her. He looks at me, panicked, and I shrug, unsure of what to do or how to handle this situation.

"So, this is where you've been all this time? In my sister's house? Avoiding us? How did you even know Margot?" She's walking around the villa, examining the shelves, her frenetic energy like a fourth presence in the room.

Oliver juts in before I can respond, sensing that I am about to say something biting and awful. "June, can I get you some coffee?"

"Sure, that would be nice," she says, throwing a look in my direction that implies I should have offered it to her instead of this stranger. I don't tell her that Oliver was probably just looking for an excuse to leave.

Before he does, he comes over to me and lays a soft kiss on my forehead and whispers, "Just breathe, Pop." My mom stares at me as if I'm a stranger, too.

When he's out of earshot, she comes close to me. I haven't moved; I'm stuck on the outskirts of the living room.

"What is going on here?" she asks me, in a low whisper. Her eyes snag on the hummingbird necklace and she gives me a pointed look I can't read.

"It's really none of your business," I say, leveling a devastating look in her direction. "Margot left this villa to me. I knew her. We used to see each other every year."

"Behind my back?" She is seething with contempt. "So, you plan to live here and shack up with this man your family has never met?"

"If I choose to, yes," I say, crossing my arms across my chest.

"You can't be serious. What about your life back home? A job? A family? Poppy, really, this is ridiculous…even for you."

"What's that supposed to mean?" I scoff. "Mom, don't come here when you weren't invited and talk to me like I'm a child. I'm really done with that. And I don't deserve it." The words feel hollow as I say them.

She flinches. "I'm trying to understand why you'd come here to Margot's home and not tell me."

"Because I didn't want you to ruin it," I say, my voice cracking. Her face contorts, and she looks like she might cry. "I think you should go, Mom. I'm not prepared to have this conversation right now."

She starts to speak, her face scrunching up, until she sighs heavily. "I'm staying at the Delcloy Hotel, nearby," she says. "I'll be here a couple weeks. Sightseeing. Trying to understand why *my* daughter would choose the sister that betrayed me over her own mom." I breathe in the blow. She turns on her heel and walks out, the tension in the air diffusing when she does.

I breathe out loudly once she's gone and the door is closed. I collapse on the couch, Beau coming right next to me to snuggle against my side. Oliver sits down on the other side.

"Are you okay?" he asks, stroking his hand across my cheek, and pushing a strand of hair behind my ear.

"No," I say.

Oliver puts his arm around me, and I find that I am tearing up, my anger turning into grief now. Tears for Margot. For my fractured relationship with my mom. She couldn't have arrived happy for me? She couldn't have showed up and said "Poppy, darling, what fun you've had! Tell me all about it!" It had to be a slight against her. It had to be about her. It had to be me in the middle of some thirty-year battle she's had with Margot, like I had any part in it. Like the worst thing I ever did was remind my mom of her sister.

I'm caught in their crossfire. And truthfully, being here at Margot's villa, I'm on *her* side. Whatever happened, I'm sure it was my mom's fault. Whatever broke them, it was my mom. Because she's done it again. She's broken us, too.

"Maybe you should talk to her," Oliver finally says, pulling me out of my thoughts.

"I really don't want to," I say, and then I add something even truer, "I'm not ready to."

"There has to be a reason she showed up, though," he says. "She might be angry, but she loves you, Poppy. Otherwise, she wouldn't have come all this way."

I don't want to tell Oliver why I am so angry. I don't want to say "that's my mom, the person who convinced me I was hard to love, that my dreams were too big, that I was too big for my dreams." I don't want him to see me that way. As someone he should be ashamed of.

I came to France and reinvented myself. To Oliver, I am confident, sexy, exciting. And if I lay bare all of this, if I suggest to him that maybe my body is an impediment to love, that maybe I believe that too sometimes—he might see me differently.

And so, I don't share my shame with him.

It's hard enough to let him desire me, to let his hands rove their way across the parts of my body I've hid away and sucked in and carefully concealed through strategic clothing. It's hard enough to stand in the shower and let him see me and touch me. It shouldn't be. I shouldn't have those thoughts. I wish I could just fall in love, like a normal person.

But I can't.

My mind is crowded. And my mom showing up only makes it more suffocating.

I let Oliver hold me, and Beau comfort me. And then I realize: I'm a week out from December fifteenth. And for the first time in months, I almost want to take the escape hatch.

TWENTY-SEVEN

Cap Ferrat, France

The next evening, I'm still trying to escape the torrent of negative thoughts that have come rushing in since my mom arrived. After she left yesterday, I couldn't write anything. Today, it's the same. I haven't been able to look at either of my books. I've been testy and annoyed with everyone, including Oliver. I feel like my mind is crowded with the doubts I've been staving off, like her arriving here has shattered some illusion I didn't know I was under.

I'm sitting at the kitchen island halfheartedly reading a book while Oliver chops vegetables for a stew. It's raining torrentially, and I can hear the hard sound of water hitting the pavement outside. It's befitting my stormy mood.

I take a long sip of my red wine and in the relative silence, the chime for a new email startles me.

When I look at my phone, I take a sharp inhale. It's an email from Claudia. About my romance novel. I feel myself go cold, my heart yammering in my chest. This could be it. Finally. An agent. Good news to salvage this day. I clutch my phone to my chest. Oliver looks up from the cutting board, knife in hand and says, "What's up?"

"It's from Claudia," I whisper.

His eyes widen. "Shit," he says. "Open it. Read it!"

My hands are shaky as I get to the email. I take a deep steadying breath. I start reading aloud.

"Thank you for sending me your partial draft of *You Had Me at Bonjour*. As you know, I was keen to read a book from Jackson's sister and hoped the material would reflect his level of talent. Unfortunately, and I say this with regret and only respect, it's not where I need it to be to consider you for representa—" I stop and fling my hand over my mouth, a sob bubbling up from my throat.

I hear the clang of the knife as Oliver quickly comes around the island, over to me, but I am already off the stool, darting out of the kitchen, embarrassment burning on my cheeks.

"Poppy," he says, tone worrying and urgent.

"Just," I say, nearly choking on the words, "give me a second." I hold up my hand and race to Margot's office, lock myself inside, and sit on the floor against the door with a loud thud. I am vibrating with panic. I can hardly see through blurred vision to read the rest of the email. I feel nauseous and dizzy, like I'm plummeting into an unknown. *This is why you don't have fucking hope*, I think to myself, bitter, spitting. I force myself to read the rest of the email.

…I say this with regret and only respect, it's not where I need it to be to consider you for representation. If you want to continue working on it and send me a revised version, or if you end up writing something else, I'd be open to reading. For right now, I cannot take you on as a client. I am very sorry, Poppy, and I wish you all the luck on your journey.

My head hits the back of the door. I feel my shoulders slump and sink. I close my eyes, clench my jaw. This is what I'm used to. This is what I should have been expecting. It was foolish to believe anything else would happen. I don't even feel tears threatening. I'm just...numb.

So, that's it, then. I'm not as good as Jackson, clearly. Absolutely nothing is different about this time. Nothing. Yet another rejection. Yet another time I got my hopes up and found them shattered on the ground.

I shake my head, feeling ridiculous and foolish. There's a perverse familiarity to this feeling. I was right earlier this year to give up. I should have just stuck with my original plan. I shouldn't have even come here. I find myself indulging in an irrational anger at Margot, her forcing me to come here, trying to instigate her will. I know it's stupid, but I'm mad at everything right now, most of all myself.

A few moments pass, my eyes still closed, my fists clenched in my lap. I want to evaporate into thin air. I want to blink and pretend none of this happened, be back in my apartment in LA, trying to find some job that won't break my heart.

Then I hear another email chime. This time, from Jackson.

Hi Pop,

Please call me right when you get this. It's urgent.

Love, J

My heart drops. Urgent? Jackson hardly ever emails me, and I haven't spoken to him since I arrived in France. I get a horrible feeling and say a silent prayer to the universe that nobody is hurt, that nobody is in the hospital, that my nieces are okay. I take a deep breath and call him, my nervousness washing over me.

"Hey, Pop," Jackson says, his voice uninterpretable.

"Hey, Jackson," I say, already feeling raw and not ready for the news to come. "What's going on? You have me worried."

"Do you know a Claudia Drake?" he asks, and I'm hit with

a wave of surprise, because that's the last thing I thought this call would be about.

"Yeah…" My stomach bottoms out.

"Are you working with her or something? Is she your agent?"

"No," I say, feeling nausea rising up. "I wrote a novel, and she was considering me as a client."

"That's amazing, Pop, that you're writing again," he says, and I feel a little taken aback by how genuine he sounds. "What kind of book is it?"

"A romance novel," I say, my voice low, almost a whisper.

"No kidding? But you always wanted to write thrillers." He laughs, not in an unkind way, but it still grates on me.

"Well, Claudia wanted a romance novel, so I decided to give it a try." I don't tell him about the other book. I don't want to talk about my writing any more than I have to. Jackson pauses, a long pause, and I can tell he's weighing how to say what he needs to say. I try to help him along. "Jackson? What was so urgent?"

"I don't really know how to tell you this, Pop, but you deserve to know," he says, sighing and deliberating.

"Just say it, Jackson."

"This Claudia Drake person called me out of the blue yesterday and started pitching me. She wanted to represent me and poach me from my current representation. She said she knew you? I was so confused. But, she's a snake, Pop. Agents like that are not worth your time. I wanted to make sure you didn't agree to work with her."

I sink back against the door, and my whole body goes even more numb. This can't be true. I feel dizzy. Everything is swirling around, like I'm on one of those spinning carnival rides. I feel the urge to throw up. This is…my worst nightmare come true. That Claudia would be a fraud, and that I'd have to hear it from Jackson. That I'm the fool, once again. I feel so small and stupid. I can't speak. There's an interminable pause between us, and I don't know how to fill it.

"Poppy?" Jackson finally asks. "Are you okay? I'm sorry if she fooled you with her act. I had to let you know. You deserve better."

I don't tell him that she doesn't even *want* to sign me.

"I don't need your pity," I spit out. "Claudia was just one connection I was fostering. And I wasn't even sure I was going to sign with her anyway." I lie, but it's better than the pathetic truth, even if I'm certain Jackson doesn't believe me. I need to leave this conversation with a half ounce of my dignity still intact. I feel as though I'm about to break open.

"Sure, of course, Pop," Jackson says. "You're a ridiculously talented writer. I'm sure you have them lining up for you."

"Don't patronize me. That's worse than pity."

"I'm not patronizing you, Poppy! Who do you think was the inspiration for my own writing? *You.* You got me into reading. You got me into writing. I've always thought you're an incredible writer." He sounds genuine, but I can't translate it into a compliment. All I can see is Claudia telling me I'm not good enough, not as good as golden boy Jackson Banks. Looks like my mom bet on the right kid after all.

"Okay, Jackson," I say, my voice monotone. "Thanks for letting me know. I'll take it from here." I need to get off this phone call.

"Are you going to be okay?"

"Of course," I say. "Why wouldn't I be?" I can't show weakness. I don't want Jackson, of all people, to see me like that. It's prideful. It's stupid. But I am done looking like a fool in front of my perfect, accomplished brother.

"Okay," he says, uncertain. "Call me if you need anything, even if it's just to talk."

"Sure, will do," I say, buoyantly, doing anything I can to end this conversation without breaking down.

"Bye," he says, as if he wants to say more.

"Bye," I say, and end the call.

I sit there, completely stunned. I can't even cry. The numbness seems to harden me. There's an unpleasant buzzing in my body, a torrent of pulsing anxiety. I feel my jaw clench, my eyes gloss over. I'm disappointed and hurt and embarrassed, but the prevalent feeling is rage. I am so fucking angry. At Margot. At Claudia. At my mom. At Jackson. At myself. I should never have come here. I should have followed my original plan to give up on writing. The feeling I have right now is somehow worse than all the other disappointments I've felt before.

Because I truly believed things were going to be different, and it's clear—clear as ever—that they aren't, they won't be, and I was stupid for having hope.

Now I just feel embarrassed I told everyone I'm staying. Because I don't want to stay. I wish I could take a flight out to LA right now and pretend this was all a dream. I don't care if I'm being weak and brittle. I'm exhausted.

I think about my meeting with Booksmart coming up. That December fifteenth is only a week away. I feel like my brain is jumbled and static. The escape hatch calls to me. I could take it. Pretend none of this happened. But then I realize, even if I want to sell the villa, I have to stay until the six months are up. And I have to finish a book.

My jaw clenches. Margot and this ridiculous scheme.

I want to scream, feeling trapped and frustrated by this whole arrangement.

Oliver knocks on the door, reminding me of another complication that I tried to avoid, but stupidly didn't. Oliver. He turned down that job. I told him I was for sure keeping The Colony. *Fuck*. This is exactly why I tried to stay away from him.

"Are you okay?" he asks tenderly through the door.

All I want to do is run away. I hate that I want to run. But I do. I really, really do.

"Yes, I'm okay," I lie. I stand, wipe the tears from my face, and open the door.

Oliver's arms are open and I fall into him.

"I think I need to just be alone tonight," I say, trying to stave off all the worries that are threatening to take over.

"Are you sure?"

"Yeah."

"Okay," he says, uncertain. "Well, I'll leave you dinner."

"Thank you."

And at that, I go upstairs to my room, fall onto the bed, and stare at the ceiling, worrying and worrying for hours, until I am finally tired enough that my eyes close on their own.

TWENTY-EIGHT

Cap Ferrat, France

When Brent and Cody arrive a few days later, I've somehow rearranged myself into someone businesslike and serious. It takes a great deal of effort to do it, but I steel myself. I am unpierceable. I am a fortress. Which doesn't mean I didn't spend all last night tossing and turning, questioning my every decision across ten different axis points.

Everything has suddenly become messy, with a hundred threads tangled together. Even now, I can't tell if the part of me that wants to stay only wants to stay because of Oliver. This is exactly why I wanted to keep things from progressing with us. This is why I was trying to be smart and not reckless.

I just need things to be simple.

Selling the villa to Brent and Cody seems like the simplest answer to everything, as long as I can finish my thriller. I've abandoned the romance novel that I can now admit wasn't even that fun to write. I was doing it for Claudia. I'll just figure out a way to finish this thriller, stay here until February, get the deed, and cut out. That's the only answer.

I meet Brent and Cody in the village down the hill to avoid

them running into anyone. I feel like I'm lying to everyone and in some way, I am. When I arrive, the two men are waiting patiently at an outdoor table. It's a bright blue day, sun shining high, and yet it's cool enough that I need a sweater.

"Poppy!" Both Brent and Cody greet me in unison, standing up and shaking my hand.

"Thank you for meeting with us again," Cody says, smiling genially.

I don't really have a lot of energy for small talk, so I just get right into it.

"So, I wanted to ask some follow-up questions," I say, opening up my notebook to a list I made last night. "This was my aunt's residency, and I don't want to see all of it gone if I do sell to you. Will you still have women and nonbinary folks come here to work on their books? Will you still make sure to include a diverse range of people? Will you offer scholarships to people who might not be able to afford the cost of a 'literary spa'?"

Cody looks at me with bright eyes and says, "Love these questions, Poppy. And, yes, certainly, anyone can come here to work on their books. If they can afford it, of course." I narrow my eyes at him. "Well, we can't all be as charitable as your aunt, but if one of your stipulations is that we offer a scholarship spot, we can do that. Sure. Why not?"

"What Cody is trying to say, and bungling it horribly, is that of course we want to keep the general vibe of the place," Brent cuts in. "That's why we love it. But it needs to be updated. To the twenty-first century, you know? Social media presence. More focus on the location. Not making it so secretive. Do you know how hard it was for us to even locate The Colony? It's a total mystery. I mean, look at this view." He thrusts his arm out behind him. "How can this place be a secret?" He smiles at me. "I also don't think all the focus would be about the books. People come here, they enjoy the amazing villa, they read books, and maybe they have time to write. Less rigorous."

"But that's the essence of The Colony. It's all about creating books, and giving people space and time to write, which they don't ordinarily have," I say. "You have to preserve that part."

"We'll try," Brent says. "But we can't make promises. We have to make this place profitable first and foremost. This is a business that works with Booksmart's other goals."

"But," Cody says, his eyes glinting. "We think you'll be happy with our updated offer. A million, even. All in."

A million...dollars? I gulp. Well, that would definitely make giving up on all my dreams easier. But, I still don't know if Margot would be upset if I sold her villa? I start to feel anxious.

"Like we said, December fifteenth is our hard date and it's approaching fast," Cody says, his face serious. "This is our top choice, but there's another villa owner we've been talking to. We've been waiting on you to decide. Ideally, we'd like to know right now if you accept our offer. We could buy a villa anywhere, but it's the name and the reputation of The Colony that brings the value."

"Okay," I say, small and low. I'm so tired. Tired of trying. Tired of blow after blow. And I'm done getting my hopes up. I was fooling myself thinking I could make a life here. And the idea of having to be here, year after year, as residents write their books and get publishing deals and I just have to take a back seat to all of that—I'd rather be doing anything else, anywhere else.

"Okay?" Cody asks, excited. "Does that mean you're in?"

If Margot really didn't want me to sell, she wouldn't have given me that option. This is the kind of money that can change my life.

"When we first met, you said Margot talked to you about selling. You told Caroline that Margot arranged the meeting with me. Did she?" I have been wondering this for months, because if Margot was willing to sell and had arranged all of this, maybe she really was open to me keeping or selling the villa. Maybe she really didn't have a preference either way.

Brent and Cody exchange guilty glances.

"Not exactly," Brent says. "We got the information about The Colony from a past resident."

"So, you never talked to Margot?"

"No," Cody says. "Is that a problem?"

I have a moment of hesitation. Guilt nearly propels me to turn them down, but I remember the mess I'm in, how much I need to get out of this situation.

"I guess not," I say limply.

"So, does that mean you're in?" Brent asks, eyes hopeful.

"Yes," I tell them both. "But I can't sell officially until February, as you know. I don't have the deed." I don't tell them that I have to write a book in order to get the deed and that, currently, I haven't been able to write a word in days. It may not seem like a long time, but that's how my last bout of writer's block started—a few days turned into years.

"No problem," Brent says. "We can get everything ready on our end so that by the time you have the deed, it will be a smooth handover."

"Is it okay if we return on the fifteenth so you can sign an agreement to sell?" Cody asks. "It won't be an official document, but that can get us going on our end."

"Sure," I say, with absolutely no passion in my voice. I just want this to be over. I want to go home. I want to give up, for real this time.

They might ruin this place, but I don't know if I even care anymore.

They leave and I return to the villa only to spend the rest of the day with the curtains closed, in bed, avoiding everyone, and watching Netflix until I feel numb.

TWENTY-NINE

Cap Ferrat, France

Days later and I'm sitting with the residents at the dining room table, their keyboards clacking. My hands are still. It's happening again.

I try to work on my thriller, but I haven't been able to write a word since my mom showed up. Nothing. I've been watching a blinking cursor for days. It's the same as it was before. When I sit in front of the document now, all I feel is this buzzing in my head, the all-encompassing desire to run.

Oliver keeps asking if I'm okay, and I feel this gap between us building and building. I don't know how to tell him that I've agreed to sell. Or tell Sebastian. Or Caroline. Or anyone. Are they going to hate me? My mind is against me. It's hitting me with a constant rush of fear and anxiety.

I shake my head in frustration. I read back over the last scene I wrote before inspiration dried up. I hate it. I can see all the mistakes glaring at me. Can hear Claudia's words from her email rattling around in my brain. *Not as good as Jackson. Not good enough.* I shut my laptop with a thud and stand up quickly before any of the residents can ask me what's wrong.

I go to the front door to take a walk, get some of this frustration out, try to clear my head if that's even possible. The moment I get to the door, it opens, and Oliver walks in, colliding with me.

"Oh," he says, smiling, giving me a quick kiss. "Hey."

"Hey," I say a little too sharply.

"You okay?"

"I was just about to take a walk."

"You want some company?"

"No," I say, distant. "Or, sure, if you want to."

I see him wince. He takes my hand and leads me into Margot's office, shuts the door, and when he looks at me, his eyebrows are stitched together with worry.

"Can you talk to me?" he asks delicately. "You haven't been yourself since your mom showed up and you got that email from Claudia. I'm here for you, Pop. Let me in."

I chew on my lip, look at the ground. What do I say? Whoever Oliver fell for is not who I am. *This* is the real me. Negative, jaded, bitter, hopeless. I'm aware that I'm in a self-sabotage spiral right now. I've been here before, and thought this was behind me. All I want to do is destroy anything in my path, especially anything good. I can't seem to stop myself.

I don't know what to tell him except for the truth.

"I'm selling the villa," I say, my eyes downcast, my voice a whisper. "And I'm going back to LA in February."

The silence is a roar. I don't dare look at him.

"Wait, what? What do you mean?" His tone is lethally calm.

"I'm sure you're disappointed. I'm sorry. I just can't do it. This isn't for me. This isn't my life."

"Disappointed? I—" I hear him pace the room and when I finally look up at him his face is all anguish. "Poppy, let's talk about this before you make such a big decision."

"All you're going to do is try to talk me into keeping it."

"Well, yes," he says. "I want you to keep it. Not for me. For us. For you. You've seemed so happy. You told me you wanted to stay. Aren't we building something here?"

"We could sell the villa and go do anything else together," I say, not even sure that's something I'd want. "And then…if for some reason, we don't work out, we can go our separate ways." I shrug, thinking this is reasonable.

"Do you hear yourself, Poppy? I'm trying to not get upset right now, but it's almost like you don't know me at all."

"It's a good idea. A clean break. A fresh start for us both."

"A fresh start—it sounds more like you're planning for an ending."

"Oliver," I say, a little too coldly. "We just started dating. It would be crazy for me to stay here just for you. We have no idea where this is going, and I don't want to keep The Colony." I cast my eyes to the ground. "I *can't* keep it."

"But… I'm falling in love with you," he says, low, pained.

I should be thrilled to hear this, but I just feel numb.

"It's too risky," I say.

"Poppy, please don't sell." He's pleading. "This would break Margot's heart. How—" Oliver stops, strangled. "But…how can you do this to Margot?"

"I'm not *doing anything* to Margot," I say, finally letting loose the indignation. "She saw something in me I don't see. Maybe she wanted it to be there so much that she imagined it. Whoever she thought I was, I'm not her." I feel the weight of everyone's expectations finally drop off my shoulders. I feel the weight of hope drop, too.

Whoever Oliver was falling in love with was just a role I was playing anyway, a person I was convincing myself to be. I am not her. I don't get a life like this, even if I wanted it. And things with Oliver will probably end the same way everything else does: with me heartbroken, trying to put myself back together.

"I can't do this," I say.

"But why, Poppy?"

"Because I can get my life back on track with that money. I can go start over. I can finally give up on writing and go find something else to do with my life. I can't stay here and watch everyone publish their books when I'm just stuck in the same place I've been in for years and years. Don't you get that? This is bigger than you and me."

Oliver's eyes on me are like daggers. "Are you going to meet with those Booksmart guys again?"

I can't lie to him.

"I already did," I say.

"You what!"

"I told them I would sell it."

"Poppy…" His face is tortured.

"You can't look at me like that. How can I have a clear head when you look at me like that?"

"Just…stay."

"I can't," I say, choking out the words. "And if you will only be with me if I stay, then I think we have our answer."

"So that's it, then? My fate is in your hands?" He throws his arms up. "This could be amazing. You and me. All of this. How can you throw it all away?"

"Is that what I'm doing? If I sell, you don't want to be with me?"

"I can't be with you if you would do that to Margot."

I feel like I'm sinking, drowning.

"Then, that's it, I guess," I spit out. Not enough. *I'm* not enough.

He doesn't get it. Doesn't understand what it took for me to come here. I am so tired of trying to believe in myself. Exhausted by it.

"I think you should go to New York," I say. "Maybe you'll love that job. Maybe this was just a stopover on both our journeys." I hold back the sob that is threatening to come out.

"You can't mean that. I said no to that job for you."

"I didn't ask you to!"

"But I wanted to," he says. "I wanted to do all of this *with* you."

I groan, struggling, push myself against the closed door with a heavy sigh. I want to be the type of person to tell him "okay, let's try it, I'll give it another shot," but I'm so defeated. I can't even muster a lie.

"This is a clean break," I say, my voice cracking. "I go back to LA, you go to New York, and neither of us gets our heart broken."

"That's what you think? A clean break," he repeats under his breath, looking at me with such sadness and longing, my will and conviction is tested again. And then he moves through the sadness, I see it happen on his face, and he replaces it with anger. He looks like the man I met in the airport now. The one who hated me on sight. And I feel a sick wave of relief to see him appear. "You know what? I guess you're right. You're not at all who Margot thought you were. And, obviously, you're not who I thought you were, either." His words pierce my softest places, but I take it.

I nod. I deserve this. He's right. He's been right from the beginning. Now he sees the real me.

"You think this won't break my heart?" he asks, angry. "You think I can walk away like it's a fresh start? Nothing ever breaks clean. Especially not this."

I will myself not to cry. I fear if I cry right now, he'll comfort me, his goodwill winning out over his anger, and it will shatter me. If he puts his arms around me, I might splinter into pieces. I might never be able to put myself back together.

"It's better this way, Oliver."

He watches me for so long, I have to look away. His eyes are searching. He's waiting me out, hoping I'll change my mind. Minutes pass. Maybe hours. Who knows? It feels infinite.

I settle into the perverse comfort of who I used to be. Of

not having my heart out there for him to break. Of not risking anything, of not having to be brave, of not having to expend any more effort in believing I get to have everything I want. See? I broke it all. I lit it on fire.

I'll slip away as quickly as I arrived. And I'll get back to the comfort of being invulnerable. The whole thing feels nearly poetic. Like these last few months were a fever dream.

At least, I won't get hurt.

At least, I won't be heartbroken.

At least, I won't have to keep convincing myself I deserve good things, or love, or a life that is beautiful.

I tell myself the lies until they sound like truth.

Oliver's eyes are glassy when they finally land on mine.

"Wow," he says. "Okay. So that's it, then."

And he walks out.

Once I hear the door shut, I collapse to the floor.

THIRTY

Cap Ferrat, France

Four anxious days pass and I've spent the majority of them avoiding everyone and staying in my room as much as possible. I haven't seen Oliver at all. I've been binge-watching shows on my laptop, trying not to think about what I've agreed to. I sneak down to the kitchen late at night and early morning so I never have to come in contact with anyone. I can't face the residents and their well-meaning questions right now. Stella tried to talk to me a couple days ago and I couldn't do it. I feel so stupid for telling them I was staying and letting them get excited for me.

It's December fifteenth in a couple days and that'll be the end of it. I'll sign the agreement. I'll give up.

But, those two stipulations to inheriting the villa weigh on me constantly. I have to somehow stay here until February, even though I wish I could leave right now. And I have to finish a novel. It doesn't have to be publishable, or even that good, just finished. But I haven't been able to focus enough to work on my draft, and the idea of not completing it—and missing out on all that money—haunts me. To think I came all this way and now I won't be able to sell the villa, either, it makes the writing even more fraught.

I'm flailing. There it is. Flailing. Which reminds me that my mom is still in France. And the idea of seeing her when I'm like this makes me sick. She'll probably tell me she knew this would happen all along, confirm all my worst fears about myself. And she'd be right.

There's a soft knock on the bedroom door. I hear Sebastian's calming voice and the sound of Beau's tiny paws. As much as I don't want to talk right now, I can't ignore Sebastian or Beau.

"Kiddo," I hear Sebastian say. "Let's talk."

I open the door and Beau races to me. I pick him up and hug him close while Sebastian enters.

He surveys the chaos of the room and me, disheveled, eyes rimmed with red.

He whistles out and says, "Oh boy. I see I've come in the nick of time." He looks at me imploringly, and goes in for a warm hug, squishing Beau between us, and my heart is about to break in pieces.

"Your face is a storm of worry, kiddo," Sebastian says. "Come on, let's go for a walk." He gestures toward the door. I want to turn him down, but I can't.

After we put Beau on a leash, we head outside. I turn to Sebastian, finally able to speak. "How did you know?"

Sebastian shrugs and says, "I had an intuitive moment. And Oliver left without an explanation, so I figured something happened."

"Where did he go?"

"New York," Sebastian says softly. "He ended up taking that job. The position was still open, even though he turned it down before. I haven't heard much from him since." I knew Oliver was gone, but hearing it confirmed, my heart feels as though it's in a vice. I just want to lie down on the ground and howl. But I don't deserve to. I did this. I ruined everything.

It's a sunny day, almost blinding, and yet it's cold enough to warrant a jacket, the wind off the ocean coming in strong on top of this bluff. Sebastian and I walk, winding ourselves down the picturesque street that will land us right in the middle of town. I don't know what to say, or even if I did, how to say it.

"We can walk in silence for as long as you want, but I think you'll feel better if you open up, Poppy," Sebastian says, stopping for Beau to sniff a bush.

"I don't know what to say," I say slowly.

"Okay, I'll talk," Sebastian says. "Margot was going to give The Colony to Oliver. That was her plan for a long time. She never told Olly that, but it was clear enough by how Margot taught him everything. He'd read everyone's manuscripts, if he had the time, and he'd give great feedback. He would sit in on workshop sessions, cook up pasta dishes while everyone wrote in the dining room. He had plans when Margot got ill. Plans to keep her legacy alive, and then she passes, and he finds out she has left it to you.

"When Margot got sick, she knew she had little time left. She and I talked a lot about the villa, the residency, about Olly, and about you. She told me she kept having this vision, this dream, that you and Olly would run it together. I thought Olly would have no interest in sharing any of Margot's legacy with you, or anyone. He's lost so much, The Colony would be one more thing for him to grieve. But then Margot had this hare-brained idea to bring you here."

I listen in silence, hungry for any insight into Margot's thinking.

"She thought that if you came here, her vision would come true. You'd love it, and Olly would see what a great team you two are." Sebastian laughs and shrugs. "She told me she saw so much of herself in you. But she didn't think you'd come if it wasn't under mysterious conditions." He rubs his hands over his chin the same way Oliver does. "She thought that if she revealed her grand plan, you'd never take the leap. And maybe she was right."

A long pause hangs between us and I finally say, "She was. I would never have come had I known she was trying to give me a whole new life. Margot definitely got *that* part right." I laugh dryly, and Sebastian chuckles, his eyes still glistening.

"She made a real mess of things, though," he says.

We've made it to the town and suspend our conversation for a moment while we find a café to sit at. It's late afternoon and the village is teeming with activity, groups of people gathering around tiny tables, sharing bottles of wine and aperitifs. We find a spot on the outskirts of a café and Sebastian orders us a carafe of cabernet, which the waiter brings with a flourish, dropping a bowl of mixed nuts and olives on our table, as well. A small bowl of water is placed next to Beau, by our feet, and he laps it up happily.

"If I sell," I start saying. "Would Margot hate that?"

"Poppy," Sebastian says, turning to me with a serious look after he's poured two glasses of wine for us. "If you're selling because you really don't want this, I understand completely. And I know Margot would, too. I know she'd want you to do what was right for you. But if you're selling because you're afraid, because you think you can't handle it, or because you feel like you're not living up to Margot's expectations—then I implore you to stay. Don't walk away in fear, kiddo." His eyes are kind and I can tell he means every word. "That's how you grow up with regrets."

I don't know what to say, but I hang my head in shame. I don't know why I always do this—run away when something feels difficult. Why can't I be brave enough to face it? Why am I always so quick to give up on myself? And on others? I don't know how to fix any of it.

"It just seems like lately all I've received are signs I should give up," I say.

"Well, that's your problem right there," Sebastian replies. "It's not about signs. There's always going to be a reason to give up. What matters is continuing on when things *aren't* going your way. It's easy to keep going when it's all working out. The real grit comes from believing in yourself when you have no evidence you should. Writing the book if you don't know it'll be published. Loving someone when you don't know if it'll work out. Taking on a new adventure like moving to France when you don't know if you'll be able to do it. *That's* what builds resolve, Poppy."

"Resolve," I breathe out. "That's something I've been sorely lacking."

"Just like anything else, you build that by believing in yourself over and over, especially when times are hard and things aren't going your way."

I sit back in the chair with a heavy thud.

"How do you do that?" I ask, shaking my head in disbelief. "How do you know exactly what's going on with me, even better than I do?" I give out a small laugh, a huff of air.

"Because, Poppy, you are so much like Margot when I first met her," he says, smiling. "It's like I've been transported back a few decades. You have no idea how alike you two are. Margot was not always the fearless woman you came to know in your twenties. I told you she had to do a lot of scary things and take on big risks to become the woman she was."

"Somehow I still don't believe that. Like my fears are worse than hers and I don't have what it takes to walk in her footsteps. Margot was a whirlwind of a person, so confident you couldn't help but feel braver in her presence. That's a gift I'm not sure you can cultivate."

"You sound exactly like Margot." He shakes his head, laughing. "I promise you, given the same circumstances, she would have tried to run away from this, too. But you haven't run yet, Poppy. You can stay. You can see it through. You can choose to be brave. That doesn't mean you won't doubt yourself or be afraid. Margot was always afraid when she took a leap of faith, but she just didn't let that stop her. She always said it's not about being fearless—it's about doing it afraid. Do you know how scared she was to start The Colony? She was certain nobody would apply. But she did it anyway. Because she'd rather *do* the thing than regret *not* doing it. And you can choose to do the same."

"How do I tap into that courage?" I ask, suddenly feeling a tiny sense of resolve build within me.

"It's easy," Sebastian says with a smile. "All you have to do is stay. And when you feel the urge to flee in fear, you don't. You stand firm. And you choose courage. You keep choosing courage over fear, until it feels natural. Until you realize you're the bravest person in the room."

"Is that what Margot did?" I ask, my body feeling less burdened. I thought that I had to wait until I didn't feel afraid. I always thought that fear meant inadequacy, that confident people just feel capable all the time. But maybe I've had it all wrong. Maybe Sebastian's right. Maybe the fear never goes away. Maybe what changes is your *response* to it. Maybe you just keep choosing to be brave, every single day.

"That's what Margot did," Sebastian says, nodding his head. "She got disappointed and life didn't always go her way, but she kept going. She kept trying. She didn't let herself get defeated for too long. And there is no doubt in my mind that you are stronger than your fear. Margot made a choice to live boldly, because she knew at any point she only had two choices: back away in fear or choose courage."

Sebastian lowers his voice and dips closer to me. "And you know what, Poppy? When Margot decided to choose courage, a funny thing happened: she always got braver. Fear doesn't like boldness. And regardless of what decisions you've made in the past, you can choose again. Choose courage, Poppy. Don't settle for less than what lights you up. If there's anything Margot wanted from you, it was that. Only that."

I nod, not trusting my own voice yet.

"And hey, just look at me," he says, grabbing my forearm gently. "I've reconnected with the love of my life in my seventies. Life can continue to surprise you right up until the end, if you're brave enough to take risks."

I'm crying now, right in the middle of a busy café, and I don't even care. Because what Sebastian has just said—it's exactly what I needed to hear. Because I have been living in service of my fear for too long. And I did it again. Cowered in the face of it.

I need to be bold.

I need to find a way forward, without running away.

I need to be the main character in my own life. For good this time. No matter what external circumstances might get me down. All it takes is one loving and brave step at a time.

"Thank you," I tell him, my voice unsteady. And he nods, like he knows he's gotten through to me.

The first thing I do when I get back to the villa, after hiking up the large hill with Beau and Sebastian, is take a shower and get dressed in real clothes. And then I do something even more unexpected. Something that seems like the most urgent thing to do right now, given Sebastian's wise words.

I call my mom. I tell her I'm coming to her hotel tomorrow. It feels like I can't move forward until she and I talk. Suddenly, I feel ready to finally face up to the fear of what needs to be said between us.

THIRTY-ONE

Cap Ferrat, France

I'm standing outside the door of my mom's hotel room the next morning, holding a bag of *pain au chocolat* and two takeout espressos, taking deep, steadying breaths. I know I need to do this—talk to her honestly—but that doesn't mean I feel ready for it. I am raw with emotion. But after my talk with Sebastian yesterday, I realize that my fear doesn't mean I am incapable. It simply means I am afraid and I can live with that. It doesn't have to kill me.

This isn't going to be easy, and I'm going to have to draw on a vast well of strength to face my mom, but I think I'm ready. I tell myself I'm ready. I breathe in ten more breaths before I knock.

My mom lets me in, her face unreadable. Her room is small, with a queen-size bed, but it has a fantastic view out the window, where there's a balcony, a small table, and two chairs. We're on the top floor, so the view is unobstructed, and I can see the blue of the Riviera, boats clustered in the distance.

"I brought breakfast," I say, showing her the bag, and she just nods. She looks tired, and worn-out, and I don't know how to broach the conversation I know needs to happen between us. Instead, I hover in small-talk territory.

"How has your visit been?" I ask her, sitting at the small table on her balcony, both of us casting our eyes out to the view.

"Good," she says, curtly. She takes a bite of her pastry and closes her eyes, making a small satisfactory sound. "God, they sure know how to make a croissant here." She grins, and some of the tension deflates between us. "Nice of you to finally show up," she adds, revving the tension right back up.

I shake my head and feel that familiar anger bubbling up inside of me. "Why do you have to do that, Mom?"

"Do what?" She looks at me.

"Guilt-trip me, like always," I say, feeling like I'm losing the thread of this visit already. This always happens. One slight comment from her and I'm off, incapable of seeing anything but red. Every little barb from her piercing a part of me that believes I am unworthy, inadequate, not good enough.

"I don't guilt-trip you," she says, as if I've completely exhausted her already. "I can never do anything right with you. Everything I say is wrong. Everything I do is wrong. I'm obviously not a good enough mom, according to you. You chose Margot over me."

I sit quietly.

What she just said is a whisper of my own mind. This is exactly what I say to myself. I let the pause linger in the air, eyes narrowed at the space where the sea hits the sky, the color blinding. An exhale of breath leaves my chest quickly, and the tension between us drains from me entirely.

Because suddenly, her words hit me in a whole new way. She is me. I am her. She is not mean, or cruel; she is afraid. She has insecurities, too. And I have done nothing but confirm her worst fears about herself. That she is wrong. That she isn't good enough.

I decide, in that moment, to take the risk and hand her an olive branch, to end this battle between us.

"Mom," I say, breaking the silence, my voice cracking on the word, her eyes meeting mine in surprise when she hears the emotion. "I'm really sorry you feel that way. I never wanted you to feel that. I want us to be good. I want a real relationship with you. How can we fix this? I miss you so much." I watch her finally soften. I haven't seen softness in her face in so long, it almost makes me cry.

"Oh, Poppy," she says, grabbing my hand across the table. "I do, too." And we both let out a sigh of relief.

"How did you know where I was?" I ask.

She looks down at her hands, fidgets, then casts her eyes out to the horizon. She then sits up and reaches into her back pocket to reveal a folded piece of paper. She holds it up to me and says, "Margot sent me a letter."

My eyes widen.

"What?" I say. "Wow. What does it say? I mean, you don't have to tell me if you don't want to."

"No," she says, her voice distant and...sad. She sounds exposed and vulnerable, a remarkable change from her usual demeanor of being cold and impenetrable. "I think it's time I tell you what happened between us."

"Okay," I say, my heart racing.

She takes a long sigh. "There's a reason I never told you. First, I was angry at Margot. Then, I was embarrassed. And then, I worried you or your brothers would get the wrong idea. But my keeping this from you has caused way too many problems and it's time you know the real story. Give us a do-over."

"Mom," I say, pleading. "I'd love that."

"Me too," she says. Her voice is shaky. I can tell she's nervous. "Here goes." She takes a deep, steadying breath.

"I was pregnant with Jackson when your father and I got married. Did you know that?"

"No, I didn't."

"Yeah," she says. "Not too far along, but I don't want to lie to you anymore. It's part of the reason your father and I decided to get married. At the time, it seemed like the right thing to do. After my mom died, all I ever wanted was a family, to not be alone. That's what my mom drilled into me. Get a man to provide. Margot went the other direction. She didn't want to get attached. It was always an issue between us. She thought I was playing life too safe, and I thought she was being too reckless."

"And we know Margot had her opinions…"

"So many opinions," Mom breathes out, chuckling very lightly before her face falls. "Well, it was my wedding day. Margot was my maid of honor. It was a small wedding, as you know. And it was a bittersweet day for me. You always want your mom there on your wedding day and she wasn't. Anyway, Margot was getting ready with me, and once my makeup and hair were done, we were alone in the hotel room. It was only an hour until the ceremony. She sat me down and said 'I don't think you should marry him. You're not happy. You deserve better. Don't do this just because you're pregnant. I will help you. You won't be alone.'" She exhales loudly, turns away from me. "An hour before my wedding, Poppy."

"Oh," I say into the silence. "Oh no." I place my hand on hers and she looks at me as if she's surprised I'm still here, like she's lost entirely in the memory of that day.

She wipes at an errant tear on her cheek, steels herself.

"I was so angry. Embarrassed. I screamed at her. All that had been unsaid between us, all the jealousy and pettiness that had racked up over the years, it all came out. I called her selfish. Told her she was just jealous. After our mom died, she went off and had a life, but I felt left behind. Abandoned. Like she was so much better than me in every way. And now she was telling me to leave my fiancé? To raise my child alone? Rely on her? Margot, who would probably be on a flight to Europe the next day! I couldn't do it. She had always made me feel ashamed for choosing stability and comfort, and so I doubled down."

She shook her head. Fidgeted more in her lap.

"I told her to leave."

"No," I say. "And did she?"

"She did," Mom says, her voice pained. "I got married without my best friend, my sister, my maid of honor. And without my mom. It was…not really a great day, to say the least."

"Oh, Mom," I say. "That's devastating."

"Yeah," she says, heavy tears falling now. "It was."

I wait for her to continue. This is not an easy story for her to tell and it's been locked away for more than three decades for a reason.

"I couldn't forgive her," she says. "To forgive her would mean she was right about my marriage, and I didn't want her to be right. And I didn't want to tell you or your brothers, because I never wanted any of you to think I regretted my life. Or being your mom. Because I haven't."

"We would never have thought that, Mom," I tell her. "Ever."

"Yeah, well," she says, resigned. "It was easier to pretend I didn't have a sister."

"That makes sense," I say, because it really does. All the pieces are coming together.

"But—" Her expression is agonizing. "She *was* right." And suddenly my mom—my mom, who is a fortress of no emotion—is sobbing into her hands, making sounds that break my heart.

"Mom," I say, standing up and pulling her into a hug that she pliantly falls into. We stay locked together like that for a good few minutes, and after she pulls herself from my arms, she wipes her tears and apologizes.

"Don't apologize," I tell her. We both sit back down, and I face her again. "But, what do you mean Margot was right?"

She doesn't reply. She just opens the letter and starts reading.

June, I'm so sorry for what I said at your wedding. It wasn't my place. But trust me when I tell you that I thought I was looking out for you. You didn't seem excited or happy to marry Frank. He wanted a traditional wife, and I didn't think that was what you wanted. If you have had a happy and fulfilling life, then I was wrong and for that I will forever be sorry. I take that regret to my grave.

Mom folds the letter, tears streaming down again. "There's more, but that's the important part. I wasn't happy with your father. I don't feel fulfilled. I love you kids, don't get me wrong. Please don't ever think otherwise."

"Mom," I say, stilling her. "You are your own person. I can understand that who you are as a mom and who you are as a woman are two different things."

She looks at me then—like, really looks at me—and her face is the picture of gratitude, like a weight has been lifted.

"I thought I was doing the right thing, marrying your father," she says. "I wish I could have told Margot that I should have listened to her. Or maybe not. I don't know. But… I can't stay with your father, Poppy. I can't. I'm sorry."

"There is nothing to be sorry for," I tell her. "Please, go find your happiness. It's your life, Mom. You go do whatever makes you fulfilled and I will be there, cheering you on. Promise."

"You really mean that?" she asks, childlike, as if she is the daughter and I'm the mother.

"Absolutely."

She squeezes my hand across the table and gives me the first genuine, unguarded smile I've seen from her in a long, long time.

Later, we have lunch at a little outdoor café near her hotel. It's sunny and brisk out, and all the tables around us are filled.

After we've finished eating a delicious meal, both of us order coffees and chocolate mousse.

"I have something I need to say," Mom says, stilling the spoon at her lips.

"Okay," I reply, setting down my spoon, as well.

"I'm sorry, Poppy," she says, her voice cracking. "You reminded me so much of Margot. I should have been a better mom to you. I should have been able to put how I felt aside and be supportive of you. I feel so much shame for the way I treated you. I think I was jealous that you seemed to be choosing Margot's life over mine, which only made me feel like my life was less than. It was irrational. I tried to bring you down to make myself feel better, to justify my choices. Thinking about it now, it doesn't even make sense. Like if you got trapped in an unhappy marriage, then I would be happier? And when it comes to the body stuff, I hated that Margot seemed happier and I was always on a diet, thinking that if I was thin I'd be happy. It just made me so angry. Please know it was my own shit. I'm so sorry."

"It's okay, Mom. I actually understand now."

"You are so talented and wonderful, honey," she says, covering my hand with hers. "I am so sorry if I ever made you feel like that wasn't true. I was always trying to earn my love from others, Poppy. If I was thin enough and good enough and perfect enough, played by the rules, was a good wife and a good daughter and a good woman, I'd be okay. But Margot, she didn't play by those rules. And I didn't understand how she did it. And instead of trying to learn or take inspiration from her, I hated her for it. I judged her. I made her wrong so that all my pain would be right."

"Thank you for saying that," I say, and it feels like something deep in my core has shifted. It's so humbling, how much I need my mom. And I feel like I haven't had her for so long. "And I'm sorry you've felt that way about yourself, Mom."

"I should have encouraged you. I should have brightened you up, instead of making you feel inadequate like I felt." She shakes her head and takes a tentative sip of her coffee.

"Mom, all I ever wanted was to know you believed in me," I say, the vulnerability crackling around us both.

"I've *always* believed in you, honey," she says. "I've just had a very bad way of showing it." She meets my eyes again, and we both give sideways smiles.

"It's okay, Mom. I haven't been the best daughter, either." I shrug and add, "I'm sorry, too. I'm sorry I lied to you about seeing Margot. And for anything else I've done to hurt you."

She looks pensive. "You know, moms have feelings too, Poppy. I think you kids forget that. We're just people like you."

"Mom…"

"No, let me say this," she says, stopping me gently. "I'm human. No one really tells you the disappointment you'll feel when your daughter doesn't want your life."

"But, Mom—"

"The disappointment in *yourself*, Poppy. Not in you. In me. I felt like you looked at me like I was just some silly woman, and it's exactly how I thought Margot saw me. But really, it's kind of how I saw myself, if I'm being completely honest."

"Oh, Mom," I say. "You kept us all together. You gave us a happy childhood. You did…you do…everything. You're a great mom."

"I was furious when I found out where you were," she says, looking down at her lap. "I hate that. I thought you chose her over me. My worst nightmare."

"I love you both. But you'll always be my mom."

She smiles, her eyes shiny with tears.

"I'm going to divorce your father," she says.

"You should. Start over. You deserve that."

"Do I?" She's fidgeting with her hands.

"You absolutely do."

"You inspired me, you know. I forgot what that was like, to just start over. I told your dad all of this, and he all but shrugged at me. I think I would have stayed with him forever if you hadn't left, honey. I think I stayed with him to prove Margot wrong. A stupid reason. But I can be stubborn."

"No shit," I say, and we both burst out laughing.

Then her face turns serious.

"It's like I've come out of a long daze," she says. "And now I'm awake and I miss my sister." Her voice cracks with sorrow.

I reach for her hand, and we stay there for a while.

"She knew you loved her, Mom. She must have."

"Maybe. I hope so."

"I'm sure of it. From what I've learned about Margot over the past few months, she knew everything. But I'm sorry you didn't get to reconcile."

"Me too, honey. Me too." And then her hand goes to her mouth. "You're not upset, though? About the divorce? Divorce can be tough on the children. I never wanted to upset you all."

"I'm not upset, Mom. Not at all. Sometimes, you have to choose yourself. Besides, we're grown-ups. I'd be more upset if you didn't let yourself be happy."

"You're something else, Poppy," she says, looking at me with tears in her eyes.

"I'm proud of you, Mom," I say, meaning it. "What will you do now?"

Her face breaks into a blinding smile. It's stunning. "Wow, I don't know. Anything, I guess?" Her hand goes to her heart. "Definitely going to start painting again. I've missed it. I haven't felt like this in a long time. Or ever."

"Possibility," I say.

"Yes, that's it. *Possibility*."

"A great, big scary feeling."

She looks over at me and our eyes catch. "Exactly." A long,

comfortable pause stretches between us. "I don't know why we didn't do this before. It's like I forgot we could just talk it out."

"Being angry was easier," I say.

"Yes, being angry was easier," she says. "I guess you got that from me."

"I got a lot from you, Mom," I say, smiling widely now.

"Can we promise we'll always be honest with each other from here on out?" she asks, her face hopeful.

"Promise."

"Now, tell me everything," she says. "Starting first with the beautiful man with his arm around my gorgeous daughter. My goodness, Poppy. Who was *that*?"

As we walk back to her hotel and then sit at the balcony while the sun sets, I divulge everything, no detail left untouched. I tell her about Oliver, the good, the bad, and the breakup. I tell her about the residency, the villa, about Booksmart, about Margot's wishes, about everything Sebastian told me the other day. And I tell her about Mauro, about Claudia, about Jackson's phone call, and I flinch going over it, feeling so exposed and embarrassed.

I wince, waiting for her reply.

We may have just had a heart-to-heart, but I still have no idea how she's going to respond to all of this. I don't know who this new version of my mom is, or what our relationship will become.

I find that I'm holding my breath, waiting for her to process everything, her eyes narrowed at the horizon, clearly in deep thought.

"I'm trying to find the right words," she says, looking over at me. "But the first thing that comes to mind is, wow, I have such a brave and incredible daughter. I'm so proud of you." She grabs my hand again, and I'm crying, large drops cascading onto my shirt. "You're my hero."

"Thank you, Mom," I croak out, overcome. I can't believe how much it means to me for her to say that. "But...what do I do?"

"What do you *want* to do?" she asks, and I have to catch my breath. I've been waiting for her to ask me that for what feels like a decade.

"I want to be bold," I say. "And courageous. I want to be the person Margot thought I was. I want to make her proud. And you, Mom. I want to make you proud, too. And, more than that, I want to make *myself* proud." The words come out crystal clear, without any obfuscations.

"Well then," she says, clapping her hands together and wiping the last remnants of tears from her eyes. She stands up with resolve. "Sounds like you've got a plan."

That evening, I order room service, both of us famished by this reconciliation, a vulnerability hangover settling in around us. I ask for two cheeseburgers, cooked medium, with fries. I order everything in stunted French, and my mom looks at me, eyes wide, the entire time. When I hang up with a *"merci beaucoup,"* she's looking at me like I'm a total stranger.

"Okay, so you speak French now?"

"Oui, madame," I say, laughing. *"Un petit peu.* A little bit." I shrug.

My mom laughs and says, "Poppy, I am so proud of you." Her eyes go misty again. "This is going to be a whole new chapter for us." She crosses the room and sits down on the bed, and I'm at the tiny desk in the corner. "I'm glad we got everything out in the open."

"Me, too," I say. "Honesty, from here on out." And we both nod, and my heart fills with warmth.

"I can't believe you thought you wanted to write romance," she says, shaking her head and giving out a chuckle. "I've never once seen you read a romance novel. You were always reading PJ Latisse or Agatha Christie, or what's that one you loved with the unbelievable twist, the one with the *Good Will Hunting* guy in it?"

I laugh and say, "Ben Affleck? *Gone Girl*, Mom."

"*Gone Girl,* yes, that's it," she says. "You do love a good plot twist."

"I really do," I say, just as there's a knock at the door.

Room service sets out our plates on the balcony table, a chilling breeze coming off the water. We both dig in, dipping our *frites* in creamy mayonnaise, as you do in France, and eating our messy burgers, ketchup and Dijon mustard dripping down our chins, the tinny sound of our laughter a soundtrack. I feel such a rush of happiness. Being here, in the south of France, sitting across from my mom telling me a funny story, her head whipped back in laughter.

"Where did you get that necklace?" she asks.

I lift the hummingbird off my neck. "I found it in Margot's closet. Apparently she wore it all the time and hardly ever took it off. Why?"

My mom's eyes go glassy again.

"She wore it? She wore that necklace?"

"That's what the villa's caretaker, Caroline, told me."

"Wow," my mom says, wiping at her eyes. "I gave that to her after our mom died. Our mom loved hummingbirds and whenever we saw one, we thought it was a sign from her."

My eyes widen. "Oh my god." Tears fall to my cheeks.

"Yeah," she says. "I can't believe all these years later she still wore it."

"See? Margot didn't hold it against you, Mom."

"I guess not," she says, lost in the moment.

And then, my phone beeps and I see a text from Caroline. The guys from Booksmart are at the villa with the agreement. My stomach lurches. Is it December fifteenth already? I've been so caught up in my downward spiral, I didn't realize.

Wait, it's not. It's the fourteenth. They must be early, eager. It just comes across as pushy, which is, I recognize, how they've been this whole time.

I feel an involuntary shudder of fear at the thought of having to face them, but it leaves as quickly as it arrives. Because, I remember, looking up from the remnants of my burger, that I don't have to do it alone.

"Funny enough," I say, through a mouthful of fries. "The Booksmart guys are at the villa right now."

"Oh, are they?" Her eyes narrow. "Let's head over there. Time to deal with those fuckers once and for all, no?"

I nod emphatically. "Let's do this."

THIRTY-TWO

Cap Ferrat, France

We head to the villa, and on the taxi ride over, I point out all my favorite spots, so happy to be able to share this part of my life with my mom. We laugh and giggle through the ride like best friends, and it's startling to me how much more fortified and at ease I feel with my mom by my side. I knew we were broken, but I could not have predicted how I would feel after we repaired our relationship. I feel a tight pinch of sadness that Margot and my mom never got to reconcile, thinking of all the memories we missed out on, the three of us together.

I steady myself before entering the villa, my mom's hand in mine. I can't tell in this moment who hates Brent and Cody more—me or her. And having her anger on my side for once, well, it gives me a rush of boldness. I can't believe I even considered selling the villa, and, worse, to these guys, who seem hell-bent on ruining everything Margot has built. I must have been truly out of my mind to have said yes to their offer.

I introduce my mom to Caroline, who's in the kitchen, her eyes darting to the backyard. These guys are such assholes, and it feels good to finally admit it.

"You're not going to accept, are you?" Caroline asks tentatively.

"Hell no," I say. "I had a moment of weakness, but I'm not going anywhere."

"Thank god," Caroline replies, letting out an exhale. "I was worried for a second there."

"Me too," I say. I hug her tightly and leave her and my mom in the kitchen.

Before I go outside, I take a breath in. I look back at them, who both give me a reassuring thumbs-up.

Brent and Cody jump up out of their chairs to greet me, their faux charm dialed up to a hundred. My stomach recoils at them. How could I have *ever* considered selling this beautiful place to these two guys? No wonder Oliver was so upset. Now that I see the villa and the residency with the same fondness that he sees it, I would probably lose my cool at anyone who wanted to give it away, too. Especially, to two douchebags who want to turn it into some inaccessible spa weekend for rich white ladies. Even for a million dollars, it's not worth it.

Before Brent and Cody can even launch into whatever spiel they have prepared, I put my hand up to stop them, and both of them go quiet. I walk around the table to face them, a silent tension hanging in the air, and I don't sit down. All three of us are standing, and they are both waiting for me to speak.

"I've changed my mind," I say, in a clear, even voice. Both of their jaws hang open, and I continue, "I had my doubts about selling to you guys, and you *almost* convinced me. But I'm not going to let you take my aunt's legacy and destroy it." Both widen their eyes in surprise.

"Poppy, be reasonable," Cody says, pleadingly. "You already agreed."

"I didn't sign anything," I say, defiant, chin tipped up. "The answer is no."

"Wait just a minute," Brent says. "Let's talk about this."

"No," I say.

Brent seems to lose his composure, leans over the table quickly and says, "Wow. Okay. That's very unprofessional."

"We had a deal," Cody says, rude and biting. "You can't fucking go back on it now."

And before they can continue, my mom comes to my side, surprising me. Caroline is close behind.

"My daughter here has given her answer," my mom says, lethal and calm. "The villa is not for sale. Not anymore. And even if it was, you'd be the last people on earth we'd sell it to." She crosses her arms over her chest. That *we* makes me smile broadly. She and I, a team. I feel almost dizzy with relief. To know she believes in me, it gives me the last boost I need to really believe in myself.

"Time to go, boys," Caroline says, with a smile that makes her eyes crinkle. *"Au revoir!"*

They stumble out, not saying another word, their big egos silenced. Once they're gone, all three of us look at each other, and start laughing.

"Caroline, Mom?" I croak out. They both look at me, quieting down their celebrations for a moment.

"Yeah?" my mom says, taking my hand.

"In case I haven't been clear, this is it. For real this time. I'm going to keep the villa, move here, run The Colony," I say, my voice rooted and grounded. "This is my home. And I'm going to finish my thriller manuscript. Maybe I'll find the perfect agent for me and publish it. Maybe I won't. Either way, I'll be good. And I'm going to use The Colony to help other writers follow their dreams. And I am done—really, truly done—with giving up on myself."

Both of them break into loud cheers.

Sebastian and Andrew come outside, letting themselves in through the villa, Beau at their heels as always.

"What's all this?" Sebastian asks, stepping into our little celebration. Beau is so excited to see all of us that he can't decide who he wants to jump on, so he's moving from one pair of legs to the next.

"We just told the guys from Booksmart to take a hike," I say, grinning. "Oh, and this is my mom, June Banks. Mom, this is Sebastian and Andrew. He was Margot's best friend and Andrew is his partner. They live down the street."

"It's so nice to finally meet you, June," Sebastian says, taking my mom's hand in both of his, eyes shining. "I've heard so much about you from Margot."

"A pleasure to meet you, June," Andrew says and before he can even finish his sentence, my mom pulls them both into a hug.

"You have to tell me everything about Margot," my mom says, her voice cracking. "I want to know everything. I was supposed to leave tomorrow, but I'm extending my trip. I can't leave now!"

"Wait," Sebastian says, turning to me. "Does this mean *you're* staying?"

"Yes," I say. "I'm staying. I'm staying!"

Sebastian claps his hands together and whoops, so loud that Beau starts barking. "Beau is clearly very excited," Sebastian says, laughing. "We need champagne. This is cause for celebration!"

We all agree, and I see Sebastian hook arms with both Andrew and my mom, walking inside the villa, and I am tickled to see it. Caroline procures a bottle of chilled champagne from the fridge, and pops open the cork to a festive "hurrah." The residents finish their writing time and join the celebration. They knew I was having a crisis of confidence, so all four of them are thrilled I've made a final decision.

I look around, feeling full of life, clinking glasses with these people I love so much. But I can't help but feel a sharp pain that is illuminated, even more, by how happy we all are. Tears spring into my eyes, and Caroline, seated next to me, squeezes my hand under the table, telling me she understands.

Our togetherness in celebrating can't help but highlight the absences also present.

I wish Margot were here to see this, and hope that somewhere, she is.

And I wish I hadn't pushed Oliver away. It feels wrong being joyous without him. The thought of calling him to tell him about my decision passes through my mind, but I can't. I don't want that to be the reason he comes back.

The rest of the night passes in that way: bittersweet joy, and the overwhelming feeling that someone crucial is missing.

THIRTY-THREE

Cap Ferrat, France

The next few days pass by in a blur of snippets. Mom and Sebastian go on meandering walks, her arm in the crook of his, the two of them like old friends. He even took her to his favorite museum—their shared love of art bonding them together. My mom cooks with Caroline in the kitchen in the afternoons, while I write feverishly, the tap of inspiration miraculously flowing again. The residents take to my mom like fireflies to the night, asking her for advice, or ideas, and my mom gives it readily and with abandon.

Three times a day, she comes by with a meal. And in between, she fills my water glass, makes me espresso, fetches a croissant for me in the morning, and whispers encouragement in my ear as she passes. "You've got this, Poppy."

"Bestseller status right there."

"Never doubted you for a second." It's almost a little much, but I relish it. No battles. No harsh words exchanged. Something unlocked between us, and I feel like I have a mom again. A support system. And her encouragement, her being here and helping out wherever she can, it's lit a fire under me. My first draft is nearly done. And… I don't even care if it's good. I'm just happy I'm writing again.

It's a Friday, another workshop day, and I've been noncommittal about joining, but at the last moment, I head downstairs from my bedroom desk to the dining room.

"Yay, Poppy's here," Jasmyn exclaims.

"I finally made it," I say, laughing. "Thanks for being patient with me."

"We love you, Poppy," Evie says. "You definitely have been on a wild ride here."

"Yeah, no kidding," I say.

"And you're here now, that's all that matters," Kerry adds. "We've all been waiting to hear about this elusive thriller novel you've been working on."

"Yeah, we need details," Stella says. "I vote for Poppy to go first."

"Go ahead," Janelle prompts from the head of the table. I take a deep breath in.

I look at all of them watching me expectantly, with kind eyes and openhearted faces. I feel brave enough to want their feedback, to trust them, and to no longer worry if I'm good enough. I now know fear is not a sign of inadequacy. It's a sign of courage.

"This is the first scene of my book. It's called… *You Think You Know Florence James*," I say, gauging their reactions to the title and feeling good that everyone is smiling, listening intently. I give them a quick overview of the synopsis, then start reading the scene. When I'm done, I lower the pages, and look out at Jasmyn, Kerry, Evie, Stella, and Janelle, who are all rapt. I'm shaky, nervous, terrified.

"That was…" Evie starts and claps her hand over her face. "Oh my god, Poppy, that was so good. I honestly cannot wait to read the rest."

"Really?" I ask.

"You're an incredible writer," Kerry says. "What's the big twist?"

"I don't want to ruin it," I say, shrugging. And all of them cajole me into telling them, so I do.

"Well, the twist is that Florence James, the sultry actress that everyone compares to Marilyn Monroe and treats like a sex symbol with no brain, who seems innocent, and who everyone is distressed, trying to find—" I pause for dramatic effect "—actually fakes her own death. All to go live on a farm with a man she met in Montana, whom she fell in love with, after hating every second of the spotlight and the fame that went with it."

Gasps ring out around the room.

"No!" Evie exclaims.

"STOP IT," Jasmyn screams out.

"That is…incredible!" Stella cries.

"You think?" I ask.

"That is so intriguing and fresh," Janelle says. "To be honest, it sounds like something PJ Latisse would write." I beam as the rest of the group nods in agreement.

"Well, that's the highest compliment I could ever receive," I say. "You all know how I feel about PJ."

"Even your writing style is a little like hers, now that I think about it," Janelle says, pondering. "Not like a copycat. It's just… stylistically, you two are very similar."

"Again," I say, "highest praise."

We all fall into a contented chatter, and then the workshopping continues, and they offer some constructive edits that make the scene even better. The rest of the residents take their turn. As I listen to everyone's scenes, I don't feel any jealousy. No competitiveness, or self-loathing.

All I feel is that, here, at this villa, surrounded by creative, intelligent, and gifted writers—I'm *exactly* where I'm meant to be.

After the workshop disperses, my mom comes in from yet another long walk with Sebastian, her cheeks pink from the cold. She walks right up to me and asks, in a whisper, "So, how was it?"

"They really liked it," I say, locking eyes with her. She beams at me.

"Of course, they did," she says. "You're Poppy Banks. Future bestseller. The next *Gone Girl* lady. They'd be idiots if they didn't recognize talent when it's sitting right in front of them."

"I love you too, Mom," I say, through a tittered laugh. And she stops, and looks at me so sincerely, I freeze in place.

"I love you, Poppy," she says, her eyes glistening. She pulls me in for a tight hug. "You're my favorite daughter," she whispers in my ear.

I giggle. "I'm your *only* daughter," I say back into her ear.

"And still, my favorite one."

Her love, the workshop feedback, my own belief in myself, it has a catalyzing effect on me. I feel strong. Stronger than I've *ever* felt before.

THIRTY-FOUR

Cap Ferrat, France

A few days later, the first draft of *You Think You Know Florence James* is finished. I've printed it out, and I'm sitting alone at the long dining room table, with a cup of peppermint tea, just holding the warm pages in my hands, cherishing all 90,654 words that are in this book.

Writing it feels like a triumph, that I dug deep within myself and extracted these words. I find that I truly do not even care what happens next. If this book goes nowhere, okay. If it's not good enough to be published, okay. I'm just proud that I *finished*.

Kerry and Evie trickle in and sit at the table with me. It's early evening, all of us feeling fairly exhausted after months of writing. We are all weary, but it's a good tired. Stella joins us, with a cup of tea of her own. Jasmyn comes in from the backyard. We've all finished the first drafts of our books. They'll leave soon, and I can already tell that each time the residents go, I'll feel some type of way about it. It makes me excited, though. I like how The Colony already feels like mine.

Piercing through our comfortable silence, a surge of activity explodes through the front door, and all of us exchange glances.

Sebastian and my mom come through first, Beau screeching through the foyer and past the living room to jump up on my lap, and then... Is that...?

I stand up quickly, and poor Beau leaps off me just in time.

"That's Jackson Banks," Stella says, in a reverentially loud whisper, and I stare in awe.

"Surprise!" Liam shouts out, coming in through the living room, heading straight for me, then wrapping me in a hug. Jackson follows closely behind, and he's a lot less animated than Liam, but I see him smiling tentatively. I'm excited to see both of my brothers, actually. It's funny how all my previous tension with my family dissipated once my mom and I repaired our relationship.

Liam and I break apart, and Jackson comes in for a hug, too. "Surprise, Pop," he says, as we hug a little longer than we typically do.

I look at them both and glance over to Sebastian and my mom, who are behind my brothers with delighted smiles. It's pretty clear the two of them set this up. I look past Liam and Jackson and shake my head at them, pretending to be chastising, but actually feel quite special that my brothers have come all this way to surprise me. I hear the residents whispering about Jackson, and I don't unleash them on my big brother quite yet.

"What are you guys doing here?" I ask.

"Mom called us," Jackson says. "She told us we had to come and see what our amazing sister was up to in France."

"Yeah, and damn, Pop," Liam says, looking around the villa. "This place is sick."

My mom steps forward between them and says, "I just wanted us all to be here together." She smiles almost sheepishly, and shrugs. "I hope you don't mind."

"Mind?" I ask, wiping an errant tear from my cheek. "I couldn't be happier to see you guys."

Finally, I introduce Jackson to the residents, who commandeer his attention for a solid hour, asking him every question they can think of—how to get an agent, navigate the publishing process, write bestselling books. I stand away from the fray, and his patience in answering their questions surprises me. I think maybe I've misjudged my brother.

My mom and Sebastian are on the couch, talking about who knows what, the two of them practically inseparable at this point. Caroline returns to a full house, and after meeting everyone, quickly steps out to get provisions for dinner. I go into the kitchen and find Liam there, and we hug again for good measure.

"This suits you, Pop," he says, knocking me on the shoulder. We're leaning against the sink, side by side. "You seem at home here."

"Really?" I ask. "Yeah, it feels that way, actually."

"I haven't seen you this happy and relaxed in a long time."

"I haven't felt this happy and relaxed maybe ever," I tell him, exhaling a deep breath. "How are you?"

Liam takes a few minutes to update me on what's going on with his new job as a software engineer for Apple—his dream job—and then tells me that he and the girlfriend he'd been seeing for a few months broke up. "I'm fine—the spark just wasn't there," he explains. "Speaking of, where's that guy you texted me about? Is he not here?" I'd texted Liam on Thanksgiving to say hi, and I told him about Oliver. I had forgotten, until now, that I'd done that. My heart drops, and Liam turns toward me, noticing the way my face has changed suddenly. "Uh-oh, what happened?"

I will myself to not cry, fearing that if I do, I might never stop. I don't want this day to be about Oliver, but it seems like no matter what I do, I can't stop thinking about him. It's like he's embedded in every single nook of this villa. I could try to call him, track him down, but I'm embarrassed about how I ended things. I feel awful. He probably hates me. I don't even know if I deserve his forgiveness. And considering his history, and the people he's lost—I should have known better. I don't know how, but I should have done it all differently. And I wouldn't blame him if he never wants to see me again.

"We broke up," I eventually say.

"Oh no, Pop," Liam says. "Why?"

"We just wanted different things, I think," I say, trying to remember why it felt so urgent to break it off with him, and then trying to forget the look on his face when I did.

"What, he didn't want to stay in France?"

"No, he actually did. He wanted me to keep the villa and it was this huge barrier between us. I was indecisive about it."

"But...you're keeping it?"

"I was scared," I say, thrusting my face into my hands. "I got in my head about it."

"Damn," he says. "Maybe it's not too late. Where is he? Is he here? Let's go find him."

"No, it's too late," I say. "He's in New York now. He took a new job there. I told him to go! How stupid is that? He's starting a whole new life. I don't want to upset that for him. It was complicated between us. He only wanted to be with me if I kept the villa. Or that's how it felt. But I want someone who will choose me regardless of anything else."

I realize how true those words are, and I'm surprised by this feeling of self-worth, respect, and trust I've stepped into. Regardless of the fact I'm keeping Margot's villa, I wanted Oliver to choose me over that. To want me, no matter what.

"I get it," Liam says. "But, that still sucks."

I let out a tight, breathless laugh. "*Sucks* doesn't even begin to cover it." I give him a pained smile.

"Not to completely change the subject, and sorry if this makes it worse, but, uh, is that woman Caroline single?"

"Liam!" I cry, hitting him playfully on the arm. "Yes, she's single. Go for it. You two would be cute together." My little brother is truly the best person in the world and so is Caroline. I ship this completely.

"Whoa there, *together*?" Liam laughs, putting his hands up in front of him. "Can I start with a first date, please?"

"I guess," I joke.

Jackson pops his head into the kitchen and gestures to me. "Can we talk?" he asks and then adds, "Alone?"

"Sure thing," I say and follow Jackson into Margot's— actually, now *my*—office off the foyer.

Jackson walks in and looks around in awe, as I did the first time I came in here. He scans the books and finds the Jackson Banks collection.

"Aunt Margot had all my books," he says, in a tone that suggests he's very touched. "And of course, she has all these mysteries. Mom was right. You two are so alike." He turns around and looks at me.

"Mom called me and told me everything, by the way," he says. "Honestly, I didn't know how hard she was being on you. And I couldn't have helped with that. I feel awful, Poppy."

"No," I say forcefully. "I'm the one who's sorry."

"For what?" he asks, surprised.

"Oh, I don't know, for being a jealous little sister who couldn't be happy for your success. For blaming you for not being able to write, as if it was your fault. I've been angry at you for a long time. And honestly, for the life of me, I can't understand why, except that I was blindingly envious of you."

"Well, Pop, thanks for saying all that, but I have to say I don't think I've been a perfect older brother, so don't take it all on." He gives me a rueful smile. "I'm competitive, and I did like being better at writing than you. I hate to admit it, but it's true. You were *always* the smart one, Pop. And I was the stupid jock." He shrugs and continues, "It felt good getting all the acclaim."

He adds, "I thought you'd hate me for telling you about Claudia, but you're my little sister. I have to protect you."

"Claudia didn't want to sign me," I say. "In the end, it didn't really matter."

"I'm sorry," he says. "But maybe that's better? Romance isn't really your thing."

"I was desperate." I shrug. "But now I realize I don't need an agent or a book deal for validation. I can just…write because I love it."

"That's how it started for me," he says. "Passion first. That's the only way you can keep writing books. It's a labor of love every single time."

"I'm starting to understand that."

"But, does that mean you're not going to do anything with your writing? Because I, personally, think that would be a disservice."

"I don't know yet."

Jackson just nods, maybe understanding how delicate this all feels for me. Maybe all this time I could have had Jackson as my ally instead of my competition.

"Can I read your book?" Jackson asks gently. "I give good notes."

"You want to?"

"Of course," he says. "Have you forgotten that I was the number-one member of the Poppy Banks Fan Club growing up?"

"You did read a lot of my short stories," I say, laughing.

"Every single one!" he says. "You got me into reading."

"Okay, you can read it if you actually want to," I say. "Don't feel obligated. But if you really want to, I'd love your notes."

He takes a step back and places his hand over his heart. "It would be my honor, Pop," he says. "It means so much to me that you'd want my opinion. Honestly."

And it's in that little office, surrounded by beloved books, that Jackson and I start to learn how to create a new relationship—

one of literary peers and supportive siblings—without envy and animosity.

We walk back into the jumble of activity. Caroline and Liam playfully flirting while chopping vegetables for dinner, Sebastian, who is now joined by Andrew, and my mom at the dining room table with the four residents, the mood lively.

I grab my printed manuscript and hand it to Jackson, who takes it from me and holds it to his chest. "I'm proud of you, Pop," he says. "It's an achievement just to have finished writing this. Believe me, writing is hard work, and you've done the hardest part." It's not a condescending compliment. I feel a smile spread across my face.

"Thanks, Jack," I say. "I hope you like it. I really, really do."

"No doubt in my mind, it's going to be incredible," he says. He takes a red pen and a pile of Post-its and holds them all up in the air and says, "Off to read now."

And I watch him go to the couch and find a comfortable spot. He notices me observing him and gives me an encouraging thumbs-up. I finally turn around to sit at the dining room table, letting the nerves roll off me, and trusting, for once, that my big brother actually has my back.

What a difference it makes, to have my family here in support, to not have to do everything alone, and to let them back into my life.

To forgive, and forget, and leave room for people to change.

To leave room for me to change, too.

THIRTY-FIVE

Cap Ferrat, France

The next morning, I wake to the sound of heavy rainfall battering against the villa, and it casts a feeling of coziness. I shower quickly, get dressed in a comfortable thick sweater and sweats, and head downstairs. There is only one person seated at the dining room table, and it's Jackson with his back to me, gazing out at the backyard. Jackson looks as if he hasn't slept all night. There are Post-its scattered around him, and four mugs. His hair is sticking up on the right side, and I feel a bloom of fondness, just looking at him sitting there.

I also get a wave of nerves. I care about Jackson's opinion of my book, perhaps a lot more than I ever considered—and my heart is thumping underneath my sweater. What if he *hates* it? Am I strong enough to be able to withstand his criticism?

Yes. I can do this. I can get feedback. I am changing my own narrative. I am not letting fear dictate my life. I take a steadying breath in.

I put my hand on Jackson's shoulder and he jumps, takes off his headphones.

"Good morning," I say softly. His eyes are red, and I look at him quizzically. "Are you okay?" I sit down in the chair next to him.

"I'm more than okay," he says. "Poppy, I didn't sleep. I couldn't put your book down. I stayed up all night reading it."

"I stayed up all night reading your book" is the highest compliment an author could ever receive. I practically beam.

"You did not," I say, shocked. I exhale hard. Relief. I feel almost light-headed. I would have been able to survive his criticism, but his praise? It's so unexpected. So…lovely.

"It's so damn good, Pop, oh my god," he says, his eyes bright now. "I just finished the last chapter before you came down, and it made me cry. This book is amazing!"

I sit there, stunned into silence. Of all the feedback I thought Jackson was going to hurl at me, this was not even in the top one hundred.

"Are you just saying that?" I ask, still not believing these words are coming out of my big brother.

"I'm serious, Poppy. It's beautiful. I don't know how many more effusive adjectives I can use. Brilliant! Incredible! Awesome! Mind-blowing!" He laughs and I just shake my head, unable to fully wrap my mind around this.

"I'm shocked."

"Really? Come on, you know you're a great writer."

"I thought I was, and then I got rejected hundreds of times and lost all faith in myself."

"I got rejected, too," Jackson says. "I only had one agent interested in my book and that was after a year of looking. That book got a six-figure deal. Rejections don't mean anything."

"I didn't know that…"

"Well," he says softly. "You never asked."

I nod and smile at him.

"I need coffee," I say, and go into the kitchen to make a double espresso. I grab two *pains aux amandes* from the pile of baked goods that Caroline already set out for all of us. It suddenly hits me that I don't have to leave Caroline. If I'm staying at the villa, that means she still has her job. I'll miss Mia, JoJo, and my family terribly, but this just means they have a villa in the south of France to stay and visit anytime they want. I think they're up for the trade.

"Okay, I can think now," I say, bringing out the coffees and pastries for Jackson and me. "So…" I point to my manuscript on the table in front of him. "You were saying? You love my book and think I'm the greatest writer in the world?"

Jackson grins. "I have to say, I had high expectations, and this exceeded them. You've managed to write both a mystery and a romance, without compromising on either of them. I could see this as a movie, like, tomorrow."

"I hear you saying this, but all I see are a million Post-its sticking out of the manuscript, taunting me. Looks like you have some changes."

"I have a few changes," he says. "But really, they're small. Most of the changes are things to remove to make the story even tighter. I'd like you to kill some of your darlings, Pop."

"I'm open to it," I say. "I'm trying out this thing called: letting people help me. It's new, but I think I'm doing well, so far."

"Finally. You've been a bit prickly the past few years."

"I know," I say, putting my face in my hands and shaking my head. "But here I am. I'm open, and I want to make this book better. And I trust you. You're a great writer, Jack."

Jackson's eyes travel up to mine, and his face is drawn. "That's the first time you've ever said that to me." I feel my heart physically wrench in my chest. "I always thought you hated my books."

"Never," I say, laying my hand on Jackson's shoulder. "I loved your books and cried at every single one. And at every single movie." I roll my eyes playfully, and Jackson's smile doesn't reach his eyes yet. He's serious, running his hands through his hair.

"Thank you, Pop," he says. "That means a lot to me. I know I seem all tough and cool, but your opinion matters a lot."

"Well, I never said I thought you were cool…"

He laughs on an outtake of breath, and I go in for a hug, pulling his broad chest into mine.

I pick up the manuscript and do a cursory look through his notes.

Jackson drinks his coffee and goes into the kitchen for another cup. I scan through the Post-its and realize there's a system. Of course, there's a system. Organized, put-together Jackson always has a system. He has it written on a notepad. His key. Yellow for places where text can be removed. Green for things to change or add. And pink for parts he loved.

The manuscript is a sea of pink.

I clasp my hand over my mouth, just as Jackson walks back in and I stand up, hugging him so hard he almost spills his coffee.

"All these Post-its are things you like," I say into his shoulder.

"Told you I loved it," he says. "But it is a first draft, so there are revision notes in there. All my books have gone through revisions, often multiple rewrites. But I have to say, I don't think I've ever written a first draft as good as this. I'm impressed and, honestly, a little jealous." I laugh and settle myself at the table with my laptop and manuscript, starting with Jackson's notes on the first page.

The rest of the morning passes with me making changes on my computer, while Jackson naps in a spare bedroom. It'll take me a good amount of time to finish the first revision, but I thought I'd start right away. The residents join me, making edits to their books before they leave next week. I can't imagine being here in the villa without them. We've all become so close.

I have several meetings set up already, scheduled for the week after they leave. With Janelle, to start preparing for the spring semester. We skipped the fall to help me get my bearings, but I already have some plans to make The Colony my own. The biggest one is that I want to set up excursions, dinners, and fun activities for the residents to all do together.

Part of what I love about The Colony is the camaraderie with the residents, so I want to add that into the package. Do wine tastings, beach clubs, visits to other cities in the region, host dinners out on the town, maybe even a couple weekends away to Provence or up to Paris, budget permitting.

I also have an idea of asking previous authors from The Colony to give workshops on Zoom and talk about their experiences with publishing, maybe even become mentors to new residents.

I already talked to Caroline about it all and she effusively wants to help, so we have a bunch of meetings to make plans for the spring. I do wish Oliver was here to give his input and do this with me, but I know now it's not my place to get in touch. I hope he's happy in New York and I hope eventually I'll stop missing him.

When Jackson emerges a few hours later, the residents pounce on him with even more questions, requesting his feedback on various scenes. He is so obliging it makes me proud that he's my brother. That's a new one. I used to loathe when anyone even brought Jackson up, and now, here I am, full of sisterly pride.

Finally, when the residents have released him, he sits down with me, and we start crafting a query letter which I'll need if I want to try to get an agent.

"Just in case you want to use it," Jackson says. "You don't have to publish this book, but I think you should. It doesn't matter how many rejections you've had in the past, it only takes one agent to see your vision."

"Okay," I say. "I'll think about it."

"Where's Liam, by the way?" I ask, suddenly realizing I haven't seen him since last night.

Jackson smiles. "I think he's with Caroline."

My eyes widen. "All night? Already?"

"Yeah," Jackson says. "They were up late here and then left to go to her place."

"Well, that happened quick," I say, laughing.

"Sure did," Jackson says, eyebrows raised. "Get it, Liam."

We laugh at that.

"I'm so glad you came," I say.

"Me too."

I spend the rest of the afternoon, and well into the evening, revising, while Jackson reads a PJ Latisse book, *The Dark Room*. It makes me think of Joan, my friend from the plane, who said it was her favorite. If only she could see me now. I don't even remember that version of myself. It feels like years ago, not just a few months. She thought I was brave then, getting on the plane without any idea of what was to come.

Joan had no idea just how brave I could be.

And neither did I.

Until now.

THIRTY-SIX

Cap Ferrat, France

A few days later, I say goodbye to Jackson, Liam, and my mom, who are all flying back to Los Angeles together. We have a group hug in the foyer of the villa, exchange tears and words of love, and I assure them I'll return to LA to both visit and retrieve all the stuff I've left behind. I've asked the subletter if they want to take over my lease, and just my luck, they do. I plan to go back to Los Angeles at the end of February, so I'll tie up those loose ends.

Closing the door as they leave, I realize I'm going to genuinely miss them. Finally, my relationship with my family is not fractured, and yet it happens at the exact moment I've decided to move across the world. Life has a funny way of giving you exactly what you want at the exact wrong time.

The next night, I am an emotional live wire yet again during the goodbye party for the residents. Over the past few months, I've become so close to all these women. It feels like we've done battle together, slayed our creative demons, and come out the other side, victorious.

The backyard is decorated the same way it began, with twinkling lights strung across the trees, and heavy candles encased in glass on each table. The champagne is flowing, and there's a spread of food that Caroline prepared. Everyone is here, except Oliver, of course.

I must look downtrodden, because Stella approaches and says, "Hey, this is a party, you know?" She smiles softly at me, and I perk up. "Cheers," she says, and we clink glasses.

"I know," I say. "I'm just emotional."

"Me too," Stella says. "I can't believe this experience is over. It has changed my life completely."

"Mine too," I say, and we meet eyes, and smile.

"Are you going to try to get an agent?" she asks. She and the other residents are already plotting their path to publishing, and it's been all anyone has talked about. Jasmyn and Kerry already have interest from agents, while Stella and Evie are still working on their revisions.

"I don't know," I say. "I haven't decided yet."

"I really think you should."

"It's nice right now to not care about whether I get published or not."

"I love that," she says, squeezing my forearm. "But I still think you should go for it."

"I know," I say. "Thanks, Stella. I'm going to miss you."

"Me too," she says and pulls me into a hug. "Let's join the group."

We walk arm in arm, holding our glasses, and pull up to Evie, Jasmyn, Kerry, Sebastian, Andrew, Janelle, Caroline, and Beau. I smile at all of them, tears pooling in the corners of my eyes. Thankfully, I only have to say goodbye to the residents. I'll be working closely with Janelle and Caroline, and, of course, Sebastian, Andrew and Beau are down the street. Without them, I think I'd be falling apart right now at this great exodus.

"I'm so proud of all of you," I say, holding up my glass. "We all finished our books. We stuck together. We helped each other. We vented our frustrations like wild women." They break into tittered laughter.

"Hashtag feminist rage," Jasmyn says, raising her glass. We all smile, and wipe tears from our eyes.

"You know," I say. "Six months ago, if I had to be around four amazing women who were all going after their dreams, I would have been intimidated. But I've realized that another person's greatness takes nothing from my own. And that the bravest thing you can do is support people and celebrate their success with as much excitement as it deserves. It's funny, the more you celebrate *others*, the more you celebrate *yourself*."

"That needs to be made into a poster and put up in the dining room, Poppy. That's so true," Stella says.

"It is," Jasmyn says. "Society tries to tell us that women only get one tiny sliver of pie, and we need to fight each other for it. But it's a lie. By supporting each other, we make a new pie. We make endless pies."

"Anyone else really want pie now?" Evie asks, and we all erupt into laughter.

A bit later, I'm sitting alone by the pool in the same spot where Oliver told me about his job offer in New York, and I'm wondering how it's going, if he misses home, or me. I'm trying not to think of him too much, but I have so much guilt that he isn't here, seeing off this season of residents. He really should be. I wish he was.

Tomorrow, I'll be in the villa, completely alone for the first time since August. Soon, it will be Christmas and then New Year's. I'll have a book to revise, and a life to begin, without the one person I want to share all the details with. All I can do is hope that wherever he is, he's happy. I've come to terms with it. I ruined it, ruined us, and even if at the time, I felt it was the best for both of us—it's unforgivable. I let my fear get in the way.

I think about reaching out to him all the time, but I keep coming back to the feeling that it's not my place. He may even hate me, and that's not something I want to know right now.

I just have to hope that if Oliver ever does come back, he'll be willing to be my friend.

JANUARY

THIRTY-SEVEN

Cap Ferrat, France

I spend New Year's and the first couple weeks of January revising my novel and exploring the south of France on my own—time that I needed to process the last five months and prepare myself for what's to come in February, when I officially take The Colony over.

I'm heading over to Sebastian's, since he asked me to stop by earlier. I put on a heavy jacket for the short walk to his house. It's now officially cold in the south of France, and especially on the top of this bluff, the wind is howling.

Once I arrive at Sebastian's, I take a deep breath. I know Oliver isn't here, but I still take a moment to catch my breath. I miss him so much sometimes it hurts.

Before I can knock, Sebastian opens the door with a flourish, Beau yipping at me and waiting for me to pick him up.

"Beau sensed you were here five minutes ago," Sebastian says, pulling me into a hug. "Why are you standing out here in the cold, kiddo?" He ushers me into his beautiful and tasteful modern villa, vibrant artwork filling every single open space of his walls. His kitchen is all updated, with sleek appliances and forest green–and–silver accents. It's Sebastian, through and through.

"Tea?" Sebastian asks, holding up the stainless-steel kettle. I nod.

"Where's Andrew today?"

"Gone to London for a few days," Sebastian says dramatically, pouting.

"Don't tell me you miss him already."

"Terribly," he says, laughing. "I feel like a teenager."

I shake my head. "That is way too cute."

Sebastian smiles and goes back to the kettle.

"It was great to spend time with June, by the way," he says, pulling out teabags and placing them into two heavy mugs. "Healing."

"I'm so glad you two bonded. She needed that. She needed all of this." He nods and hands me the mug of tea, and I spend some time doctoring it with milk and honey. "Have you… heard from Oliver?" My voice is low, shaky.

"Only by email. He seems okay. He's not saying much."

"Oh." I don't know what else to say. A few beats of silence pass. I look up at him. "So, you wanted to show me something?"

"Yes, yes," Sebastian says, heading for a hallway off the kitchen. "I'll be right back."

I sit down on a stool at the breakfast bar. Sebastian returns with a white envelope and a fat stack of printed papers.

"I'm breaking a Margot rule," he says, leaning across the kitchen island and looking at me conspiratorially. "Technically, I was supposed to give you this at the end of the six months, but I'm following my intuition here. I think now is the right time."

He hands me the envelope and slides the papers toward me. My throat drops into my stomach when I see the handwriting on the front. "A letter?" I ask. "From Margot?"

"*Oui*," he says. "A pretty important one, too."

"Wow," I say, my voice low. "I'm suddenly very nervous. What other surprises are there left?"

Sebastian only pats me on the arm and chuckles. "I'll leave you with it. Have your tea, kiddo." He pats the envelope once. "Come on, Beau." They both walk off to another area of the house, and I'm left alone with Margot's last message to me, trying to catch my breath.

My heart is beating so loud. I place my hand on my chest and take five deep breaths in.

The front of the envelope says "To Poppy: For when you decide to stay…"

I open the seal carefully, tenderly, as if everything about this Margot gift is sacred. I pull out a typed letter with Margot's elegant signature at the bottom. My eyes are already misty with tears, and I blink them away, trying to focus on the words of the letter. I take a sip of my tea, readying myself, and then I begin.

Dearest Poppy,
The last time I saw you, it was clear to me that you were at a crossroads, and you didn't know it. I wasn't always going to leave the villa and the residency to you. I wanted you to know about it, and to visit, but I didn't want to lay the responsibility at your feet, even as a choice. But then, the last lunch we had, I felt a lurch of worry for you. I knew exactly where you were in your life, because it's the exact crossroads I'd found myself at before I moved to France. I didn't realize at the time that I was staring down the barrel of two vastly different life paths. Either choose to live in hiding of my truth, my gifts, and my honest self. Or to be courageous enough to embrace it.

A lot of people choose to hide, and I have to admit, Poppy, you were actively choosing that path. I think you know that now. At our last visit, I decided, on my drive back to the hotel, that you were the person I would leave

my legacy to. I knew you'd struggle at first. It would be
a roller-coaster of emotions for you, questioning whether
you deserve it, and wondering just what the hell your
batty Aunt Margot was thinking. But I have the utmost
faith in you, and I know that if you're reading this letter, it means you've stepped into your power, that you've
chosen the hardest, most rewarding life path: to be brave
and authentic even when you are afraid.

"Do it for the plot" wasn't just advice I doled out to my
wonderful niece. It was what I lived by. To me, it meant
do it afraid. Do it anyway. Go for it. Try. Don't stand on
the sidelines of your own life. I thought the only way to
shock you back into your life would be to bring you to
France and force you to step up. If you're reading this, I
guess I was right.

I don't have a crystal ball, as some might presume, but I
knew you would make this choice, because I was around
the same age as you when I made my choice, and you and
I, Poppy? We're soulmates. I realized it from the first moment I met you. You might question yourself and doubt
your potential, but eventually you step up, just like me.
And what is courage, if not that?

However, the villa and the residency is not the whole
of my legacy, my darling girl. There is something else
that only four people in this world know about. You will
now be the fifth.

My books.

Darling, it made me so happy when, at our first lunch,
you told me who your favorite author was. It took everything in me to not let the truth spill out right there, but
I knew it wasn't the right time. I knew you had to write
your book before you could know about mine. Congratulations for finishing your manuscript, by the way. You

just needed space and time for your writing to flourish, and the belief that you could do it. I'm so proud of you.

So, are you ready for my biggest secret?

I am PJ Latisse.

I wrote my first book *The Midnight Colony* at the villa, before I started the residency. That's why I named it The Colony—it was an homage to that book and the bravery it took to write it and get it out into the world. (And if you think PJ Latisse wasn't rejected by over a hundred agents, you'd be wrong.) It warmed my soul to know you loved *The Midnight Colony* and my other books, not knowing that your own aunt had labored over and written them. Writing was the ultimate act of courage for me. That is why I knew I had to leave you this legacy, so you could start building your own.

Which is why I have just one more gift for you, if you want to take it. The last manuscript I ever wrote. My last book. The last book PJ Latisse will ever publish, if you do it for me. It's a rough draft I finished early last summer. It probably isn't very good. Edit it for me, my darling niece. Publish it. I trust you will do PJ Latisse (and me!) justice.

Writing runs through our blood. Go forth in the world and give it your magic. And take care of mine.

I love you forever,

Margot

P.S. PJ Latisse is PJL. Poppy. Jackson. Liam. You three were always with me.

I set the letter down, my face covered in tears. I let out a long exhale. Margot is PJ Latisse?

MARGOT IS PJ LATISSE?

I run my hands over the stack of papers, which I now understand is incredibly precious: PJ Latisse's last-ever book. In my hands? Right here? That Margot—no, my favorite author PJ Latisse—thinks I am capable of editing?

I feel like I could actually fall through the floor. I am so dizzy with shock.

I don't even know what to think or say or do. There's so much to process from this letter.

No wonder she had a collection of first-edition PJ Latisse books to give me! They were her own! It's like all the pieces of this puzzle are coming together at once, the picture finally clear.

Sebastian pokes his head in and says, "Quite the big reveal, no?" He smiles devilishly, his eyes bright and full of fondness. "Margot did always love a good plot twist."

"My mind is *blown*," I say, through an outtake of breath. "I have no words. No words, Sebastian!"

"She thought you might react that way," he says. "She did always have a flair for the dramatic."

"My favorite author in the world, my hero, my inspiration, my muse…is actually my Aunt Margot. Is this for real?" I can't stop whirling it around in my head. It's so unbelievable. "Did Oliver know about this?"

Sebastian shakes his head. "Nope. Margot was secretive about it. She hated fame, but she loved writing books. This was her way of maintaining the life she wanted. Plus, if it got out that Margot Bisset was PJ Latisse, can you imagine how different the residency would be? She said you can tell Oliver and your family, but advised you to keep it to yourself beyond that so the residency can remain focused on the authors."

"She really had a very specific way she wanted to exist in this world," I say. "God, I wish she were still here."

"Me, too," Sebastian says, walking closer to me and putting his hand on my shoulder. "Every day, kiddo."

"I can't believe Margot was PJ Latisse," I whisper, still in total disbelief. "Now I get where the money comes from for The Colony." I laugh. "Margot was rich."

Sebastian laughs and says, "Of course the person who never believed writing would ever make her any money got rich off of it."

"Margot didn't think she could make a living from writing?"

"Not really," he says. "I told you she was a lot like you."

I sit back, stunned again. The parallels between us—I had no idea. It makes me trust in Margot's vision for me even more. But I have to say, I'm glad to have found out this plot twist after I decided to keep The Colony. It makes it so much sweeter that I said yes to all this and wrote my own book first. Not for Margot or to get a book deal. But for *me*.

I run my hands over the manuscript. I get to read a rough draft of my favorite writer's last book. My aunt's last piece of her legacy. I feel overwhelmed.

"We need wine," Sebastian says. "I'm going down to the cellar for a good red. You hold tight."

He walks away, Beau following closely behind, and I lean back in my chair and let out a gust of air, shaking my head, still reeling from that letter. I pick it up again, hold it in my hands, and I trace my finger over Margot's signature. It's the last thing I'll have from her, and it feels like the most exceptional gift of all. Yes, she's left me a legacy. Yes, she's left me a whole home and business.

But she's given me even more.

Her belief in me.

What she saw in me before I saw it in myself. And her wisdom to know exactly what I needed to become the person I'm meant to be.

Whatever else she's given me apart from that, it's all just extra. My soulmate, her unshakable belief, her literary talent running through my blood—that's *everything*.

I spend the next few days reading Margot's letter over and over, chewing on a decision that feels like a leap of faith. I go to my computer on a rainy afternoon, set up a mug of tea next to me, and start reading through the agent query letter that Jackson and I drafted together. My novel is fully edited and in a place where I feel confident about it. I go back and forth. I feel like I could be happy if I never get published, but there's a part of me that wants to try. That wants to give it a shot again.

So, that's what I decide. Over the next few hours, I send out a few dozen emails to literary agencies, just like I did years and years ago. When I sent those emails way back when, I was so nervous and terrified. I wanted to prove to myself I was good enough. I wanted some agent and then a publisher to finally validate me. But now, I feel like I have all the validation I could ever need, from within.

I send the emails, close my laptop, and notice there isn't a single stitch of worry or panic within me. If I'm meant to find an agent, I will. If this book is meant to be published, it will be. Whatever happens, I know I'll be good.

And just like that, I begin again.

Stronger. Happier. More confident than ever. Trusting in myself. Knowing that whatever happens, I've got my own back.

I get ready to meet Andrew, Sebastian, and Caroline for dinner in the old-town part of Cannes and find myself feeling buoyant, trusting that whatever is meant to happen will be.

FEBRUARY

THIRTY-EIGHT

Cap Ferrat, France

The beginning of February in the south of France is desolate and quiet, with so few tourists. It's only a few days into the month and I can already tell it will be my favorite time of year here. Sure, the summer is glittery and hot and beautiful, but something about walking through the village with just the locals makes me feel like I belong.

I'm not some transient American here to take pieces of the French culture for my own gain. I want to be a part of this town, as much as I want to run the residency. My French is improving, too, and I can now do a full market day without needing English at all. I'm not having any deep and philosophical conversations with the butcher, but I can successfully ask how he is, order my meats, and pay without reverting to English.

I've got a large jacket on, a scarf, boots, and jeans. It's a sunny and cold day at the market, and I'm a regular now, darting in and out of my favorite stores and stalls with a wheelie basket at my feet, gathering up a few days' worth of groceries. I smile and wave at all the people who have become friends over the last six months, my cheeks and nose red from the chill outside.

If someone had told me back in August, when I quit my job, that this is where I'd be in February, I would have laughed in their face. It's amazing the difference a lot of courage and self-worth makes.

Earlier this week, I'd emailed Joan, my friend from the plane. I told her about the last six months, every detail. She emailed me back within a few hours and told me that she'd decided to stay in Europe for the foreseeable future, as well. She's in Rome now. She bought a baby pink Vespa. She sent a picture of it to me and wrote, "You're not the only brave cookie around these parts." I told her she must come visit me, and she emphatically promised she would.

I lug my basket up the hill, only slightly out of breath by the time I make it to the villa.

I feel joy in the most uncomplicated way. Sebastian and I went to Margot's lawyer the other day to sign the papers, so I'm officially the owner of the villa and The Colony, and the recipient of PJ Latisse's legacy. I felt so much gratitude to my aunt, signing those papers. And I know with full certainty, this was the right decision.

I am not the victim in my own story anymore. Or a supporting role. I am the main character—and I step into that energy every single day.

I open the door of the villa and Beau comes trotting toward me. Is Sebastian here? Caroline? Beau wasn't here when I left this morning. I wasn't expecting anyone, but Caroline and Sebastian are usually in and out these days.

I hear noise and movement in the kitchen.

"Where did you come from, Beau?" He looks up at me and tilts his head, as if he would very much like to answer me right now. I pet him softly and then he lopes along with me. I wheel my basket in the direction of the kitchen, thinking Caroline is probably wearing her headphones and can't hear me.

I arrive at the entryway to the kitchen and stop completely, my heart beating wildly in my chest when I see who's at the sink, his back to me. I gasp so quickly that I drop my basket with a loud clang.

He whips around to see what the commotion is, and our eyes land on each other with a startle, an electric shock.

"Oliver," I whisper.

I take a step backward, almost tripping over the contents of the basket that are now splayed out on the floor.

He's wearing a cream cable-knit sweater, rolled up to reveal his tattooed forearms, the delicacy of his wrists, his long, tapered hands. His hair is grown out, the tendril swooping over his green eyes longer and even sexier than I remember. I try to say something but have lost my voice.

He looks so good.

What is he doing here? Maybe he's back visiting Sebastian. But why is he here, in my kitchen?

Oliver hasn't moved at all. He's still holding a dish towel in his hand, and his face looks about as shell-shocked as mine does. But I can't read him. Or his energy. Or really interpret anything that's happening right now.

"Hi," I finally croak out, feeling like it's an insufficient word for the surge of emotion I feel. I thought I was getting *over* this man? That I could be his *friend*? That's hilarious. It was never over. For me, at least. I realize that in a split second.

"Hi," he says, moving toward me. He pauses, then steps forward a bit more, and I step forward, as well, until there's only a few feet between us. I can smell him now, and it hits me in waves. I made myself forget him as much as I could, but now it's all coming back, intense and undeniable.

"I'm sorry, Poppy," he says, his voice low and shattered.

"What?" I ask, incredulous. I move even closer. "I'm the one who's sorry, Oliver. I should never have broken us up. I was such a mess."

"I was a mess, too," Oliver says. "And I was still angry and grieving over Margot, and I felt too strongly about what you should do with the villa. I should have let you decide on your own. I should have at least heard you out, understood where you were coming from."

"I ruined everything," I say, coming even closer to him and laying my hand on the kitchen island to steady myself. "I thought for sure you hated me."

"Hated you?" he asks, his voice low. He looks at me through his eyelashes. "I could never hate you."

"Oh," I say on a breath. "Well, it's good to see you. Are you here visiting Sebastian?"

He looks at me quizzically, like I'm missing something crucial. I don't know what to say.

"Sebastian?" he asks. "Poppy," he moves forward and closes the distance between us. "I'm here for you."

All the air rushes from me and my body seems to sway.

"Am I too late?" he asks tenderly, his voice fragile as glass. "I know I have no right to tell you this, and if you've moved on, I'll understand. But I'd regret it forever if I didn't tell you that I want to be with you. Even if it's not at this villa. I don't care where. I'll be with you in Los Angeles, or New York, or Thailand. I just want to be with *you*." He closes the space between us, pushing a tendril of hair out of my face.

I break into pieces. I cup my hand across his cheek. His head falls into my hand, and he closes his eyes, letting out a deep sigh.

"You're not too late," I manage to say. "Thailand is tempting, but I'm just wondering if you'll be with me…here? And run The Colony with me? And, maybe, I don't know, never, ever, ever leave again?"

His eyes tear open, and his gaze burns into mine.

"You're keeping it, then?"

"I'm keeping it," I say with a shrug, pretending it's no big deal, and yet the look on his face tells me it's monumental, that he's not messing around anymore.

He throws his arms around me in a tight hug, and then pulls away quickly. He grabs my face in both his hands, then gives me a kiss that is so good, so urgent, I actually feel myself melting into him. It's tender and gentle, yet so burning hot, that I have to find the kitchen island behind me so I can keep myself upright; my back against it, and Oliver pushing into me, as if this kiss might save his life.

The world spins, everything goes quiet, and I feel his hands on my neck. My hands roam up his sweater to his back, and I hear him groan into my mouth. He kisses my neck and nibbles my ear and I gasp, his other hand touching my skin anywhere he can find it, both of us hungry for each other. When he gets to my left ear, he whispers, "no more leaving," in a breathy voice that sends shivers all the way through my body.

"God, I missed you," I say, when we finally break apart, his face so close to mine I can feel the outtake of his breathing on my lips.

"I promise you I missed you more," he whimpers.

"Where did you go?" I ask, running my hands through his hair.

"New York, at first," he says, kissing me in the middle of his story. "I ended up taking that job. They hadn't found anyone to fill the role yet. But I hated it." Kiss. "I was miserable." Kiss. "So, I quit, and then I went to Spain for a while, got really drunk, and thought about you." Kiss. "For every minute of every day, until I couldn't take it any longer." Kiss. His eyes search mine, and he swipes away one of my falling tears. "I wanted to come home."

I nod, and then before I can answer, he adds, "To you, Poppy. *You're* my home."

And then I splinter completely, sobs escaping from me. It's not out of sadness. It's happiness. That we've found each other again. And I know this time, I won't ruin it. I know this time I deserve it. I'm allowed to have this. I'm allowed to be this loved.

"Oh, Poppy," he says, holding me to him tightly, letting the tears move their way through me. Once I regain my breathing, I pull back from him and look deeply into his green eyes, those flecks of gold mesmerizing.

"I love you," I say, and his face breaks into the most blind ingly gorgeous smile.

"I love you, too," he says.

He grabs my hand and pulls me upstairs, not saying another word, and leads me to what will now be our bedroom, at the end of the hall. He undresses me wordlessly, kissing down my body at every piece of clothing he removes. My nerve endings feel as though they're on fire, and everywhere he touches is a blaze of heat. I take his shirt off and drag my hands across his tattoos.

Undressed, we go to the bed, where I climb on top of him, positioning myself above him. And then, without speaking, his eyes trained on me with an inferno of intensity and passion and emotion, we come together, and he's right: it feels like home.

Later, entangled together, my head resting on his chest, his legs flung around mine, I prop myself up on him and say, "By the way, a bit of news."

He opens his eyes and looks at me with such adoration, it takes me a moment to catch my breath.

"Tell me," he says.

"You remember my favorite author?" I ask nonchalantly.

"Of course," he says. "PJ Latisse."

"Well," I say, shrugging, pretending to be chill. "Turns out PJ Latisse is actually our very own Margot Bisset."

He bolts upright, jumping out of the bed.

"What?" he screams out. "How? What? Oh my god!"

I break into a wide smile. "I know!"

"This explains a lot of things," he says, laughing. "The money. Locking her office to do 'secret work.' Why she was so good at helping the residents shape their books. That's wild!" He shakes his head ruefully. "I'm in total shock."

"Yeah, same. She also left me her last manuscript and wants me to edit it and have it published for her."

"You'll do that and publish your own book too, right?" he asks, concerned.

"Of course. If I get an agent and a book deal."

"Good," he says. "I don't want you to give up on your dream of being published."

"No," I tell him, resolutely. "I'm not giving up on *anything* this time."

That pulls a beautiful smile from him, and he plants a soft kiss on my lips before lying back down on the bed.

"Good," he says again, with finality.

He pats the spot on his chest where my head was before, bringing me back to him. I slide in next to him, the sturdy feel of his body next to mine like a gift.

I can't believe I ever convinced myself I could live without him, because now that he's back, I realize just how in love with him I've been for months. Every bit of good news that comes my way is better when I get to tell Oliver about it.

We spend the next many hours in bed, swapping stories from the last couple months, sharing insights and epiphanies, deep diving into the feelings we'd kept hidden away from each other. I fall asleep with the bedside lamp on, a printed copy of my book in Oliver's hands, his face scrunched with concentration. And it's there, in the haven of that bedroom, while the day turns to night, that we start to build something wonderful...*together.*

AUGUST

THIRTY-NINE

Cap Ferrat, France

It's a balmy evening, and the late summer humidity has settled over the villa like a veil.

"Enjoy this peace and quiet, because this time next week, it's going to be mayhem," Oliver says, sipping a fresh glass of rosé, watching the sun sink into the horizon.

"I can't believe it's time already," I say, drinking my wine, and swatting away a mosquito.

"This is a good group," Oliver says. "I'm excited."

"Me too," I say, looking over at him and feeling nothing but contentment. The new cohort of residents arrives next week, with four wildly talented people. I feel ready. Energized. Prepared. Caroline and I have a whole host of exciting things planned for them, not limited to a glitzy excursion at a beach club in Cannes the day after they arrive, to welcome them in style.

"There you two lovebirds are," Sebastian says, walking out into the backyard with Andrew, Beau jumping up on my stomach so hard I let out a breath.

"Hi, bud," I say, fluffing his fur as he licks my hand.

"Are you two ready to go?" Sebastian asks, looking dapper as hell in a light linen suit.

"They were *busy*, darling," Andrew says, laughing.

Oliver and I exchange guilty glances. We were supposed to be going to dinner with Sebastian and a group of people out in Antibes, but we forgot, too caught up in each other to remember.

"We messed up, my love," I say, giggling at Oliver, who gives a cheeky grin.

"You'll have to tame yourselves once the residents arrive." Sebastian shakes his head playfully.

"Will we?" Oliver asks, looking at me with heat. "I seem to remember that I have a room at your place still."

"Oh no, Olly," Sebastian says, covering his ears with his hands. "Alright, get changed. Get decent. Get your heads out of the gutter. We're leaving in twenty."

Both Oliver and I rush into the villa to get dressed up.

"He's maaaaaaad," I say, poking Oliver in the stomach. "You don't cross a Libra, Olly."

"He's fine," he says, waving him off. He eyes the bathroom. "Quick shower?" I get goose bumps and nod.

Standing in the shower, face-to-face, Oliver looks at me in that intense way of his, like I'm the object of every fantasy he's ever had.

"Stop looking at me like that," I say. "We have to go, Olly."

"Looking at you like what, Pop?" he asks innocently.

"Be good," I warn.

He lets out a flirty laugh.

We get dressed and descend the staircase, holding hands.

"Remember when I died of jealousy here, when you wore that red dress to go on a date with another man?" Oliver asks, roving his hand over his stubble.

"I remember," I say, as he pulls me close to him in the foyer and starts kissing the soft space below my earlobe.

The door opens so fast we both just dodge it. Sebastian narrows his eyes at us. "I get it. You two are madly in love and can't keep your hands off each other, but we really do have to head out." He taps his foot, and tries to maintain a serious face, eyes twinkling all the while.

We three walk outside, Beau following behind as always. Sebastian and Oliver join Andrew by the car. I stop for a moment and look back at the villa.

That first day, I arrived so bitter and closed off. I was sure that nothing was going to work out for me. I look back at Sebastian, Oliver, and Andrew, tears in my eyes, at these three wonderful men I get to love. And little Beau, whose face is turned upward toward mine, as if he understands, somehow, the gravity of this moment.

This is the same spot as where it all began, but it's so different. The villa, a home to call my own. That surly man who hated me on sight is now the love of my life. And Sebastian, well, I loved him from the outset, and now I love him even more. The privilege of seeing Sebastian and Andrew find each other again and fall madly in love.

Margot gave me so much. She gave me all of this, and allowed me to step into it, to finally understand that I do deserve it. That I don't need to fight the good. That I don't need to settle.

I get to be afraid, and brave, and experience everything.

I am going to live with an open-heart, no matter how hard it is, how vulnerable, or scary. No more hiding. No more running.

I will always be the main character of my own life.

No more sidelines.

No more supporting roles.

And honestly?

It should be no surprise, but that's when the plot got *really* interesting.

EPILOGUE

Three Years Later

The *Los Angeles Times* Books

*Review: A riveting debut takes on two genres and twists it
into one*

When you read *You Think You Know Florence James* by
debut author Poppy Banks (out September 17th), you may
think it's a standard-issue domestic thriller featuring a
beautiful, famous woman who goes missing at the Cannes
Film Festival. But what you won't expect is for the story
to morph your understanding of what a thriller can be,
by providing a twist so satisfying you'll be recommend-
ing this book to every person you've ever met.

There's a lot to expect from Jackson Banks's younger
sister, considering Jackson's phenom-like literary talent,
but to compare the two would be like thinking a pineap-
ple is going to taste like a cucumber. They are two wildly
different writers. The only thing they seem to share is a

bloodline. Poppy's writing is hypnotic and prose-heavy, with a deft understanding of plot. To compare her to Jackson would be a disservice to them both.

You Think You Know Florence James is already one of the fall's most highly anticipated novels. It's equal parts timely and captivating from the first page to the last. Without giving too much away, the plot twist is fresh and guaranteed to shock readers.

Poppy Banks lives in the south of France, where she co-runs an impressive writer's residency and a highly sought-after incubator for new literary talent. She is married to Oliver Hayes, a graphic designer, and also the co-owner of the residency. They have a 6-month-old daughter together named Margot.

★ ★ ★ ★ ★

ACKNOWLEDGMENTS

Thank you so much to my readers who inspire me every single day. I wrote this book with you in mind.

Thank you to my agent Samantha Fabien at Root Literary for pulling this story from the slush pile and getting on the phone and saying, "Can I tell you what I love about this book?" You made my life.

Thank you to my editor Laura Brown from Park Row for championing this story and loving Poppy just as much as I do. Editing with you is a true joy.

Thank you to the friends who let me question myself, but didn't let me give up. Thank you to my beta readers for offering indispensable wisdom and notes. Thank you Savannah Gilbo for helping me shape the initial stages of Poppy's first draft.

Thank you to my family for getting excited with me. Thank you to my mom for somehow believing in this story more than I did.

Thank you to my husband who has never once let me doubt myself.

Thank you for all the years of questioning—they made me stronger and more convicted. I wrote this book not knowing if I could actually write it. It was a test of faith and a labor of love. It taught me so much about myself. I cherish the fall of 2020 for showing me what is possible when I put my butt in the chair for hours and just write the story I want to read.

Lastly, thank you to Poppy Banks for becoming such a strong presence in my life I could do nothing for months but write your story.